Praise for *The Planet Thieves*

"Moves at warp speed, a riveting story with characters so finely drawn that I wonder if Dan Krokos actually is an alien."
—Eoin Colfer, *New York Times* bestselling author of the Artemis Fowl series

"Krokos launches this series with skill and purpose, immediately placing readers in the action and never slowing down.... Intriguing concept, intense sense of adventure, and high stakes."
—*Publishers Weekly*

"Excitingly suspenseful and filled with intriguing plot twists, *The Planet Thieves* offers a science-fiction adventure with a lot of heart. Gripping battles, daredevil heroics, and races against the clock make for page-turning fun, but Mason also provides an endearing protagonist whose depth and relationships balance well with the more fantastical parts of the story. The text reworks imagery from some of the most widely popular and beloved science fiction of television, books, and film, but spins these elements into a unique and original space escapade, while also touching on interesting themes of the untapped power of young people and how we characterize the alien 'other.' Certain to be a crowd-pleaser, readers will wait anxiously for the next installment."
—*VOYA*

"*The Planet Thieves* is the first installment in a fast-moving, exciting new middle-grade series.... If you enjoy teens with special abilities and unusual backgrounds involved in nonstop interstellar action, don't miss this engrossing series." —*BookLoons*

"This book will appeal to science-fiction fans, especially those who are enthusiastic about the upcoming movie adaptation of Orson Scott Card's *Ender's Game*." —*School Library Journal*

TOR BOOKS BY DAN KROKOS

The Planet Thieves
The Black Stars

The Planet Thieves

DAN KROKOS

A TOM DOHERTY ASSOCIATES BOOK

New York

THE PLANET THIEVES

Illustrations by Antonio Javier Caparo

A Starscape Book
Published by Tom Doherty Associates, LLC
175 Fifth Avenue
New York, NY 10010

www.tor-forge.com

The Library of Congress has cataloged the hardcover edition as follows:

Krokos, Dan.
    The planet thieves / Dan Krokos.—First edition.
        pages cm
    "A Tom Doherty Associates Book."
    ISBN 978-0-7653-3428-2 (hardcover)
    ISBN 978-1-4668-0998-7 (e-book)
    [1. Science fiction.   2. War—Fiction.]   I. Title.
    PZ7.K9185Pl 2013
    [Fic]—dc23
                                        2013006321

ISBN 978-0-7653-7538-4 (trade paperback)

Starscape books may be purchased for educational, business, or promotional use. For information on bulk purchases, please contact Macmillan Corporate and Premium Sales Department at 1-800-221-7945, extension 5442, or write specialmarkets@macmillan.com.

First Edition: May 2013
First Trade Paperback Edition: September 2014

Printed in the United States of America

0 9 8 7 6 5 4 3 2 1

To Suzie Townsend, for always making me better

Acknowledgments

I've wanted to write a book like this since I was a kid, and now here it is, one more dream fulfilled. I couldn't have done it without the help of Suzie Townsend, Joanna Volpe, Kathleen Ortiz, and Danielle Barthel at New Leaf Literary. Thank you to Whitney Ross and the incredible team at Tor. To Dana Kaye, Janet Reid, and Rachel Silberman.

Thank you to everyone at Benderspink and Heyday Films, including Christopher Cosmos, J.C. Spink, Chris Bender, Jake Weiner, David Heyman, and David Whitney. Thank you to Steve Younger, for giving me Dodgers tickets with preferred parking.

Thank you to my friends Adam "Complexity" Lastoria, Will "15 minute Salv/DE Epics" Lyle, Sean Ferrell, Jeff Somers, Barbara and Travis Poelle (and Char Char), Joe Volpe, Sarah Maas, Susan Dennard, Josh Bazell, Brooks Sherman, John Corey Whaley, Margaret Stohl, and Jesse Andrews. You guys are okay.

Special thanks to my old man, for getting me hooked on SF and Fantasy early.

And a final thanks to you for coming on this adventure with me. I hope you have as much fun reading it as I did writing it.

The Planet Thieves

Chapter One

The prank Mason Stark pulled on his sister was doomed from the beginning. For starters, he wasn't supposed to be on the bridge. Cadets age thirteen and under were forbidden from any section of the ship deemed *combat sensitive*. Which pretty much left the crew quarters, cafeteria, gym, and certain hallways as the only places they could roam. Sometimes Mason's sister, Lieutenant Commander Susan Stark, would tour the engineering decks with him, but that was it.

The pranks were a new thing, born from pure boredom. The last one, on fellow cadet Tom Renner, who Mason thought needed to experience what Academy I called *Humility in the Face of Glory*, had ended badly. Mason's lip was almost healed, but Tom's left eye was still mottled bruise-yellow.

In Mason's defense, there wasn't much for eighteen cadets to do on a ship that was mostly closed to them. Sure, when no one was looking they raced each other down the corridors, or held mock battles, but that got old. And Mason was sick of the crew sneering at the cadets or telling them to knock it off. Mason already had years of training, but was forced to imitate cargo just to log his required spacetime for the summer quarter.

Another reason his prank was doomed: Mason hadn't known that Captain Renner would call a code yellow in the middle of the night, from her personal quarters. Her voice booming through the ship had made him drop the final bolt he'd removed from Susan's chair. The bright white light on the bridge had changed to a pulsing yellow. Under normal circumstances, the bridge was under the computer's control between 0300 and 0600 hours. Now it would be fully staffed in a matter of minutes, a full hour before it should be.

Which of course made Mason wonder what could rouse the captain, and the ship, in the middle of the night.

Nothing good, he knew.

The last reason his prank was doomed: Susan was usually the first person on the bridge each morning. She liked to set up her engineering console and drink her morning synth-coffee, all while looking through the great transparent dome that separated the bridge from cold, empty space.

She was supposed to fall out of her chair by herself. No one was *supposed* to be watching. Afterward, she would laugh, maybe put Mason in a headlock and rub her knuckles over his head until it burned.

Instead, the officers rushed onto the bridge with pillow-marked faces, and Mason dived behind the pilot console at the front left of the dome. The best place to hide, really the only place. Though now he was as far away from the two exits as possible.

"How close is the Tremist ship?" Captain Renner said. Her usually tame brown hair was frizzy. Her eyes were a little puffy from sleep, but they still appeared hard and calculating, all-seeing. "How much time?"

A few feet from Mason, Ensign Chung tapped the perimeter console a few times. Mason could only see his back and a sliver of the hologram in front of him. "Previous course was parallel to ours, but they've drifted three hundred kilometers closer, Captain. Now only forty thousand kilometers away. Recommend code red."

Crouched behind the desk-sized console, Mason broke out in a cold sweat, even though the bridge was a constant seventy-two degrees. Code reds only happened if a ship was expected to come in contact with the Tremist. *Direct* contact.

Of the Tremist, Mason knew one thing for certain, and two things not for certain.

The certain:

The Tremist were aliens bent on annihilating the human race.

The uncertain:

They had better technology and, depending on who you talked to, would probably win the war.

They were vampyres inside of human-shaped space suits that resembled armor worn by ancient knights of Earth. And they wanted to drink your blood. Since a fellow cadet named Mical said the Tremist were also shapeshifting werewolves, Mason doubted this was true.

Ensign Chung sucked in a breath. "They're putting on speed. Location thirty-five thousand klicks away, still closing. Captain?"

A good cadet would stand up, announce his presence, then walk himself to the brig and right into his holding cell. He didn't want to distract the crew, since it was very likely not everyone would survive the Tremist engagement—that was plain history. But fear held him behind the console. The vitals monitor built into his uniform vibrated against his forearm, a stupid reminder to keep his heart rate low. *You're too nervous,* the buzz told him helpfully. He clamped his palm on the mechanism to muffle it and hoped the crew didn't hear.

"Set a code red," the captain said. The soft yellow light changed to a throbbing red. The transparent dome over the bridge stayed clear, but now angry red words and numbers began to scroll down the inside in all directions, the black of space as their background.

Mason pressed his face to the console. Lieutenant Hill was sitting there now, just a few feet of plastic and metal between them. Mason looked around the side with just his left eye. Susan was near the back of the dome, diagonal from him, at the console that linked the bridge to engineering.

Don't sit down, Mason thought. *I'm sorry, I'm sorry!*

Susan sat down in her chair. Which promptly slammed back and dumped her into a backward somersault. Her synth-coffee splashed everywhere, staining her uniform from shoulder to wrist.

All fifteen people on the bridge froze. Susan popped to her feet, blinking coffee from her eyes.

"Distance?" the captain demanded, forcing the crew's attention back to their screens.

"Now thirty thousand kilometers," Ensign Chung said. "They're getting closer, but taking their time."

Mason peeked from behind the console again. Somehow Susan knew his exact location and was already glaring at him from across the bridge. Her face was red, and not just from the strobing lights.

"Captain," she said, tugging her uniform taut around her waist. It was the same uniform they all wore, Mason included—simple black pants, tall black boots, and a long-sleeved shirt, also black. Thin and tight, but able to keep a soldier warm or cool depending on the weather. The symbol of Earth Space Command, a small blue ring inside a silver ring, always went over the heart. Susan's uniform also had two blue circles on the neck to mark her rank. Mason had none.

"Yes?" the captain replied.

She never took her eyes off Mason, and Mason never moved.

"Permission to remove my brother from the bridge and escort him to the brig." His prank had upset her, and worse, *distracted* her, at a moment when she would need all her wits. Some brother.

"Granted," Captain Renner said, not once setting her steel-hard gaze upon Mason. The other officers, though, were sneaking disgusted glances. Any amount of respect the cadets had hoped to acquire this trip, Mason had just thrown away. "But make it fast," the captain added.

Mason wasn't even scared about getting in trouble anymore. A code red kind of put things in perspective. Trying to stay calm, he reminded himself of the facts, because that's what a soldier did. Facts were calming, Instructor Bazell once told him. *Logic is a salve to the infection of fear,* she sometimes added. Whatever that meant. But it was worth a shot.

So, the facts:

The SS Egypt was the flagship of the fleet, the most important ship, even though it didn't carry an admiral. It was 745 meters long, almost half a mile, and shaped like a giant letter *H*. The left part of the *H* was a massive, continuous cylinder comprised of twenty levels where the crew lived and worked and went to jail if they embarrassed their sister in front of her fellow officers. The right side of the *H*—all 745 meters of it, a cylinder identical to the left side—held the engine they used to travel through normal space. The crossbar of the *H* connected the two cylinders, and right in the middle of the crossbar was the clear dome that covered the bridge. If you looked out the front of the dome, you could see the two cylinders of the Egypt jutting forward like twin gun barrels. Gun barrels the size of skyscrapers.

It was the SS Egypt, and she was ready for battle. The crew wasn't floating around in some weak civilian shuttle. If there was going to be a code red, *this* was the ship to be on.

Mason decided Instructor Bazell had no idea what she was talking about: the facts didn't make him feel any better. Probably because his sister had crossed the bridge and now stood in front of him.

Susan grabbed Mason's arm and dragged him out from behind the console. Every eye was on him until Captain Renner barked, "I want a shield test while the Tremist are out of range!"

Susan pulled Mason off the bridge and across a hallway, to a

set of stairs that took them one level down. A sign on the wall pointed the way left to general crew, and right to engineering.

When Mason looked up, his sister's eyes were shiny with tears and coffee. "I'm sorry, Susan. I really didn't mean it."

"What did you mean?" she said in a calm way that was worse than yelling. Susan pulled him left, to general crew. The lights in the ceiling flickered red every few seconds, painting the walls in blood. Almost like the Egypt was showing the crew what would happen if they failed her.

"I thought you'd fall when no one was watching. I didn't know there'd be a code yellow."

His sister was all Mason had, and if he played a trick on her it should be one they could both laugh at, not one at her expense. That's how he'd intended the Great Chair Collapse of 2800 to play out, anyway. Susan resembled their mother, and he their father; her hair and eyes were so dark they were almost black, while Mason's hair was sandy, and his eyes were a blue as bright as the Egypt's engine at full thrust.

"How could you know?" she said. "That was really mean, either way. You're lucky I like my coffee lukewarm."

Mason didn't think it was possible, but he felt even worse: here she was, wasting her time dragging Mason to the brig. She should've been on the bridge, mind focused on the incoming Tremist.

An alarm began blaring up and down the hallway, in time with the red lights.

The captain's voice broke over the shipwide com: "All personnel who aren't at their stations, find a place to buckle up."

Mason felt his sister tense through the grip she had on his arm.

Susan never showed fear, never got rattled. Mason didn't know what the alarm meant specifically, but if it gave Susan a physical reaction, he guessed *his* reaction should be to start crying.

"We have to stick together, you know?" Susan said over the

noise. She led him to an elevator, which would drop them another two levels to the brig. "So I want you to think about what you did."

"Susie—" Mason began. He never called her that. Not ever.

Susan winked but didn't smile. "Don't worry about me. I'll be fine."

Mason didn't say anything. In a few hours, Susan would forgive him with a smile, and maybe get him back in some way. Not because she wanted to, but because she knew evening the score would let Mason know there were no hard feelings.

The lights suddenly flashed quicker—a code red 2, which meant direct contact within thirty seconds. Mason's heart was thumping so hard it hurt. He wanted to be anywhere else, anywhere he could help. *Punish me. Put me on a gun.* His greatest fear was happening now: he was waiting to be blown into space, with no way to put his training to use.

"We have to hurry," she said. She released his arm and they broke into a jog. "You'll be safe in the brig."

"Safe?"

"It's a code red, dummy. This area is secure," his sister said matter-of-factly.

"We'll blast them out of the sky?" He said it almost like a question, like a little kid asking big sis for reassurance. Mason clenched his jaw against the shame—A1 last years weren't supposed to need comfort.

His sister smiled then, but it was the saddest one he ever saw. It made Mason feel cold all over, especially when she didn't immediately assure him they would win. They just kept running.

The brig was empty, like it usually was, because soldiers on a ship run by Captain Renner knew better than to break the rules. There was a small unoccupied desk for the jailer, and a long narrow aisle that had three cramped cells to the right and left. Susan jabbed a quick series of numbers into the keypad, and the first plastic door on the right slid into the ceiling. Mason started toward it, but Susan grabbed his arm and spun him around, face-to-face. She was only a few inches taller than him now that he was 5.5 feet.

"I didn't mean to make you feel bad," she said. That wasn't like her. She'd usually let him worry for at least a little bit.

"Is this really bad?" Mason held his breath. "You can tell me."

"Just listen. Stay here, and wait till someone gets you." She put both hands on his shoulders and squeezed a little too hard. "You'll be safe here."

"I don't want to be safe." Though he was afraid he really *did* want to be safe, that he was glad to dodge his first combat situation. "Susan, what's happening?"

Mason felt the ship accelerating, a deep hum that traveled from the floor and up his legs. He felt himself leaning right and braced his arm against the wall.

Susan kissed his forehead and shoved him into the cell before the plastic wall slid back into place. She gave him one final look before running out the door—the way she'd looked at him six years ago. They had been on a shuttle, and Mason was getting dropped off for his first day at Academy I. Susan was going a little farther, to start her fourth year at Academy II. She had been sixteen, and she looked at Mason like she would never see him again. Mason hadn't thought much about it then; he was too excited for the Academy. But now it left him chilly and anxious. His palms were sweaty.

There were no benches in the cell, so Mason stood.

That changed a few seconds later, when an explosion rocked the Egypt and shut off all the lights.

Chapter Two

The backup lighting turned on a few seconds later, but it was dim, cold light. Mason staggered to his feet, prodding the fast-growing lump above his ear. A new alarm blared down the hallway and the Egypt tilted under his feet, pulling hard to the right. He was ready this time, catching himself with both hands.

Now that he was "safe," Mason realized it wasn't what he wanted, which relieved him a little: who wants to find out they're a coward? Instead of safe, he felt trapped, and waiting for death would be worse than going out there to face it head-on. Alongside the other cadets, if he could. Adrenaline was pumping through him hotly, tamping down fear and replacing it with a feeling soldiers called *Things are happening!* So *this* was what his instructors had been talking about the entire time. After months of boredom and inaction, a sudden threat was almost welcome to a soldier. Almost.

Mason tapped the skin below his left ear to activate the tiny com unit implanted underneath. It was standard-issue and every member of the Earth Space Command was required to have one. He thought about Tom as he tapped it, and a channel opened to him. Tom knew computers better than most cadets ready to leave Academy II, better than most general crew, too, and Mason couldn't deny it. He was the last person Mason wanted to call, but the only one who could get him out.

A soft buzz in his ear meant the com was ringing on the other end; Mason bit his lip, wondering if Tom would pick up. Tom would come if only to scold him about the dangers of tampering with equipment. He was technically a year younger than Mason at twelve, but they were really born a few weeks apart in the same hospital. While Mason's parents had died in the First Attack, Tom's hadn't. His mom was captain of the Egypt, and his dad was a vice admiral at the space station Olympus.

Mason and Tom didn't really talk much if they didn't have to. Tom seemed to think he knew everything because his mom was captain. Mason disagreed. The problem was, the other cadets didn't. *I should've called Merrin,* Mason thought as the com kept buzzing. Merrin might've had trouble getting him out, but she'd be happy to see him, at least.

Mason had met Tom and the other cadets years before at Academy I, but most of them were in different units, so Mason didn't really know them, not well. Now that Mason was graduating from Academy I, he'd been selected to log his spacetime on the SS Egypt, along with seventeen other cadets from different years. Two weeks earlier, the Egypt had left the space station Olympus with eighteen cadets on board, for a routine patrol that would end with the cadets getting off for a new year at Academy I. Or, in the case of Mason, Merrin, Tom, Jeremy, and Stellan: Academy II. The big show, where training got real.

There was an incident ten days ago, when Tom lost a foot race because Mason turned on the magnetic flooring on Tom's side of the hallway. The cadets had been bored in the middle of the night, and Jeremy had mentioned how he was a good sprinter, and Tom had said something like, "I bet I'm faster."

To which Jeremy replied, "I bet you're really not."

During the race, Mason used a wall console to activate the magnets, not really knowing why he was doing it. The magnets were only activated for a split second, so it appeared like Tom fell on his own. *Humility in the face of glory.*

Tom stood up and looked at his skinned palms, then pressed them against his uniform. "Who did that?"

Mason raised his hand. "I did."

Tom nodded while frowning, like he was considering this information. Then he stalked forward and executed a perfect straight punch to Mason's chin. Tom had clearly been paying attention during hand-to-hand combat training. Mason took the hit because he knew everyone was watching, and then he swung his elbow into Tom's cheek.

Then Jeremy knocked their heads together, hard enough to make them stop. "You're gonna get *all* of us in trouble," he said.

"Whatever," Tom said. "Mason's only here because his parents died and they had nowhere to put him."

A few cadets gasped. Mason felt something cold open inside his chest.

Tom took a breath, looking stunned.

"I didn't mean that," he said. "Hey, I didn't mean that. I'm just mad."

Mason nodded and fought hard to keep his eyes on Tom's face, not on the floor.

"Shake hands," Jeremy commanded.

They did, firmly. Mason knew what it was like to say things you didn't mean, to just have them vomit out, and then feel that crushing ache when you realized you could never pull them back.

It was only two years ago when Susan was visiting him at Academy I and trying to offer some helpful advice that Mason said, "You're not Mom. Okay?" Susan's eyes had glazed shiny with tears, and Mason had apologized a thousand times after, but his words still stuck in his lungs when he remembered them.

Anyway, Tom hadn't acted so superior after their little brawl and handshake. Wasn't that the kind of progress the ESC was constantly striving for?

.   .   .

⫸ Tom finally picked up after nine buzzes and said, "Cadet Stark," in a flat tone that seemed to convey all the annoyance anyone had ever felt toward Mason. Or anyone else in the galaxy.

"Tom, hi. I need you to come break me out of the brig. Please." He became light on his feet as the Egypt began to dive, until the synthetic gravity compensated. If they were diving, did that mean they were trying to escape the Tremist? Why not just drop a cross gate and disappear? Then again, there was nothing to stop the Tremist from following them right through the gate, if they were already close. And clearly they were close.

"What are you doing in the *brig*?" Tom's voice crackled with impatience, like Mason had caught him in the middle of some huge project that required all of his attention.

"My sister put me here."

"Then I think it's best for you to remain there until your sister or my mother comes to free you. I highly doubt they gave you com privileges."

Typical Tom response. Mason wanted to punch the wall. Six days into their journey, Mason and a few others talked about raiding one of the kitchens because the cook had made actual cake that day, with real eggs and sugar. Tom had looked bored, then recited the codes they'd be violating from memory. No one got cake. Then, as if to prove he wasn't all about codes and rules, Tom went to get the cake himself. Anticipating this reversal, Mason got to the cake first. It earned him a few points with the other cadets. But Mason still couldn't tell if Tom was a stuck-up, icy cadet or someone who might be relaxed and capable of fun.

He should've known better than to ask for help from the captain's son.

"Please, Tom. What if we're boarded? The Tremist would kill me on the spot." He said it to help convince Tom, but it was also probably true. Unless the Tremist thought a young cadet was a useful hostage, they'd turn Mason into a tasty snack. The thought of seeing one in the flesh gave Mason a chill that was a cross between excitement and pure, sick fear. He wondered what they looked like under their mirror-masks. It was rumored the ESC knew exactly what they looked like, but wouldn't share with anyone. It didn't seem fair to hide an enemy that, if the rumors were true, wanted to drink Mason's blood, or shapeshift into a werewolf, or whatever the current rumor was.

"They'd *kill* me, Tom." Mason injected a little more desperation into his voice.

Tom said, "The Egypt has only two access ports, both heavily guard—"

"*Tom.*"

"Only if you call me Thomas. I keep asking you to do that." His words were garbled by shouting cadets: *Look look! The claws are unfolding! No, pull up a different angle!* Mason's desire to see what was going on outside was now a physical itch.

"Fine, *Thomas*! Get me out of here!"

The link went dead. Mason wondered if Tom wasn't really coming, but it only took about thirty seconds for him to show up with Merrin Solace. Just the sight of her made his stomach unclench: Merrin was his only true friend, the only cadet onboard he really knew.

He'd known her since before Academy I. Mason had stowed away on a cruiser to join the academy a full year early; as a member of a military family, he'd been guaranteed a spot. Staying on Earth for regular schooling was not an option: Mason wanted to learn about space, to be a soldier like his sister. Susan had already graduated to Academy II, and Mason was sick of waiting for his turn. But his plan didn't work: the ESC sent him home, with a meaningless fine, since he didn't have any parents to pay. But Mason and Merrin promised to meet up next year, when they started Academy I for real. And they did. They'd been friends ever since.

Merrin was . . . different. Her long hair was dyed violet to match her eyes, and her skin was so pale sometimes Mason could see the veins underneath. Her blood looked as purple as her eyes and hair, if the light was right. Mason had asked her once if she was sick, if that's why her blood was a different color and her skin was so clear.

Her eyes had gotten all wide. Then her brow furrowed. *"No,"* she said. "Are you?" And that was the end of it.

Tom, on the other hand, looked more like Susan's brother than Mason did. He had dark hair and eyes, and always seemed to be studying whatever he was looking at. It made him look, in Mason's opinion, untrustworthy. Calculating, like his mother. Not a bad quality in an ESC soldier, really, so Mason couldn't blame him for it. But he'd never seen Tom smile, or at least one that wasn't a smirk.

Mason nodded at them. "Hi guys." The backup lighting dimmed suddenly, then returned to normal. Somewhere in the ship, metal whined, reminding Mason of the whale song recordings he heard while studying Earth animals.

"So . . . you're in jail," Merrin said. "I knew it was only a matter of time."

"Surely that's not the most interesting thing happening right now," Mason replied.

Tom ignored them, heading straight for the port in the wall, where he plugged in his personal dataslate.

"I expect the full story later," Merrin said, shaking her head. But she looked amused. The ship was under attack, but Merrin Solace was amused.

Tom cleared his throat. "Let it be known I am only breaking ESC regulation because your life may be in danger."

"Let it be known," Mason echoed, legs tingling with the desire to move move move. He imagined the Tremist making it on board, so he could try out some of the hand-to-hand combat moves he learned in his fifth and sixth year. As soon as he thought it, he took it back: if Tremist made it onto the Egypt, it would mean they were losing.

The ship had been accelerating over the last minute, but now it was slowing, and Mason had to brace himself against the left wall. Tom started to fall but Merrin's hand darted out and grabbed Tom's sleeve, holding him in place.

"Thank you, Merrin," he said. Not *Cadet Solace,* Mason noted. *When did they become friends?*

"No problem." She turned away to watch up and down the corridor.

Tom pressed a few symbols on the dataslate and the door to Mason's cell slid open. He stepped out and clapped Tom on the shoulder. Tom looked at Mason's hand like it was covered in barf.

"Thanks," Mason said, removing his hand.

"You owe me."

"I know it."

They left the brig, and Mason breathed as a free cadet. Something smelled off with the recycled air. It tasted burnt.

"Let's get back to the others," Merrin suggested. They rounded a corner and passed the opening to the crossbar, the long narrow section that connected the two halves of the Egypt.

"Cadets, hold up!" Commander Lockwood was jogging toward them. Mason froze as ordered, a reflex. So did the others.

"Now you've got both of us in trouble, Stark," Merrin whispered from the corner of her mouth.

Lockwood was a thin, wiry man, mostly bald, with a ring of jet-black hair around his head. Mason thought he looked like an eagle, with a hooked nose that resembled a beak, and fierce eyes that saw everything. But despite his intense appearance, Commander Lockwood at least made eye contact when he passed cadets in a hallway, unlike some of the officers who didn't seem to know they existed.

Tom tensed up, shifting from foot to foot.

"Don't look guilty," Mason whispered.

Lockwood stopped a few feet away and narrowed his eyes.

"Where were you going? Stark, you're supposed to be in the brig."

"We were—" Tom began.

Mason cut him off with, "I tricked them into helping me out. I didn't want to stay there."

Lockwood sighed. "Yes, well, that's not important now. Come with me."

He marched down the hallway toward the front of the ship, and the three cadets followed. A door opened to Mason's right, and three crewmen wearing battle vests and carrying rifles burst through the doorway and ran in the opposite direction, toward the crossbar and the bridge.

The rifles were a red flag. The soldiers planned to be shooting *inside* the Egypt, or were at least preparing to.

Tom opened his mouth to ask a question, even got so far as to making a *W* sound, but Lockwood barked, "Keep walking!"

"What can you tell us, Commander?" Mason said quickly, as they began to jog.

"Nothing at the moment," Lockwood said. Mason noticed the top of his head was shiny with sweat, and it caught the red lights whenever they flashed. "I need you cadets to do something special for me, can you do that?"

"Yes, sir," they replied in unison. Responding to an order was the easy part; it was the following through that Mason was still working on.

Lockwood didn't tell them about the *something special* right away. First they rode an elevator down two levels, then stepped onto a long, narrow moving walkway that sped them forward at twenty miles per hour. It took them all the way to the left front of the ship.

The segments of track slowed until they were able to easily step off next to the cadet quarters. The door opened automatically, and Lockwood basically shoved them inside. The cadets lived in an officer's room that had been converted just for them:

all the luxury furniture had been replaced with stacks of bunk beds. Until the Egypt returned to Mars to drop them off at Academy I and II, it was home.

Since it was an officer's quarters, there was a floor-to-ceiling window at the front, giving an unobstructed view of space. Unobstructed except for the fifteen other cadets, ages seven to thirteen, who were crammed against the glass. They were all staring at something outside, and the window was tall enough to see what it was.

The Tremist ship was speeding toward them, bright and alive against the complete blackness of space.

Merrin inhaled softly, and Tom's dataslate slipped from his fingers. Mason could only stare. It was a Hawk, a ship he'd studied inside and out at Academy I. Big, open, swooping wings connected to a narrow main body, coming to a point at the front, sharp as a hawk's beak. The wings were twelve levels thick. The engines underneath even resembled curved talons tucked under the body. Right now they were bristling with purple energy, sending the Tremist ship into a circle above the Egypt. Like a bird circling her prey.

"Don't be afraid," Lockwood said behind them, quietly. "The Egypt can take care of herself."

"I'm not," Mason said at once. A lie, but only half of one—he was also in awe. He'd seen vids of the Hawk, of course, but to see one alive, pulsing with energy, moving effortlessly, making the Egypt look as clumsy as a bathtub in a lake . . . that was something else. It was smaller than the Egypt, but the swooping wings and weapon clusters under those wings more than made up for it in menace.

Tom asked, "Commander? Why aren't we firing?"

Lockwood was about to say something—his lip twitched, and he made a noise in his throat—the start of a word—and Mason knew right away that whatever it was, it would be a lie.

Merrin gave Mason a look: *He's definitely about to lie.* Merrin was better than anyone at reading people, but Mason had slowly been learning from her over the years.

Instead of lying, Lockwood just shouted, "Cadets! Attention!"

The cadets spun around and scrambled to stand at attention in front of their bunks, forming two lines on either side, seven on the left and eight on the right. Mason, Merrin, and Tom joined them.

"At ease," Lockwood said. The cadets relaxed but didn't move. "I don't want any of you to worry. Captain Renner believes the Tremist ship is trying to make contact. I wish I could say more, but you're to remain here until an officer comes to retrieve you. Is that understood?"

"Yes, Commander," the cadets replied in unison. Mason had his fingers crossed, realizing Lockwood's "special" task was just to stay put. Next to him, Merrin tapped his thigh with her own crossed fingers. "Good. The cadet who disobeys this order will do time in the brig, and possibly be sent back a year in school."

With that he left the room, manually shutting the door behind him.

They all heard the lock thunk down inside the door.

"Son of *Zeus*," one cadet mumbled, a curse that could earn him five laps up and down the ship. Another cadet laughed, and a few seconds later they were all pressed against the window again, searching for the Hawk.

Though the Hawk was no longer visible from this angle, an eerie light filled the room, painting the cadets' faces a ghastly green.

It was growing brighter.

Mason knew what it was instantly: the weapon clusters under the wings were charging up. A few of the cadets who paid attention that day in class seemed to know it too—they were backing away, hands automatically reaching for things to hold on to.

"Brace—!" Mason began to yell. He barely had time to grab hold of a bunk before the Egypt made a terrible sound somewhere between a roar and a scream, and the floor dropped out from under them.

Chapter Three

 The war came about, as Mason was taught, because two races were really bad at taking care of what they had.

What both races wanted was a planet: Nori-Blue. It was one of three known planets in the galaxy that humans could thrive on. Nori-Blue was covered in forests from pole to pole, with a single ocean smaller than the Atlantic back home. The temperature ranged from fifty to seventy degrees year round, because the planet's axis was the same tilt at all times. Some creatures lived on the surface, but none like humans, and certainly none like the Tremist. Which meant it was the perfect place for humans to go now that the population was over eighteen billion: Earth was simply running out of places to put people, even with the dozens of minor settlements in the galaxy.

Nori-Blue had rivers and lakes and edible plants that grew fruits more delicious than any on Earth. The air was nineteen percent oxygen, perfectly breathable. It was only slightly smaller than Earth, too, so the gravity was suitable. It was rumored that you could jump twice as high on Nori-Blue, but Mason did the calculations in his advanced math class, and it would only be around one and a half times.

Nori-Blue was perfect for a race that had outgrown its own planet.

Which is exactly what the Tremist had done, too.

Not much was known about them. First Contact with the Tremist happened in 2640, exactly one hundred and sixty years ago. An earlier version of the Hawk was seen circling an ESC installation in Neptune's high atmosphere—the first ever sighting of an alien spacecraft. The installation sent a radio message to the Hawk, just a simple ping, in the hopes of saying, *Hey! We see you! Want to chat?* The Hawk didn't want to chat: it sped away and disappeared.

Then came Second Contact four years later, when a trio of Hawks bombed Academy I on Mars. Thirty-eight cadets were exposed to the atmosphere and died.

Immediately the Tremist were designated hostile.

But one hundred years passed before they were seen again.

It wasn't until Nori-Blue, or Earth II as some called it, was discovered. The ESC built a massive cross gate in the low altitude of this new planet. People would step through a gate on Earth and onto a platform a mile above the ground on Nori-Blue. A city was being built on the surface, near the water. They called it Hope. It would run on energies that wouldn't adversely affect the planet and atmosphere. Humans were going to do it right this time.

In 2740, when the gate neared completion, the Tremist arrived in 286 separate ships. Hope was destroyed, literally. The gate was vaporized, along with any hope of a colony. The SS Norway received a call, and on the viewscreen the crew watched as a Tremist with shimmering plate armor and a mirrored mask for a face decreed that Nori-Blue belonged to them now.

Tell everyone, the Tremist said.

The Norway crew sent out its final transmission to Earth, and then it was destroyed too.

After that, there was only war.

In the following decades, after countless skirmishes and attacks, just one Hawk was ever captured. The ESC bristled with excitement at the possibility of finally learning about their enemy's biology. But the Tremist aboard had all died in some kind of superheated explosion, which destroyed all their DNA, which destroyed any hope of finding out what they looked like under all that armor.

Susan wouldn't give Mason any more details. She scared him one night by saying she could be court-martialed just for sharing that with him. The *official* story was that the Hawk had been empty all along.

The Tremist homeworld was a mystery too, although ESC scientists claimed it had to be similar to ours, simply because the Tremist had evolved in much the same way as humans. They had two legs and two arms, and presumably two eyes behind their oval masks.

But who really knew?

➤ The Egypt was under attack; there was no doubt of that now. The quarters suddenly seemed too small, with too many bodies breathing too much air. Mason hadn't left the brig just to become a prisoner here.

Clearly the commander didn't mean they had to stay there no matter what—that would be dangerous. Clearly the commander would've added this stipulation, had he not been so distracted.

Mason was the first to his feet. Merrin was sitting on the floor, holding her palm to a purple bruise on her forehead. "I *really* wish they'd stop knocking us down," she said.

She jumped to her feet before Mason could help her, and together they jogged for the door. It was sealed, as expected. Next to the door was a computer terminal that linked to the ship's core. He could access it and sift through menus to find a way to override the door lock, but Tom was faster and Mason knew it.

Merrin put a hand on his shoulder. "Remember what Lockwood said. You don't want to miss a year of school."

"I know," Mason said. Yet that didn't seem to matter now.

The younger cadets stood up and looked out the window again with minimal words. Tom joined them at the door, followed by Jeremy and Stellan. Stellan was the tallest of them, and bone thin, with hollow cheeks, like he never got enough food at mealtime. His hair was so blond it was almost white. He was from a country called Sweden (the SS Sweden, another ESC ship in the same class as the Egypt, was destroyed by a Tremist Isolator two months ago) and Mason wondered if all people from Sweden looked like him. At Academy I, people looked different, but they seldom talked about what country their ancestors came from. Millions of miles away, it didn't seem to matter.

After Mason's fight with Tom, Stellan took Mason aside and sprayed some anti-bio fluid on Mason's split lip to keep it from getting infected. Mason squinted at the sharp taste, and Stellan said, "Next time, maybe use your words." Mason figured that Stellan's willowy frame meant he used words more than fists when it came to cadet disagreements. Mason admired that; everyone had to play to their strengths.

At the time, Mason had wanted to point out that Tom had swung first, but he only said, "I'll try."

Jeremy was short and muscular and liked to brag he could grow a beard. Mason had watched him do it over two weeks at A1, but it had grown in patches and an instructor eventually made him shave it.

Mason and Jeremy were bound by a shared fight. Two years earlier, Mason was scrapping with four cadets from Academy II. They'd been picking on a thin-limbed A1 second year in the gym, pushing him around, shoving him against the equipment. Mason said to the group, "Stop." Just once, because he wanted to give them a chance.

They didn't stop. The biggest kid just backhanded the second year casually and knocked him to the floor. So Mason waded in, fists and legs lashing out at their weak spots, but it was still four on one. Jeremy showed up just in time, and their combined fury drove the four cadets away with injured knees and black eyes.

Afterward, as they were helping the younger cadet to his feet, Jeremy said, "It didn't look fair." He shook both their hands, then left.

The cadet told Mason, "You shouldn't have done that. Thank you and all, but you embarrassed them. They're only going to come back at me harder. I would've taken the beating."

The idea baffled Mason; he hadn't stopped to consider that his help wasn't welcome.

Mason told this to Jeremy in a message, and the two of them visited the four attackers in their quarters later that night, to make sure they knew what would happen if they retaliated against the second year. As they were leaving, Jeremy said, "That's neat. We didn't even have to hit them."

"Sometimes you can talk to people," Mason said. "Or maybe they're just afraid of us."

Mason only saw Jeremy whenever units would join together for group exercises, but they seemed to automatically remain friends.

"You try the door?" Jeremy asked now, cracking his knuckles.

"Uh, Commander Lockwood just told us to stay here, like five seconds ago," Stellan said. He was hovering behind Jeremy and Tom, wringing his hands nervously.

"Relax," Mason said. "We are. We just want to make sure we can get out if we need to. You know, in case the Tremist show up."

Merrin smiled with one side of her mouth. "I almost believe that."

"Quiet!" Tom hissed. His fingers danced over the terminal. The screen flickered for a second, then flashed red. "It won't let me out. Which is actually okay, since this means we can follow orders for once."

"See what the ship is doing," Mason said, peering over Tom's shoulder.

"Is that an order, Captain Stark?" Tom said. He raised an eyebrow.

"You know you want to see too, so don't give me a hard time."

Apparently Tom did want to see: he pulled up a new screen, which showed a top-down image of the Egypt. A small red dot at the very front of the port cylinder showed their location. On the far side, the starboard side, near the engineering level, it showed the Tremist ship connected to the Egypt's main hatch.

"That's not good," Jeremy said. "We should be out there cracking Tremist skulls."

"No, we shouldn't," Tom said. "We should follow orders like *actual* soldiers."

Mason put a hand on Jeremy's shoulder. "Relax, Jer. We don't have weapons, and we don't know where the defenders are deploying—"

"We'd get in the way," Tom said, less delicately.

"So we just wait here?" Merrin asked, hands on her hips. "What if they overtake the ship?"

"Waiting here is a fantastic idea," Stellan said. He didn't look afraid, exactly; Stellan just respected authority. He figured the fastest way to captaining his own ship was to follow orders, always. Mason could respect that. He tried to be the same way, but sometimes following orders was nearly impossible for him. Or rather, he found himself questioning every order, and he found the dumb ones hard to follow. He would ask himself *Why?* and if there wasn't an obvious reason, he had to grit his teeth while carrying the order out. Why clean the urinals in the boys' bathroom? They were just cleaned twelve hours earlier by another cadet and were still utterly spotless. It was discipline, Mason knew—they were trying to teach him discipline. But there had to be another way.

Once, Instructor White caught Mason laughing at a joke in class, and then ordered Mason to stand in one spot for six hours, out in the hallway with his hands held above his head, so everyone passing would know why he was out there. He made it thirty minutes before he left, because it was stupid. It was a stupid order. But his refusal had only gotten him sent to Headmaster Oleg, where he got another order to reorganize the headmaster's library of actual paper books. Mason took hundreds of the covers off and put them on other books, so no cover matched what was within the pages. That was three years ago, and still the headmaster never sent for him. And Mason never expected him to—the books had been so thick with dust it was clear they were never read. Stupid orders.

Small blue dots began to flash on the Egypt's starboard side, right next to where the Tremist Hawk was connected.

"What does that mean?" Merrin said. They were all crowded around the screen.

Tom visibly paled and his mouth fell open. "They're firing weapons inside the ship."

"Attention all crew," someone said over the shipwide com. "All able hands report to an armory. The Tremist have boarded."

No one spoke for a few seconds. Mason's mind spun, and his heart hammered: having the enemy inside the ship was so different than fighting them on a planet's surface. Here there was metal surrounding them, like a cage. No place to run. And if one of the energy weapons somehow melted through the hull . . .

"We're able hands," Jeremy said. "That's us."

"We're trained," Mason added immediately, hoping the idea would catch.

Stellan stepped back. "Lockwood's orders supersede any thoughts of heroism you might have. You saw his face—he was dead serious."

Tom nodded absently. "You are correct. I'm not even going to cite the code on that one."

Mason clenched his teeth. There had to be some loophole in the codebook, some way they could avoid a punishment that severe.

"Can you tell who's winning?" Jeremy asked quietly, which meant he was frustrated. Jeremy only got quiet when things weren't going like he wanted.

Tom shook his head. "No, but I'm sure we're winning. Engineering is a maze of levels and corridors that only *we* know. We have the advantage."

He tapped the screen again and a video expanded from one of the security cameras. It showed a catwalk with steam rising in the background, red lights flickering on the metal. It was the coolant level on the engineering deck, where the Egypt's pumps were located. Susan showed him once, pointing out the massive tubes that ran parallel to the engine, keeping it from melting the rest of the ship.

Right in the center of the screen, two Tremist crouched in their magnificent armor. It resembled plate, like knights in ancient Europe once wore, but this was not dull hammered metal—the surface of the Tremist armor shone weirdly, like oil, shifting colors depending on the angle. Sometimes it had a near-mirror finish, close to silver, but most often it shifted between purple and black. The Tremist were as tall and wide as men, with arms and legs like men, with helmets that covered their whole heads. The helmets were the worst part—the face was an oval, the shape a normal face would be, but it was a pristine mirror, so to look at a Tremist head-on, it was said, you saw yourself. The last thing you saw was the terror on your face. A perfect image of your head, floating atop a Tremist body.

Watching them kneel, Mason knew they weren't men underneath. They were too graceful, slinking like wolves. The plates seemed forged and fitted for each individual Tremist. The slim suits of armor moved with ease, as if aided by delicate machinery underneath.

"The Tremist have—" the same voice said on the shipwide com, but was cut off.

The five last year cadets watched as both Tremist raised long, elegant rifles to their shoulders and fired thin green lasers at some of the Egypt's crew, who hid behind a huge tank hanging off the opposite catwalk. Mason could see the intense beams of light reflected in the nearest Tremist's mirror-face. Captain Renner was there, along with two other crewmen, firing back with short bursts of condensed, spherical light from their photon cannons. The camera flared as the white and green light flew back and forth.

Mason figured out what the Tremist were trying to do before everyone else; immediately he searched the screen for Susan.

The lasers cut into the catwalk in front of the crew's feet, slicing through the metal in a flurry of white sparks. They weren't shooting at Captain Renner anymore, or the defenders who fought with her.

The Tremist were shooting at the metal supports holding the structure up. The catwalk melted and buckled under the onslaught, and finally collapsed, falling ten levels to the bottom of the Egypt.

Chapter Four

Tom didn't say anything, just stared at the screen where the catwalk used to be. The catwalk where his mom had been standing. It was impossible to survive the drop. The camera didn't move; it just showed the now-empty space on the coolant level; it showed the Tremist glide past the damaged area like ghosts, until they disappeared from the screen.

Tom had something in common with Mason now. A few seconds ago, he hadn't. Mason was suddenly glad his parents died when they did, when he was young, before he could form the kind of memories that would last forever. Mason mostly had glimpses and sensations, a smell here or there, the feeling of his mother's soft hands picking him up. The sound of his father's laugh.

It was 2792, eight years ago, when a lone Tremist ship entered Earth's atmosphere and dropped a single bomb on the Earth Space Command headquarters in Midtown Manhattan. His parents were in the middle of giving a presentation to the admirals, trying to convince them it was possible to attain peace with the Tremist.

The bomb vaporized everything inside its blast radius. The ground was turned into a sheet of glass.

Mason had been four miles away, at primer school. The hair on his arms stood up as static electricity washed over the city. He didn't know for another five minutes that a bomb had been dropped, didn't know for another four hours that his parents were gone.

At the time, Mason was two years shy of Academy I, but at age fourteen, Susan was already in her second year of Academy II. They let her take a shuttle from Mars to the Upper East Side of Manhattan. Mason met her at the memorial service, seeing her for the first time in a year. Mason remembered her as looking older than she did now. She had bags under her eyes and her mouth never moved except to talk.

The ceremony took place on the street, next to the land that once held the headquarters. The Tremist bomb hadn't made a crater—instead it simply erased everything inside a circle the size of a few blocks. Where Mason stood, buildings were perfectly cross-sectioned, their walls sheered away, leaving them structurally intact until work crews could rebuild them. At the edge of the blast radius, he could see couches and tables and wirings and plumbing and insulation in the buildings. He could see a quarter mile away, where the glassy ground ended and the split-open buildings began again. His parents had died somewhere in there, broken down into their separate atoms.

He couldn't even think about it. His mind would turn fuzzy and gray, and he would think, *How can they just be atoms?*

Mason wanted to hate the Tremist then, and he felt guilty that he didn't. He only felt confused.

Why had they attacked? he asked himself. *For what?*

Susan had held his sweaty hand within hers, and Mason watched the president say words he didn't hear. After, Susan kneeled in front of him and said, "I don't know what they're going to do with you. I'm too young to be your guardian, and they won't let me stop my studies."

"I don't want you to stop your studies," Mason replied. He wanted his sister to become a soldier, to fight the enemy. The Tremist had made the war personal. Now he felt something. He was almost shaking. He couldn't wait until he was old enough to join her. Not because he wanted to fight or kill anyone, but because his parents defended Earth. It was what they believed in. Serving the human race in the protection of others was the highest calling, his mother had said once, when Mason asked, "What's a good job?"

For two years after that Mason was in a group foster home full of ESC orphans. He watched television and exercised like his father had, sometimes sneaking out to run on the streets at night. After one year he was through waiting: he stowed away on a ship, met Merrin, and was sent home for the last painful and lonely year. But then he returned to Academy I. There he learned how to fight, and fight well.

➤ The room was quiet. The other cadets hadn't noticed; they were busy against the window, craning their necks for a view outside.

Mason slowly reached out to put a hand on Tom's shoulder, but hesitated, stopping an inch away. He was almost afraid to touch Tom, who was as motionless as glass. Mason worried he might break the same way.

Merrin wasn't afraid; she pulled Tom into a hug, which Tom allowed for three whole seconds before gently breaking free. His eyes were bloodshot and he was taking deep, slow breaths. "I'm going to kill those alien *freaks*," he growled in a voice Mason had never heard before.

Finally, they agreed on something. The rage Tom was feeling would burn away all his fear, and it was always better to be angry than afraid.

"Then let's get out of here." Mason pointed toward the terminal.

Tom's fingers danced over the screen, opening a complex series of menus meant to be accessed *only* by the Egypt's programmers and engineers. The cadets were technically locked in, but if Tom could convince the computer it was an emergency, the door would open. Mason considered just asking Elizabeth, the ship's AI, to let them out, but she had ears everywhere, and probably knew they were supposed to stay put.

As he watched Tom type in strange commands, Mason thought about Susan. She was out there, maybe fighting, maybe dead. There would be a new captain now, automatically promoted, but Mason wasn't sure who. Commander Lockwood, maybe.

Half of the screen cycled through various cameras and showed Tremist pouring into the ship, marching along the catwalks in neat columns, laser rifles—what some ESC soldiers called *talons*—held at the ready. Tom closed the video feeds and replaced them with more menus.

"Let's be smart about this," Stellan said. "We go out there weaponless, they're just going to kill us or take us as hostages."

"No one is stopping me from going out there," Tom said, wiping his nose with his sleeve. "I dare you to try."

Mason wouldn't try. He'd be at Tom's side. If they weren't quite friends, at least they had a common enemy.

Merrin had been pinching the bridge of her nose, something she did when thinking hard. She lowered her hand suddenly, and her eyes were clear and focused. "I'm going too. We'll find weapons. If we can help in any way, the punishment will be worth it. If we lose . . . well . . . it won't matter."

That made perfect sense. And so it was decided. Tom gave her a grateful nod, then pretended to scratch his face so he could wipe away a tear.

Mason said, "Jeremy and Stellan, I need you guys to stay here and watch the rest of the cadets."

"No way!" Jeremy gave him a look like Mason had just suggested they all step through the nearest air lock into outer space.

"Who's going to protect them?" He winked at Stellan. "Could Stellan do it all by himself?"

Jeremy thought about that for two whole seconds. "I, uh, see your point."

Stellan smiled secretly, not taking offense, Mason knew.

Mason leaned in and whispered directly into Jeremy's ear. "If we don't make it back, or it looks like we're losing, get everyone to an escape shuttle. Okay?"

Mason pulled back, and Jeremy nodded grimly. He would get it done.

The computer beeped at Tom, who actually growled.

Merrin said, "Let's be smart. Where is the nearest armory?"

"Two levels down, six hundred feet aft of our position," Tom said at once.

"We arm ourselves, then figure out how to help," Mason said.

"Great plan, did you come up with that all on your own?" Tom asked, not taking his eyes off the screen. Mason had to force his mouth to stay closed; Tom was allowed to be angry and snide in the wake of his mother's death, as long as he kept it together.

Merrin tapped her foot next to the console; now that they had a plan, Mason knew she'd be itching to move. "How close, Thomas?" she asked.

"A few more seconds."

Mason nodded toward the younger cadets near the window, and Jeremy and Stellan took that as their cue to begin babysitting. The younger cadets didn't seem frightened; they were all jostling for position even though the Tremist ship was hidden on the other side of the Egypt. Mason didn't know whether they were brave or stupid. In fact, he didn't know if *he* was brave or stupid. The smart thing, the thing his sister would want him to do, was to stay put. To wait until a soldier came for them.

But waiting could bring Tremist instead of soldiers.

The ship groaned around them, and Mason felt the floor rotate under him: the ship was turning. The stars spun sideways until a bright blue sun appeared not so very far away.

"Almost there," Tom said. Sweat rolled down his face, and maybe some tears, too. Merrin kept shifting from foot to foot, lower lip between her teeth. Tom typed in another command and the words UNLOCK and LOCK popped on the screen. He jabbed the UNLOCK with his finger and the door went *plink!* "There!"

Mason grabbed the door and slid it open.

The three of them stepped into the hallway and crouched, making themselves smaller targets. The backup lighting was dim; panels flickered white and red in the ceiling. Mason's eyes darted through the gloom, searching for immediate danger. He expected screams but it was quiet, save the omnipresent whisper of the ship. Where the cadet quarters were alive with bodies and hushed voices, this felt like stepping into a tomb.

Go back, a voice inside him whispered. *You'll get in the way, you're not a real soldier, you're not safe out here, where monsters roam the halls.*

He clenched his jaw, grinding the thoughts under his molars.

To the left, the corridor ended at an elevator. To the right, the corridor ended at a sharp left turn. It would lead them back toward the crossbar, and to the bridge.

From around the crossbar corner, Mason heard feet pounding on the carpeted floor. "Fall back!" someone shouted. "Fall—" The voice cut off as a beam of green light etched the wall at the turn. The talon beam rose and fell, cutting off screams. The weapon buzzed like a thousand angry hornets, yet Mason could still hear bodies hitting the floor.

To run from the enemy was only cowardice when you had a fighting chance: the lesson echoed now in his brain, but hearing those screams made it difficult to retreat. *Be smart,* he told himself.

Merrin tugged his sleeve toward the elevator. "Move it!"

Mason began to move, but Susan's voice boomed through the ship: "This is Captain Susan Stark."

Despite the danger of being out in the open, Mason smiled.

Susan was alive. There was no pain in her voice; she wasn't injured. His little prank hadn't ruined her concentration after all.

Her microphone clicked again. "All crew—"

Susan's voice was cut off by the too-familiar buzz of a talon.

Chapter Five

Mason froze, waiting for his sister's voice to come back. Death was something they talked about at the Academy, but talk was talk, and this felt like a bucket of cold water to the face. A second passed, and then another, and she did not speak again, and Mason was paralyzed, remembering what it was like to see Captain Renner fall. *This is how Tom felt,* he thought.

Susan wouldn't leave him; she knew she was all Mason had left. Without her he was just a person, not a brother. Without her, he didn't mean anything to anybody, except Merrin, of course, but that was different. Susan was the only family he had left, and he would do whatever he could to help her.

Merrin grabbed his hand and gently pulled, then tugged when it was clear Mason wasn't moving.

"C'mon," she whispered. "She's okay. I'm sure they just knocked out the com."

Mason wanted to move, but it felt like he was going to throw up. He could taste it in the back of his mouth, the burn of acid and fear, and he didn't know how to make it go away. Susan had told him about a trick once, but something she only used rarely. Sometimes, if she was afraid, she'd take all her fear and gather it up and turn it into anger. Anger didn't paralyze the way fear did. It was the opposite of being helpless. But it was dangerous too, because you could end up being angry all the time.

Mason got angry.

He let it flow through him, didn't bother trying to temper it with logic or reason. He could feel it scouring the weakness from him, giving him the strength he would need to keep going.

Tom waited for them in the elevator, holding it open with his arm. "Get in!" he hissed.

Just as the talon stopped cutting into the wall.

"Shh, quiet," a man's voice said from down the corridor. "Listen." But Mason knew there could be no men left; the chuffing sounds the P-cannons made had faded to silence. So who had spoke? It didn't matter: facing the Tremist unarmed would help no one. Mason and Merrin padded toward the elevator as quietly as they could. Now he wanted to run, but their footsteps would give away their presence.

Then the ship's computer, Elizabeth, said, "Cadet Renner, please stop blocking the elevator door."

Mason and Merrin jumped into the elevator and spun in time to see three Tremist charge around the corner. They were at full sprint, faster than he thought men could move. Their plate armor shimmered wetly, shifting between purple and black, catching the sterile light of the spaceship and making it alien. Mason saw his own face in the flat mirrored surface that was the leading Tremist's faceplate.

Tom had moved his arm, but the door was still open. They were only thirty feet away now.

"Shut the door!" Mason yelled, pressing himself against the wall.

"Thank you," Elizabeth replied airily, and the door began to shut.

The three Tremist paused when they realized they wouldn't make it in time, and then lifted the talons to their shoulders. The soldier part of Mason's brain, the part that didn't get afraid, noted the angle at which the Tremist held their weapons, how, in the next second, each beam would slice through them at the breastbone.

The door sealed; Mason dragged Merrin and Tom to the floor as the talons' green beams crisscrossed through the door and heated the air above them until it was crackling. Then the car descended, giving the illusion of the beams rising up through the door until they disappeared through the ceiling.

The air was hot and baked and smelled like electricity.

The door opened on the next level down, into a corridor identical to the one they just left. Tom had his dataslate plugged into a port on the elevator. "Erasing our destination level . . . now! Bought us a few minutes."

Merrin took the pad out of his hand. Her fingers danced over the screen until it flashed red. "There—the elevator is frozen."

Tom scrunched his nose. "How did you . . . ?"

Mason was already out of the elevator, straining to hear anything over the background noise. It was quiet, and the ship didn't feel like it was moving anymore. They walked down the hall and passed through a doorway on the right, to a parallel corridor that would take them to one of the armories. Mason hoped his weapons training would serve him: *Weapons and Tactics* was one of his best classes. It was time to see how all that practice translated in a real live combat situation. A simple instruction came to his mind: *Relax, breathe, aim.*

The whole left side of the ship was made up of these corridors stacked atop each other, with rooms crammed in between them. A number on the wall showed this was level six. Level two held the theater. Levels four and five held the gym. Most of it was crew quarters, though: the Egypt was equipped for battle, but it was also the ship you took when you wanted to move a lot of ESC troops from one place to another. Though she was only packed with a couple hundred crew at the moment, the Egypt had room for two thousand.

They passed an adjacent, empty corridor, and Mason heard the faraway buzz of talons. Orders were being shouted. The battle was on. Once he had a gun, he could fight his way to the bridge and . . . Susan was still alive. She had to be, and he'd save her.

The armory was up ahead; the door was open. Crisp white light flickered from within.

It was quiet and still. Mason held up a hand, and they slowed their approach, making their footsteps silent on the carpet. He smelled burnt metal and something that reminded him of Steak Tuesday in the galley. The smell of charred meat. His stomach churned.

Tom was too dazed for caution, and he muscled past Mason's outstretched arm and stepped inside, no hesitation, almost like he didn't care about whatever danger lay within. So of course Mason and Merrin were right behind him.

The armory was destroyed. The walls, floor, and ceiling were once panels that gave off soft white light. Now they were cracked and sputtering. Now ESC soldiers littered the floor, eight of them, just lying there, smoke still rising from their uniforms. The walls, once lined with weapons of every kind, were mostly bare. The weapons were scattered over the floor, destroyed.

Tom spit on the ground and bent over, like he was about to throw up. Merrin put her hands over her mouth. Mason wanted to do the same things they were doing, but he recalled his sister's voice as it was cut off, and he didn't. Instead, he crouched and began going through the weapons, looking for one that was functional. They couldn't all be broken. The nearest armories were sub-armories—small caches hidden in the walls—and Mason doubted even Tom could access them.

"What are you doing here?" a man said behind them, softly. Mason spun around, almost tripping over one of the bodies.

Ensign Michael, a portly recruit not much older than twenty, stood in the doorway, frowning at them. Mason remembered him from the crew meet-and-greet when the Egypt left port two weeks earlier. He had two black eyes and a patch of burned skin on his neck.

"I know for a fact you're not supposed to be roaming the halls," he said, so calmly Mason wondered if he was in shock.

"We're last years," Mason said. "My sister—" He was about to say his sister was captain now, and he was going to help her no matter what, but that would've sounded terrible with Tom standing right next to him. "We need weapons."

Ensign Michael nodded and entered the armory, stepping carefully over the fallen soldiers; Mason hadn't quite looked at them yet, and he didn't plan to. Ensign Michael unlocked one of the still-glowing panels on the wall and swung it open. There were more weapons inside, unscathed.

"Hand P-cannons," he said, pulling out three handheld photon cannons that resembled ancient handguns, back when humans made their weapons out of explosive powder and projectiles. The plastic barrels glowed, a swirling mixture within that shifted between green, white, blue, and yellow. "They pack a punch. But promise me that if I give them to you, you'll hide and use them for defense only. We should have these Tremist dogs cleaned up shortly." His voice was watery and he was sweating through his suit. The black fabric was stained darker under his armpits and around his neck.

Mason hoped he was right, but he didn't see anyone around to help carry out that threat. They were on their own.

"Promise me," Ensign Michael said again.

"We promise," Tom said. The lie came so easily that Mason wondered if Tom had a lot of practice.

"Good. Now go hide." He looked down at the floor. "I have to take care of this."

Mason took his P-cannon and left with a nod to Ensign Michael. He needed to find his sister. Now. Tom and Merrin followed him, turning on their P-cannons. The handheld devices whined to life then quieted. Mason could feel the heat of it in his hand. The trigger was touch-sensitive, so pressing harder would create a more powerful energy burst. He planned on squeezing as hard as he could.

They passed windows on the way back, but they only showed more dark space. It was impossible to see the Tremist ship from this angle. Mason was heading toward the bridge, since that was the most logical place to find his sister. Merrin and Tom seemed on board, since they didn't ask where he was leading them. This part of the ship was quiet, but he could hear shouts from many corridors away and the constant background hum of weapons. The air moved hard, briefly, ruffling his hair; an energy weapon had probably cut through the Egypt's hull, creating a hole that sucked at the atmosphere until the auto-sealer could plug it. They'd been told on day one not to panic if there was a stiff and sudden breeze.

In the elevator, Merrin stepped to the front. "I should go first. I'm the best with a P-cannon," she said. "Last year I won the competition."

That was true, but Mason had come in second by 1.5 points, and he figured they were about equal in skill. The night before the contest he hadn't slept well because David Schatz, the cadet who slept in the bunk above him, was snoring loud enough to vibrate the water in the glass Mason had on his shelf. He wanted to go first, but if she truly was a better shot, it wouldn't make sense.

"We move fast," Mason said. "Once we're in there, take out your targets as quickly as you can. Don't hesitate." It wasn't much as far as plans went, but Mason didn't know what to do besides assaulting the bridge while they had surprise on their side.

"Worry about yourself," Tom said.

The door opened on the corridor that allowed access to the bridge, the same one Susan had dragged him across not so long ago. The first doorway to the bridge was just twenty feet away, across the hall to the left. The angle was too deep to see inside.

Mason held his breath, listening. He heard a man's voice inside the bridge, too faint for any details. No way to tell how many Tremist there were, and how many ESC.

Merrin stepped into the corridor first, but Mason stayed with her; they could go together. He reached the opposite wall first, and pressed himself to it, then inched closer to the door. The man spoke again: "Who is captain here?"

"I am," Susan said.

Mason peered around the corner. . . .

And saw his sister, face bruised, on her knees, along with a few other officers he'd seen earlier on the bridge.

His sister's eye, the one that wasn't swollen, found him peeking around the doorway, and the sadness and defeat he saw in it was enough to steal the resolve from the strongest ESC soldier.

But that wasn't what made his blood freeze.

Standing among the Tremist, talon at the ready, was the Tremist King himself.

Chapter Six

Of the Tremist King, Mason only knew that he wore a long black cape, and that his oval mask was not mirrored like the others', but rather a perfect black. Like staring into a black hole. His armor wasn't the standard shimmery purple-black, either, but dark red, like he'd been dipped in blood and left to dry. An image of him had circulated through the ESC with a kill-on-sight order. There was a rumor he once boarded the SS Italy and killed every crew member with his bare hands. When Mason was a first year, an older cadet told him the king liked to eat human skin to become stronger, but Mason hadn't believed him. Human skin probably wasn't any more nutritious than anything else.

And now here the king was, in the flesh, or whatever Tremist were made of underneath their suits. Mason ducked back quickly before the king saw him.

"What do you see?" Tom whispered, almost too quiet to hear. The three of them were crouched in the corridor, out in the open.

Mason shook his head. A choice lay before him. If he could kill the king, that might change the entire war. Like cutting the head off a snake. Yet better soldiers than him had tried and failed over the years. Would the element of surprise be enough to win out? The rest of the Tremist would certainly kill Mason right away, but wouldn't that be worth it?

In the ESC they always talked about self-sacrifice for Earth's cause, but he'd never thought about what that actually meant until now. Susan had told him once that bravery was when you wanted to pee your pants, but you kept fighting. You did the right thing, no matter how much your hands shook.

Mason could do that. He could try. Peering around the corner again, he saw no one had moved. The king had turned his back, showing his cape.

Merrin and Tom leaned around the corner above him, so if anyone looked, they'd see three heads stacked together. When they resumed crouching, Merrin and Tom were doing their best impressions of statues, wide-eyed like gargoyles.

The king! Tom mouthed.

"Here's the plan," Mason whispered. "You run back to our room and get the other cadets to the escape shuttles."

"You're not coming?" Merrin said a little too loudly, before clapping a hand over her mouth, which also made too much noise.

Mason winced, but there were no pounding footsteps heading for them; he was thankful for the continual background thrum all ESC ships made while powered up.

"It doesn't make sense for all of us to get captured." He didn't add *or killed*.

Merrin shook her head. "We all go, or we all stay."

Then, from the bridge, Mason heard someone say, "Captain, I've given you three minutes to confess."

"I don't care how much time you give me," Susan said.

"Tell me where the weapon was moved to." It was the king; Mason was sure. His voice came out oddly cold and crisp, like a computer-generated voice; it was possible he spoke the Tremist language, and the mask was translating. Two seconds later, Mason realized what the king had actually said. Judging from that sentence alone, the king was looking for a weapon aboard the Egypt. What kind of weapon, Mason had no clue.

"Kiss antimatter," Susan said.

"If you make me search, I will scatter your atoms in such a way that it will be like you never existed at all."

The same way his parents had died. *No.*

Mason started to move for the door, but Merrin grabbed him. She was strong, her grip like a vise. "Wait," she hissed in his ear.

"I don't know what you're talking about," Susan said to the king.

Mason heard something smack, and Susan moaned in pain. He wanted to move so badly, but the timing had to be right. He would know when. He had to know when.

Slowly, Mason edged around the corner once more and saw the king looming over his sister. He spoke English perfectly, with a slight accent that sounded British. The Tremist language was supposed to be guttural, and sounded like Ancient German.

"Very well," the king replied, sounding resigned. "I will ask the new captain after you're dead."

Mason watched the king lift his talon and point it at Susan's face.

Chapter Seven

Mason didn't think about what to do next; it was automatic. He stepped onto the bridge and raised his P-cannon with both hands. He was vaguely aware of the other Tremist on the ship, standing behind the other kneeling ESC soldiers.

They didn't matter. All Mason saw was the king.

Relax, breathe, aim.

He squeezed the trigger, and a ball of hot yellow light burst from the gun and slammed into the center of the king's cape, setting it smoking.

The king didn't even flinch, just slowly turned his head until Mason could see into the deep nothingness of his face. There were no visible eyes, yet Mason could *feel* them on his skin.

He fired again; this time the ball crackled greenish as it hissed across the bridge. The king sidestepped and the ball dissipated on the clear dome harmlessly.

"And what is this?" the king said, sounding amused.

He lowered the talon from Susan, who screamed, "MASON, RUN!"

Mason fired again with shaking hands, trying his best to hit center mass. The king seemed to know exactly when Mason was about to fire, though, and he simply leaned to the side. The ball shot past the king's arm, almost hitting a Tremist behind him.

Before Mason could fire again, two yellowish balls flew in from the doorway. Merrin and Tom were there, P-cannons raised. They both hit the king squarely, but he took no notice. His red armor seemed to drink in the energy; remnants of it crackled down his arms and legs before fading.

The Tremist King was gigantic, easily seven feet tall, but lithe, like one of the huge cats you could once find in Earth's jungles. The king reached over his shoulder and grabbed his cape, then tore it from his back and waved it in front of him. It caught fire as two more photon balls smashed into it.

"Grab them!" the king shouted.

Two Tremist rushed in from the sides and ripped the guns from Tom and Merrin, then pushed them to the floor.

Mason fired again, and the king dodged, dancing a step closer. The P-cannon was getting hot now. He waited, letting it cool so the next projectile came at max power. He felt the vibration building against his palm: *Almost there.*

"This must be what passes for a soldier of the Earth Space Command," the king observed, taking another stride. He turned his head toward Merrin and Tom, as they tried to struggle to their feet. Which was difficult, considering they both had a Tremist boot on their backs.

So Mason fired a final time . . .

And hit the king right between the eyes. The black oval swallowed the ball whole, not even a spark or a sputter. Much like the previous shots, it seemed to do no harm. The armor was still thirsty. Then the king was behind Mason, twisting the P-cannon away and crushing it in his palm. The gun released a small puff of blue-green light that left tattoos on Mason's retinas. The smell of the king's burnt suit filled the room, like hot, charred plastic and scorched metal. He grabbed Mason's shoulder and dug his fingers in until spears of pain shot down Mason's arm.

The hot tip of the talon nestled against Mason's ear. "Captain," the king said smoothly behind him. "Unless you want to be responsible for the death of this young cadet, tell me where the weapon is. You have three seconds."

"It's in the main storage bay," Susan said at once. "I can take you." Her lower lip trembled slightly, but then she made her face a hard mask. A tear slipped from the corner of her eye, the only tear Mason had seen her make since the memorial for the victims of the First Attack.

Mason wanted to die. Whatever the weapon was, Susan only told the king because he'd been stupid enough to get caught. The blame was on him now.

He tried to imagine what the weapon was, but that would be like trying to guess how many stars were in a quadrant. Pointless. But it made him feel cold just the same. It was important enough for the Tremist King to want it, to actually *be here*. It was important enough for Susan to make no mention of it. It was important enough to just be called *weapon*, instead of a proper name.

And now Susan was handing it over. Mason could not let that happen, no matter what.

Every eye was on the king, and Mason couldn't help himself. He twisted out of the king's grasp and looked up at his face. Up close, he expected to see damage to the mask, some scorching or smoke, but there was nothing. He couldn't tell if it was a black surface, or just a hole. Mason expected the king to grab him again, but the king paid him no attention.

He was staring at Merrin Solace.

Like he knew her.

"I don't believe it," the king said.

Chapter Eight

"Let her up," the king commanded.

The Tremist did as they were told, but stayed close. Merrin brushed herself off and glared at the king, her violet eyes blazing with defiance. There was no fear in her, it seemed, just anger. But her shoulders were bunched, and Mason knew why: having not one but two Tremist behind you, that close . . . He imagined the nearest one ripping his mirror-mask off and burying a mouthful of needle teeth into Merrin's neck.

"Your name," the king said.

"Merrin Solace, what's yours?" She tried to sound cool, but the shake in her voice was noticeable. Mason knew it was more from adrenaline, not fear.

A cadet had mistaken her tears of frustration for fear once during a hand-to-hand exercise, and called her out in front of the whole class. *Merrin Solace is a crybaby!* he said. *The Ghoul is afraid!* "Ghoul" was the nickname she was given for the near translucence of her skin. Merrin asked to be partnered with him for the rest of the day. He was very sorry by the end of it.

The king exhaled; through his mask it sounded raspy. This close, it was impossible not to wonder what the mask hid.

"Could someone let me up?" Tom said quietly.

To the Tremist behind her, the king said, "Take her to my quarters. Post a guard of three. Go." Merrin's mouth fell open. Her eyes locked on Mason's, widening, and she almost cried for help. Mason saw her about to do it: she started to form a word with her lips; a brief sound escaped her throat. But she cut it off by shutting her mouth. The two Tremist yanked her backward out of the doorway. Mason almost said *No!* out loud, almost charged forward, but he swallowed the word and kept still. His training kept him rooted, even though his body yearned to fight. It would do no good to get killed now, when he might have the chance to help Merrin and the rest of the crew later on. Why in the galaxy would the king want *Merrin* not just on his ship, but in his quarters?

"Really, I would like to stand now," Tom said.

To Susan, the king said, "Captain, lead my men to the weapon." He patted Mason on the shoulder. "Or this one dies first." The king picked up his fallen cape and reattached it at the shoulders, even though it had a gaping hole. *Men*, he had called the Tremist—*Lead my men.* They were no men. Mason wanted to spit on the ground at the idea. Men didn't threaten an unarmed soldier.

"Understood," Susan said as the Tremist hauled her to her feet.

Tom, making sure no one was about to stick a boot on his back again, slowly stood up too.

Susan left the bridge with her escort, just behind Merrin and hers, but not before she made eye contact with Mason a final time. The look said, *Don't do anything stupider than you've already done.*

The king stepped around Mason and kneeled in front of Tom, so their faces were about level. He set his talon on the floor next to his feet, showing his entire back to Mason. Clearly, Mason wasn't a threat. "And you must be the former captain's son. I regret the captain died before she could give me authorization to the Egypt's main computer. You will help me with that." He clapped Tom on his upper arms and gave them a squeeze. "And you won't make me hurt you. Let's skip the denials—I know all crew are required to have authorization in an emergency." His voice was perfectly pleasant. As if he was just asking Tom how to operate one of the quick-heaters in the galley.

The part of Mason that was a soldier before everything else, the part he hoped would grow as he got older, was thinking tactically. With the three Tremist escorting his sister to the storage bay, and two escorting Merrin, that left two Tremist on the bridge, plus the king himself. Mason knew he couldn't do anything to the king with his hands alone, but maybe he could scoop up the king's talon in time and fire another shot while the king was distracted. Maybe the talon would cut through his armor in a way the P-cannons could not.

"I could help you with that," Tom said. "But first you have to go to hell."

The king actually laughed, but it sounded like a cough through his mask. "Very good, very good. You are a brave soldier."

Mason inched closer. The talon rested next to the king's knee. Was he fast enough? Was it the right move? He tried to imagine what Susan would do. Being brave was one thing, but making a decision that would put others in harm was another. It was a question of what would happen if he *failed*.

He needed a distraction to even the odds, one big enough for him to escape with Tom.

It was too late to save Merrin: she was already off the bridge. To the king's own quarters, where who knew what would happen to her. Susan needed his help too, but she had a better chance of taking care of herself. And she would tell him to rescue Merrin first, because that's who she was.

Tom didn't laugh with the king. "You killed my mother."

The king nodded solemnly. "I've killed many mothers." The talon was still on the ground. Three feet away, at most. Mason visualized the steps he would make. Taking one big step, then grabbing the talon with both hands, then stepping away again before the king could whirl and overpower him. He would have to point it at the king and press the right button, hoping the weapon wasn't locked to a specific user the way some ESC guns were. Firing the talon might kill him on the spot.

Then Mason remembered what the king had said: in the event of a Tremist boarding, the ship was designed to unlock itself to all crew. Normally Mason wouldn't have access to any settings on the ship, but he was hoping that was no longer true. Captain Renner would have activated that function right away, and even if she hadn't, Elizabeth was programmed to do it herself if she deemed the danger level high enough. Mason thought this was about as dangerous as it got.

Now was the time. The king himself had given them an escape route.

"Elizabeth," Mason said.

There was a chirp, followed by Elizabeth saying, "Yes, Cadet Stark?"

The king looked over his shoulder lazily, like a lion amused that his prey had wandered close enough for an easy kill.

"Lights out," Mason said.

Every light on the bridge winked out, blanketing them in darkness. The stars were suddenly bright and vivid above them, mixed with the purple streaks of an ancient nebula. Each of the consoles still flickered brightly, but otherwise Mason was hidden.

Until the air lit up with crisscrossing green beams from multiple talons.

"The shaft!" Tom shouted at Mason.

Mason was already heading there. Every room in the Egypt had two points of entry, in case the normal doorway led to an area that was damaged or without oxygen. If the hallway outside the bridge was damaged and the crew couldn't escape that way, a shaft on the bridge would allow them to drop down to a level that was still sealed.

"Stop them!" the king snarled in the darkness. Mason heard his cape flutter, and imagined the king's steel-hard fingers digging into him again. The shaft was in the back of the bridge, near the exit. Mason tried to visualize the room when it was brightly lit, but he felt disoriented, almost dizzy with the rush of adrenaline. He had to make it the whole way through the darkness, with enemies all around.

"Open the shaft, Elizabeth!" Mason shouted, running in what he hoped was the right direction.

A hole of light opened in the floor, and Mason dived through headfirst. He heard Tom hit the tube behind him and yell some command to Elizabeth. The shaft dropped straight down for a level, then curved and dumped them into one of many corridors that connected the two halves of the ship. They slid out right onto a moving track, like the one outside the cadet quarters.

Mason hit the track hard, somersaulting as it scrolled under him, as if he'd jumped from a moving object. Tom landed even harder a few paces back; Mason heard the wind get knocked out of him, and when he looked, Tom was on his back, arms and legs flailing like a flipped turtle. Once he got his bearings, Mason saw that the walkway was taking them to engineering, not crew. The starboard side of the ship, where Merrin *and* Susan would be. Perfect.

"Did it seal behind us?" Mason said breathlessly. He stood up and grabbed onto the moving railing as the wind rushed in his ears, then grabbed Tom's hand to pull him upright.

Tom was grinning. "Not at the top. But I asked Elizabeth to shut the bottom, so whoever came after us is trapped inside the tube." That made Mason smile too.

The windows blurred by too fast for Mason to see much out of, but they were nearing the end, where the segmented parts of the track would slow them until they could comfortably jog into engineering.

"We need to take the track back to crew," Tom said, nodding at the parallel track moving in the opposite direction. "My mother told me that if anything happened . . ." He swallowed.

"To her. And the crew. If something happened, it was my responsibility to see the cadets safely off ship."

If anything happened. Was that a precaution, or had she expected something to happen?

Mason didn't say, *But your mother isn't captain anymore.*

"They're fine," Mason said.

"I don't *care* if they're fine—they're still on the ship, so they won't be for long. And how can you say that when you really have no clue, do you?"

The track began to slow.

"I don't. But we can't let my sister give them the weapon. That's the most important thing. You know it too."

"What was the king talking about?" Tom said. "What weapon? The Egypt is supposed to be a diplomatic vessel between rival ESC bases. She wouldn't be carrying something just called *the weapon.*"

"So you don't know everything, do you?" Mason couldn't help but grin.

Tom said nothing, just raised an eyebrow.

"You know what's more important," Mason said. "Be logical, that's what you're good at. We're going after the weapon."

The walkway slowed until they were able to step onto solid ground near the main engineering access. The door was a full level tall, almost ten feet, and opening it would be a little obvious. Mason hustled to an access port that, once opened, would give them entry to the crawl-paths through the walls, where engineers wiggled through to work on hard-to-reach electrical equipment.

"What if I refuse?" Tom said. "What if I go back to the others by myself?"

Mason tried to think of the right thing to say here. After six years of trying to manipulate his instructors, Mason knew he could accomplish more with a subtle touch. So he said, "I can't do this without you," to appeal to Tom's pride.

Tom took a deep breath. "Then I guess I can't let you get killed."

Mason nodded his thanks, but was smiling on the inside. Stellan had told him to use his words, and now he did, and it was more effective than violence. The idea wasn't something the ESC focused on very much in their cadet program.

Tom knelt by the wall and opened the access port with his multi-tool, a thin metal rod with a tip that could be morphed into any number of shapes, if one had the skill. *Molecular Manipulation and Practical Applications* was not the most popular class at Academy I.

"Where are you planning to go?" Tom asked, when they were already in the darkness of a tunnel. It smelled like hot electronic equipment. Mason could feel the heat battle with the chill of space, this close to the hull.

"I don't know. We need a plan."

"I only followed you because I thought you *had* a plan."

"You can do whatever you want. But I can't just sit around while the Tremist take the Egypt from us. I think your mom would've agreed with me."

Tom was silent for two full seconds. "Don't tell me what my mom would do. Just . . . don't."

Tom didn't speak again, but it was clear he thought it was stupid to wander aimlessly. And maybe it was. But Mason had to get Merrin back. They had a deal, a pact made when they were only in their first year. If either of them were captured, the other would stop at nothing to get them back. They had sealed it with a very formal handshake, and then Mason had forgotten about it over the years. He had figured they wouldn't come across the Tremist for many, many years, until after they were no longer cadets. It was an idea he now found ridiculous and naïve—they were on an ESC warship during wartime, after all, and had been on many before.

Now their pact was vivid, burning like a star in his mind.

Merrin was a prisoner of war now, no question. Mason had a mind to reverse that.

The tunnel led to a small door that Mason opened from the inside. He cracked it slightly, then peered through the gap. He could see a sliver of the engineering deck, probably level five. The tunnel would dump them onto one of the platforms that ringed the deck, all of them looking down on the ten levels of vertical pipes used to pump coolant and water through the ship. Railings stopped someone from accidentally falling over, but nothing kept someone from jumping on their own. Mason didn't know where it ended; he'd never been to the bottom.

Mason cracked the door wider and the hinge began to squeal. It probably hadn't been oiled since the Egypt joined the fleet however many years ago.

It was loud enough to make the Tremist standing guard on the platform turn around.

Chapter Nine

Mason didn't hesitate. His training was far from complete, but one of the first things Academy I does is scrub the instinct to freeze out of a cadet. He burst from the tunnel while the Tremist was still turning around. Mason wasn't small for his age, but the Tremist was somewhere around six feet.

Which meant his center of gravity was higher than Mason's.

Mason hit the Tremist in the legs, running at a full charge. He didn't know if he was trying to throw the Tremist over the railing or not; all he knew was that giving the Tremist time to point his talon would end things quickly. The Tremist stumbled away, arms flailing, but couldn't catch his balance. He fell backward and his head cracked on the railing, hard enough to make the metal tubing hum. Then he collapsed in a heap and didn't move.

"Did you kill him?" Tom said, wide-eyed. It wasn't clear if he was happy about it or horrified. Mason felt the same way: the rush of victory and the clench of regret, after doing an action that could never be reversed.

Mason scanned the area quickly; they were alone. The level was lit with orangish light that reflected off the forest of tubing in front of them. He knelt next to the Tremist and felt his neck for a pulse, wondering if he'd find it in the same place as a human. He felt nothing through the suit, so he grabbed the bottom of the Tremist's mask.

"Wait!" Tom said.

"What?"

"I don't know. You're really going to pull his mask off?"

"Should I not?"

"What if it's booby-trapped? What if it electrocutes you or releases poisonous gas or something?"

Mason did his best to ignore the images those words provided. "Only one way to find out."

"That's stupid reasoning, even for you."

"Maybe." Mason didn't let the comment bother him; he counted himself lucky Tom hadn't left him at the crossbar. "But we need to know if he's alive. Do you have a better way to find out?"

Tom didn't say anything. Mason's heart pounded. Sure, there were stories that the Tremist were lizards underneath, or pale-skinned space ghosts that filled the suits with their ectoplasmic energy, or even cyborg descendants from a long-dead alien race. A shivering cadet once told him the ESC's scientists had discovered that Tremist teeth were as long as an index finger, and hollow, containing venom that made you pee before filling your lungs with blood. It was hard to know which of those would be worse: lizards, ghosts, or cyborgs. Space vampyres, some of the soldiers called them, but it was never clear if the name was just to frighten new cadets, or because the Tremist actually drank blood.

Only one way to find out, Mason told himself again.

He peeled the mask off.

Mason's breath caught in his throat. *I don't believe it.*

Next to him, Tom gasped and said, "How . . . ?"

The Tremist weren't so different from humans. In fact, the face Mason saw was familiar. He didn't dare let himself feel relief: it could be some kind of trick, some outer layer of skin that hid a monster underneath.

The Tremist was gaunt, with hollow cheeks, almost like the skin was pasted onto the skull. But it was still a human face. Eyes, a nose, a mouth. Violet, flowing hair was tucked under the suit.

And the skin, so pale. Eyes the same color as the hair, Mason saw when he pushed a lid up with his thumb. Purplish, violet, whatever you wanted to call it.

Mason put his hand to the Tremist's mouth and felt moist breaths against his palm. He touched the skin gingerly, feeling bones in the shape of a skull underneath, a solid forehead, cheekbones. He held his breath and pinched the Tremist's lower lip. Peeled it down a little. Saw a normal-sized tooth underneath. Just a tooth. Not even that sharp.

It could be a trick! his training screamed. *Don't let your guard down.* But with each passing second, Mason believed more and more that the biology of this alien wasn't so different. If it had bones and skin and blood, it could be killed.

"Still alive," Mason said, slightly relieved. Killing the Tremist was one thing when he imagined them as monsters beneath their suits, but to find they had eyes and ears and noses . . . they looked too human.

"Are you seeing what I'm seeing?" Tom asked.

Mason knew exactly what Tom was talking about, had noticed the same thing right from the start, but wanted to ignore it. The idea made his stomach churn.

It was the violet hair and eyes, the semitranslucent skin.

"Merrin," Mason said shakily.

"It can't be possible," Tom said. "The Solace family is well known. Her mother is an ESC commander and her father is in charge of the Disease Control Agency on Earth *and* Mars. He stopped the plague on Mars and saved millions of lives."

"I'm not saying I believe it. It could be a coincidence." Mason could hear the hollowness of his words. He had a funny taste in the back of his throat, and the urge to seek cover.

Tom pointed at the Tremist's face. "But look."

The pale skin was like Merrin's too, laced with purplish veins. Mason had wondered about her skin for years, but Merrin never offered an explanation. Many cadets were extremely pale from the lack of sun. And he'd always assumed she dyed her hair—many people did back on Earth, and the ESC allowed it, believing individuality was an asset to a soldier.

What would it mean, if Merrin really was a Tremist? Would it matter?

No. You know her, Mason thought.

Tom kicked at the deck, making it ring softly. Mason didn't yell at him for making noise because he was too busy thinking of alternatives. "Could be a Tremist trick. I've heard they're shape-shifters."

"And I've heard they do magic," Tom mumbled. "You can't trust rumors."

Mason said nothing. The king had recognized Merrin, that had been plain. But perhaps he didn't recognize *her,* but rather what she *was.* The color of her hair and eyes was too much of a coincidence. It's not like she had dyed her hair and changed her eye pigmentation to mimic a Tremist—there wasn't an ESC member who knew what they looked like.

"I don't know if we should be doing this," Tom said, like he was talking to himself. "I think the most logical course would be to find an escape shuttle and cross to Olympus. We could try to get the fleet to cross back here."

"What happened to going back to the cadets?"

Tom sneered. "Be smart. What chance would a lone Hawk have against our might? As long as Elizabeth keeps them out of her core, the Egypt is staying in one place. I can even get the coordinates before we go."

He was right: they should try to escape. But Mason wasn't leaving. Not because he didn't want to, but because once they left it was possible the Egypt and her crew would never be heard from again.

Mason stood up straight. "That's not an option for me. By the time we tell someone and a rescue mission is approved, it'll be too late. The fleet will still have to assemble. You know that.

There might not even *be* any ships at Olympus. We can't risk losing the Egypt in the meantime. You can go, but I'm staying."

"I'm not a coward," Tom said. "And there are always ships at Olympus. Always at least two."

Mason just nodded. The ESC could be overcareful. If there weren't enough ships they might decide not to send any at all.

"What do we do with this one?" Tom asked, pointing at the Tremist with his foot.

Mason studied the Tremist's armored suit, taking in its size and shape, and an idea came to him.

"We use him," Mason said.

> Tom didn't have a problem with using the Tremist until Mason told him what he meant.

"No, no no. No. You're crazy. What if he wakes up?"

The Tremist was still knocked out, breathing steadily.

"Aim your cannon at him," Mason said, then muttered, "and don't shoot me on accident."

"What? I don't *have* my cannon. They took it."

Mason forced himself to keep his voice low. "Then use the talon!"

Tom picked up the talon and inspected it.

Mason began to remove the Tremist's suit. It felt like trying to remove an injured tiger from a trap: at any second, the Tremist could wake up, grab Mason, and heave him over the railing.

The suit came off in pieces. The arms and legs connected to the main torso piece. The metal felt cool and sturdy under his fingertips, not oily. The surfaces shifted under the lights, purple to black. Tom was pointing the talon at the Tremist's face, shaking, lips pressed into a thin white line.

"Hurry," Tom whispered. The arms and one leg were off. The Tremist wore a thinner suit of stretchy fabric underneath.

Mason worked on the last leg, keeping an eye on the Tremist's face for movement.

"You think this is the right thing to do?" Tom asked as Mason rolled the Tremist onto his stomach to work on the torso section. He was surprised Tom was asking him instead of just flat out disagreeing.

"I think someone has to figure out what's going on." He said it with more confidence than he felt.

"And it's going to be a last year cadet . . ." Tom said.

"Not too late to find a shuttle." That shut him up.

Once the Tremist was stripped of his outer suit, Mason grabbed his legs and pulled him into the access tunnel they had come through. Tom kept the talon on him the whole time, until Mason finished stuffing him inside. Then Tom locked the door using the small screen built into the wall, and enabled the locks on the first port they'd come through. When he woke up, the Tremist would be trapped in the dark tunnel.

"Can he damage the ship in there?" Mason asked while he tried putting the leg parts of the suit on. He knew the suit would be too large, but now he was worried it would be completely obvious.

Tom pulled up a schematic for the tunnel. "He can, but nothing that would really hurt us. There's no direct computer access in there. And no access to life support, I think."

"You *think*?"

"I think," Tom repeated.

Tom kept watch while Mason finished dressing. The torso piece was too big and hung on him funny. Mason was about to yank it all off and give up when the suit began to contract around him. He gasped, worried it was a defense mechanism designed to crush an unauthorized user. But then it stopped shrinking. Now it hugged him gently, the perfect size to fit his smaller frame. So that was how each Tremist's suit looked like it was tailored for them especially. He was still small for a Tremist, but he remembered seeing one on the bridge that was around his height. As long as he didn't draw attention to himself, it could work. He hoped.

Mason put the helmet on last, smelling some faint perfume

left over from the Tremist's hair. It adjusted in the back, the material—which was clearly not metal, despite all appearances—tightening until it fit snugly.

He opened his eyes and peered through the mirror-mask . . .

. . . And watched a heads-up display flicker to life, the same way the Egypt's bridge painted information on the clear dome's surface. Strange symbols scrolled in the lower right of his vision, a few of them flickering between two or three of the same symbol. Mason's vitals, perhaps. Tom appeared highlighted, with a little window next to him listing more symbols Mason had never seen before. The ESC had rough translations for a few inscriptions found inside the captured Hawk, but most of the Tremist language was not translated.

"What do you see?" Tom asked, raising an eyebrow.

"It has a heads-up display." In the top right corner of his vision, a circle pulsed once every second, showing the location of multiple white dots. Some of them were purple. He guessed the purple dots were other Tremist wearing armor, and the white ones were humans, but couldn't be sure. And straight ahead, a little window with an arrow pointed to the far right side of the ship, where Mason knew the Hawk was connected to the Egypt. It was like someone had dropped a flare he could see through the walls, the arrow appearing in three dimensions. Perfect.

When he looked down at his belt, his HUD showed grenades attached there, two separate kinds. He had three of each. That would come in handy, once he figured out what they were. They were definitely not fragmentation grenades: no one used those in an enclosed, pressurized space.

"I can't come with you," Tom said. "Obviously."

Mason nodded. "I know that. Thanks for your help. I know we don't always agree on stuff."

Tom shook his head. "I don't agree with this."

Mason stuck out his hand. Tom shook it briskly, though he didn't look directly at the mirror over Mason's face.

"I hope you . . ." Tom began.

"I hope so too," Mason said, his brief smile hidden by the mask.

"Just don't get killed," Tom added.

"Any other valuable advice?"

Tom actually laughed, and Mason did too, which was nice. Neither had laughed in a long time, and Mason figured it might be a while before they laughed again.

"Do you have a plan?" Mason said.

"Get back to the others safely," Tom replied. "From there, I don't know. It depends on what condition the port side of the ship is in. If we can get to the escape shuttles . . ." He looked at the deck.

Mason's throat tightened, but he said, "Don't hesitate. I'll find a way off if I have to."

"I know you will. Sorry about the lip."

Mason had almost forgotten about the punch Tom threw after Mason's magnet prank. It had been a solid punch. They hadn't spoken about it since Jeremy pulled them apart.

"Sorry about the eye," Mason replied.

With that, Tom Renner, son of former Captain Joy Renner, disappeared into a different access tunnel, locking the door behind him.

Mason let his gaze roam over the ship, as parts of it highlighted in his HUD. The white and purple dots glowed in the corner. He stretched his fingers and wished everything away, wished he were in the sparring room with his sister, learning a new move, or even in school, learning about the Martian Revolution. When his wishes didn't come true, he started toward the white and purple dots, pausing to pick up the talon.

Chapter Ten

The dots led Mason through a thousand feet of an engineering deck, past mazes of pipes that routed through the Egypt like roots of a tree. He couldn't help but worry that if *he* could see the dots, they could see him too, a lone dot moving toward them. Maybe this particular Tremist was not supposed to leave his post.

Mason stepped lightly, but his Tremist boots rang softly on the decks. He sweated inside the suit but refused to let fear control him, not with so many of the crew in a worse position than he was. Not with Merrin's and Susan's fate hanging by a thread. He was still free and alive, and a true ESC soldier would use that rather than hide.

After going through a narrow tunnel onto an adjacent deck, he entered the main storage bay. It was the biggest area of the ship, all twenty levels high, used to house smaller spacecraft, including the handful of Fox fighters that could be dispatched to protect the ship if her guns weren't enough. The big open space in the middle was for maneuvering, and the decks ringed that space, so a ship could fly in and land on its designated level around the perimeter, where it could be stored or repaired when needed. To Mason's right, the massive doors could open, and a force field would allow ships to come and go without losing atmospheric pressure.

This time it didn't house any spacecraft.

Now there was no open space for the ships to maneuver in. Every available inch of space was occupied by a single, massive cube of silvery metal. It appeared solid, but where in the galaxy could someone extract and sculpt a piece of metal that large? The bay was twenty levels tall, and the cube filled all of it, hiding the overhead lights from view, cloaking the perimeter levels in dim light.

This had to be the weapon. It had to be. He'd never seen anything like it and could not begin to understand what it was, or did.

When Mason looked at his HUD again, his heart skipped a beat: the dots were just on the other side of the bay now, heading toward the marker that showed where the Hawk was docked to the Egypt. Only the strange cube separated them. Mason went over the details of his disguise again, but it was hard to focus. His voice could give him away, if he was forced to speak. He was on the short side, and he moved like a human, without that animal grace the Tremist possessed; he didn't understand their technology; they might've seen he was an imposter the moment he put the armor on.

His pulse banged like Thor's hammer on metal, but he walked. One step at a time, around the left side of the cube where the perimeter deck continued. Values changed and scrolled on his HUD as the dots grew closer.

The dots began to move from left to right, where the cube ended at the "northwest" corner of the bay; whoever they were, they were walking down the tunnel that led to this area and would cross in front of him if he slowed. The cube cloaked the area with shadows. But stealth was not an option when they were probably seeing him on their HUDs too. So with sweat-soaked hands, he held the talon the way he'd seen other Tremist hold them, across his chest, tip angled up past his left shoulder.

The dots were so close now, finally entering the storage bay. And he saw that the dots represented very different things.

Some were Tremist—the purple dots—and some were captured ESC soldiers—the white dots.

One white dot was his sister.

One purple dot was the king.

➤ The king's pace became a stroll as they got closer. Everyone
stared at the cube, clearly dazzled by its size, which meant their
eyes were not on Mason, who kept walking toward them as if he
were on patrol. One Tremist made note of Mason's approach
with a nod.

The king put his hand on the cube, fingers splayed, and bowed
his head, as if he was listening to something. Mason knew a soldier should keep his eye on the enemy at all times, but it was
hard to keep his eyes off the cube too. The metal seemed to shim-
mer when it caught the light.

Mason was only about ten steps away now, close enough to
see the individual strands of hair on Susan's head, and he had no
idea what to do when he reached the group. Stop? Ask to join
them? Try to cut down only the bad guys with the talon?

Along with Susan and the king, three Tremist walked with
three high-level ESC officers in front of them. The officers' hands
were bound behind their backs, heads hanging forward. The
number of circles on the officers' collars gave them away, showing their value to the Tremist. Mason thought it was stupid to
show off how valuable of a prisoner you would make.

"I want the protocols for transporting it safely," the king said
to Susan, almost a whisper. "I want everything you have on it.
Now." He started to walk along the north side of the cube, and
Mason fell in step behind. He almost collapsed with relief: nothing had given him away so far.

The giddy feeling didn't last.

He still didn't know what he was going to do next.

"I don't have access to that," Susan said. She glanced at
Mason and her lip curled in derision. Mason wanted to scream

out that it was him, wanted to so badly that he had to press his lips together. The king turned away, showing his ruined cape. Mason couldn't help but wonder if his hair was violet beneath the bloodred suit, if his skin was as pale as Merrin's. If the veins stood out under his skin like tattoos.

"Who had access, in the event of the captain's death?" the king said.

"I don't know. Scumbag."

The king whirled, his hand rising, and backhanded Susan so hard she fell to one knee. A single drop of blood hit the deck. Her hair hung like a curtain, hiding her face. Mason's hands clenched on the talon, but he didn't make his move. Not yet. Not when the king's armor might just absorb the beam, like it had with the P-cannon. He had to be sure, even if his blood boiled while Susan rose shakily to her feet.

"Find out," the king said.

"So that's how you get things done in the Tremist world," Susan said.

The king looked like he was going to hit her again. His hand even twitched. But he just turned away and the group continued walking.

"I'll never help you," Susan said after another twenty paces. She didn't say it with venom, or defiance, just simply. It was a fact.

"We'll make you. And if you don't, I will make someone else. While you watch."

Susan didn't reply, but Mason saw her shoulders tense.

The group left the cube behind and entered a tunnel that led to the docking port. Mason's heart rate climbed steadily in his heads-up display—he was almost sure which symbols represented it, but didn't know what values they represented. It was a high number, whatever it was. Which was no good: he needed to keep it low to avoid twitchiness. Calm and steady was the way. Deep breath. No fear. After the short tunnel, they'd be on the Hawk. Enemy territory, from which there would be no easy escape.

Mason had to study the Hawk as a first year. It was the only Tremist model the ESC had ever captured and therefore the one they had the most details on. He'd gotten in trouble more than a few times his first year, so to make Susan proud he'd memorized the layout and gotten one of the highest scores on the exam. As a reward, Susan took him on a tour of the captured ship. A lucky thing for him now, because if each Hawk was identical he *should* remember where every compartment and every room was located. The biggest room near the bridge was thought to be the captain's personal chambers. He was hoping in this case it would be the king's. Still, the Hawk Mason had been on hadn't been crawling with the Tremist at the time. And he was under pressure now, which made him wonder if he was imagining the room locations wrong. He'd memorized it years ago—too long to trust anything but his eyes.

The king turned to one of his guards. "Once we break the seal, begin extraction. Don't wait for protocol. If we aren't on our way in ten minutes, each additional minute will cost you. Understand?"

"Yes, Your Grace," the Tremist replied, then handed his prisoner over to his neighbor before turning away.

Mason had to hurry. If they were opening the main storage bay to extract the enormous cube, the Hawk would have to break away so the storage bay doors could open. He'd be trapped on the enemy ship with Merrin and Susan. The cube was massive: there was no *way* it would fit anywhere on the Hawk. Which meant they would have to tow it, if that was even possible.

Two guards stood at the entrance to the Hawk, at the far end of the tunnel. Mason waited for them to call him out, to raise their talons, but they stared straight ahead, motionless. The group continued along, nearing the entrance, with the imposter—him—in the rear. Mason held his breath as he crossed the threshold onto the alien ship, stepping from the smooth, silvery metal of the Egypt to the rough, rocklike surface of the Hawk.

It was too easy. Mason had just smuggled himself onboard. He waited waited waited, muscles tense, for something to grab him from the shadows. To carry him off to some Tremist torture chamber.

Then the king stopped without warning. The group stopped with him.

He turned around slowly, and Mason could feel the king's eyes on him, though his mask was only darkness.

"You," the king said.

Chapter Eleven

Mason froze in place. Game over, he tried, better luck next time. A cold sadness filled him up; he was their last hope, and he'd failed. The only consolation was that he had tried rather than run.

Susan was looking at him too, brow furrowed. He was ready to flee, or to launch one final attack, but he forced himself to remain calm. He couldn't act until he was sure there was no chance to recover.

The king grabbed Susan's arm and half shoved, half threw her forward. "Take her to a holding cell." And without another word, the king moved forward again, turning down a corridor Mason knew led to the Hawk's own storage bay.

The relief numbed his muscles. Every inch of him wanted to hug Susan and make her hold him upright and maybe stroke his hair the way she had when he was little, when their parents were off on some long mission and he missed them too much.

But there was still work to do.

Mason was alone with his sister, save the two guards facing away from them, who were paying them no attention. He grabbed her arm and began to lead her away. Susan said nothing at all. She didn't resist, but felt weak with defeat in his grasp. If only he could tell her it wasn't over; there was still hope. But he had to get her alone first.

They marched in silence for a few moments, side by side. Until Mason couldn't wait any longer.

"It's me," Mason said. "Uh, your brother."

Susan's mouth opened slightly, as a mixture of surprise and disbelief passed over her face. Mason could understand the disbelief; it was hard for him to believe he'd made it this far, too.

"You idiot," she said softly. "What if they caught you?" She began to smile, but it fell away like it was weighed down with iridium. She was staring out of a series of windows on the right wall. Mason stepped closer and saw what took her smile away—

The window looked down at a huge open space in the belly of the Hawk. It was, Mason realized, the main storage bay.

It was filled with the Egypt's crew. They stood in columns, bedraggled, bloody, and torn, sagging on their feet. Mason guessed there were close to two hundred of them, almost all of the Egypt's crew, save the dead. The doors leading into the chamber were guarded by multiple Tremist, all of them armed. There was no way to reach the crew, no way to free them without help. Mason knew Susan was thinking the same thing.

But it was still possible to save Merrin. The king's quarters were hopefully just ahead. Mason grabbed Susan's arm and began to drag her away. "We can't stop."

"I know," Susan said. Her eyes were wide, pupils dilated, like she was in shock. "I have to disable the ship. I have to save them."

"It's impossible," Mason said. "Stop talking." He felt embarrassed, having to tell his sister that—like who was he to tell her what to do? But he didn't know who was listening.

"I want you to turn around and get off the ship," Susan said, ignoring him. "That's an *order*."

"I'm a Tremist, I don't follow ESC orders," Mason said. Susan didn't laugh at his joke. "Merrin is just ahead," he pleaded. "We can save her."

Susan didn't argue; they kept walking. Maybe if they saved Merrin, Mason could convince Susan he needed her help to get off the ship. There was no way he came this far just to leave her behind.

The hallway dimensions were similar to what one would find on the Egypt, maybe slightly narrower. The walls seemed to pulse with strange light; it made Mason woozy to look at. But it was still a hallway, with two walls at right angles to the ceiling, the same one he'd walked with Susan when she showed him the captured Hawk at Academy I. The memory overlapped with what he was seeing now. He'd walked the halls in wonder and reverence, understanding this was a machine created by aliens. It was beautiful, in a way. But now all he saw was danger. This ship was alive, not sterile and empty. This ship could kill him.

Susan let Mason lead her along, looking exactly like a shell-shocked prisoner.

Two Tremist turned around the corner ahead, marching right for them, talons held in the ready position. Mason tensed but forced himself to keep the same pace. His eyes darted over them, searching for some sign they knew who he was. His instincts screamed to raise his talon first, to cut them down before they had a chance. But the noise would surely draw every nearby enemy. The ship would register the energy discharge and alert the crew. Next to him, Susan let her head drop, and her steps shuffle. Mason followed her lead, yanking her along a little more. They were just Tremist and prisoner, to an outside observer.

And the Tremist hadn't raised their talons yet.

Closer they came, and closer still.

Until they passed.

Mason almost flinched away, but held it together. The Tremist footsteps traveled away evenly, no increase in pace.

The hallway began to curve to the right, heading toward the front of the ship. *A guard of three*, the king had said. Luckily Mason had the element of surprise.

Mason was about to try and convince Susan to stay with him again, but then they were at the door. "This is it," Mason said.

Susan touched the grenades on his belt. "These are stun," she said, touching the ones on his left hip. "And these are EMP," she said, touching the ones on his right.

"How do you know that?" Mason said. He pulled two stun grenades off his belt and handed one to her.

"Academy II," she said with a wink. "You're not *quite* done with school."

"Don't remind me."

When they got close enough, the door opened automatically, revealing a lavish living area. Everything was violet, and Mason wondered, not for the first time, what their obsession with the color was. The bed was covered in soft purple fabrics. The walls were hung with tapestries depicting odd forests and animals he couldn't identify.

The room appeared empty. Mason and Susan paused, listening hard, hearing nothing. It couldn't be empty. They took two steps forward and saw that the room extended to the left. The quarters were complete with a personal kitchen and eating area, a desk, and a chair that Merrin was currently sitting in.

Surrounded by three armed Tremist.

"Now!" Susan said. They tossed their grenades at the same time, right at the Tremists' feet.

"Cover your ears!" Mason shouted.

Merrin was quick. She clapped her hands over her ears and squeezed her eyes tight. Mason turned away, doing the same. The twin blasts were still uncomfortably loud and bright, a wave he felt through his suit, like a full-body slap. He fell to one knee and couldn't see through the static fuzzing his mask. His body braced as the sound of talons filled the room. His vision cleared in what felt like hours, and he saw the Tremist stumbling about, slowed like he was, talons cutting into the walls. Any stray beam would end them. This wasn't going as Mason had planned; they should've waited outside, to make sure the Tremist were incapacitated. The green beams cut through the air above him. One sizzled off the right arm of his suit, blistering the skin under-neath. He cried out, a distorted sound coming through the mask.

Then: a blur from his right, as Susan moved among them like smoke. She chopped one Tremist on the neck with the edge of her hand, then threw another into the wall so hard his mirror-mask splintered. The last one backed away from her, not seeing that he was backing right into Mason. Right as the Tremist was aiming his talon at Susan, Mason sidestepped and tripped him, then dropped both knees onto his chest.

"The blast will draw them!" Susan said. "Go!"

"Not without you!" Mason screamed back.

"Mason?" Merrin said. She was out of the chair, hands still over her ears.

The Tremist Susan had neck-chopped rose up and lunged at Mason, but he sidestepped again and swung both fists in a dual hammer strike at the Tremist's kidneys—or where he hoped the kidneys would be.

"Yeah, hi," he said to Merrin.

"Where did you find a Tremist suit?"

"You're asking that *now*?"

The Tremist rebounded off the wall but Susan was there. Mason crouched and Susan jumped over him, high-kicking the Tremist in the throat.

But the armor was too thick. They'd need a lot more to put them all down. Susan reached for a talon but a Tremist kicked it under the bed. Mason was still feeling the stun grenade, and he knew Susan and Merrin had to be too. He crossed the room and grabbed Merrin's hand, pulling her around a Tremist that was still trying to stand up. Susan kicked that one in the head. Another talon was smoking on the floor, destroyed.

They ran.

Back the way they came, several hundred feet feeling like miles. The lights in the walls were pulsing faster now—some kind of alarm? Mason was breathing too hard, a rasping sound in his ears. Footsteps pounded in the hall behind him as the Tremist followed.

"Don't slow down!" Susan said. "Don't slow down!"

The hallway straightened after the curve, and Mason could see past the door to the Egypt. Six Tremist ran toward them from that direction, talons raised, masks reflecting their small images in the dim light. Mason just made it around the corner, Susan and Merrin diving behind him, as green lances of talon fire sizzled down the hallway.

The two guards at the dock were ready for them, no longer acting like statues. But Mason had expected that. He dropped two primed EMP grenades. They bounced off the floor, crackling, and Mason's HUD winked out. It was destroyed.

And so were the talons the Tremist were about to kill them with. They fired without result, and Merrin was able to squeeze by on the left, hitting the ESC starship-grade metal with her feet. She spun around to help, but Mason lost sight of her as the left Tremist punched Mason so hard he fell against the tunnel wall, still inside the Hawk. He was vaguely aware of Susan engaged with the other guard, a flurry of punches and kicks, but pain throbbed in his head, blurring his vision. He knew nothing mattered, because the six Tremist had to be only seconds away now. They would be overwhelmed. If only Merrin could get the door shut, at least she would be safe.

The Tremist loomed over him, staring down, head cocked to the side as if he found Mason curious. Then he raised his broken talon high above his head, the advanced weapon reduced to a club that could crush Mason's skull—

He closed his eyes reflexively, but they flew open a second later, when Susan grabbed Mason and threw him onto the Egypt's deck. A second of pure relief while he was airborne: his head was in one piece. He could get back into the fight.

Mason tumbled hard and lost his breath, then rolled to all fours, head snapping up to see Susan now taking on the two

Tremist by herself. He was about to charge forward, but Susan elbowed the door control.

No, that couldn't be right. She wouldn't lock herself in. Mason wanted to scream but the air hadn't returned to his lungs.

He watched as the huge dock door slammed shut between them.

The green light of talons filled the viewport. A flash of Susan's midnight hair dropping out of sight.

Silence.

Chapter Twelve

With a shudder, the Hawk detached from the Egypt and began to drift away.

"No!" Mason screamed, pounding on the door. "No no NO!" All at once he understood. His EMP grenades had kept them alive, but it had also knocked out the electronic door controls. The button she'd elbowed had been the mechanical release where the two ships met. But it was located *outside* the Egypt. Someone had to stay behind, and Mason had sealed her fate from the moment he dropped the grenades.

It was his fault she was trapped there.

The flash of green light still danced on his retinas, but he didn't believe it. They wouldn't have killed her. *No.* She was outnumbered. The king wanted to talk to her still. Yes, they would keep her alive. They would make her join the other prisoners. Maybe the talon fire had been to subdue her, or scare her.

He had locked his sister on the Tremist ship.

"Mason, we have to go. Mason!" Merrin was pulling him from behind, but he kept wriggling out of her grasp and pressing himself to the viewport. He had to see. There was nothing visible through the door; the Hawk had already dropped out of sight.

"She's gone," Merrin said. "She's doing her duty." She pulled at him again, but Mason shoved her hand away. He grabbed his helmet and ripped it off his head.

"What *duty*?" he spat. "To get caught? What good can she do over there?"

"Maybe she'll escape . . ." It was weak and they both knew it. Merrin looked like she wanted to take it back.

Her violet eyes were bright, pleading. Mason knew she wanted to comfort him any way she could, but the color of her eyes reminded him of a crucial thing. He could see the faint lines of purple veins in her neck, up the sides of her face.

Mason took a deep breath. He had to know what she knew. Friends or not.

"Are you a Tremist?" he asked.

You know what she is. She's your friend. Your only friend.

"Why would you . . . ?"

"I saw one. They have the same hair and eye color as you. The same kind of skin." He tried to swallow but his throat was too dry. "Do you dye your hair? Did you change the pigmentation in your eyes?"

"No, I—"

"So are you a Tremist?"

She pressed her lips together and glared at him. His stomach clenched with regret; he hadn't meant to sound so cruel. But if Susan had just stayed behind so Merrin could be free, he wanted to know she was ESC to the core. Especially since they still had to deal with the Tremist controlling the Egypt. He needed to trust her, badly. *You do trust her, you idiot,* Mason thought. *As much as Susan. What are you doing?*

"I'm *not* a Tremist," she said finally. "The fact that you would ask me that says a lot, Stark. We've known each other since *before* we were cadets, and you ask me that?"

Mason felt a sharp sting in his chest. He made his voice softer, not as accusing. "I saw one close up, Merrin, that's all. I took his armor and saw his face." He reached up absently to touch her cheek, but she pulled away before he could. *His* cheeks heated up.

"My name is Merrin Solace. My mother is a commander in

the ESC. My father is a doctor. I was born on Mars in 2787. If you don't trust me, that's your problem."

She started to walk away. Mason grabbed her wrist.

Merrin looked at where he touched her, then let her eyes drift to his, slowly, almost lazily. Dangerously. "Let go of me," she said, voice cold as ice.

He did.

"I'm going back to the others now. They need us."

He couldn't forget what he saw. The logical part of his brain said it wasn't a coincidence. But his gut said *trust her*. It said that whatever blood ran through her, it belonged to the ESC, like his. But how could he really know? He would have to wait, and see, and keep his guard up at all times.

Tremist or not, she's on your team, and you're on hers.

He put out his hand, and she looked at it for a second. "I'm sorry," he said. "You know I would do anything for you."

She nodded stiffly, then grabbed his hand and shook it once.

Through the window, the Hawk was positioning itself outside the Egypt's storage bay. They weren't coming back for Merrin.

The weapon was more important to them.

"You'll help me find the other cadets?" she asked.

"Yes," Mason said. "But there's something I have to see first."

➤ She followed him as he retraced his steps to the storage bay. It was locked.

The main doors were open to outer space; there wasn't an atom of breathable air in the room. Through the window, the cube was visible as it moved sideways out of the bay, completely silent. The Hawk was towing it out somehow, most likely using the twin tractor beams underneath the engines.

The Tremist had the weapon now. Whatever that meant, it was a mission failure. Mason had failed to stop the enemy. The soldier part of him was shamed he chose his sister and Merrin over the goal any superior officer would've given him: to keep the weapon out of Tremist hands.

The brother and friend part of him didn't care.

"What is it?" Merrin said, her voice full of awe. The size of it still startled Mason. It was one thing to see something huge made by man, like the Olympus space station, but a different thing when you had no idea what you were looking at. It was the mystery of the thing. He had no idea how it was built, or where it came from.

"It's the reason the Tremist boarded us, whatever it is. I know it." He turned to her. "We have to be careful."

They left the door, heading for the elevator that would take them to the lowest level of the crossbar. Once inside, Mason pressed the down button. He touched the space under his ear. "Elizabeth?"

"Yes, Cadet Stark," she said in his ear.

"How many personnel on this ship? ESC and Tremist."

"There are nineteen ESC personnel on the ship. And twelve Tremist, not including the unconscious one in the engineers' tunnel."

That stole the breath from Mason. There were eighteen cadets total. There had to be a mistake, so he asked, "How . . . how many ESC of rank?"

"Commander Lockwood is the only remaining officer on the Egypt. Two hundred and ninety-six have been captured and are on the Tremist ship, thirteen have been killed. Commander Lockwood is in critical condition in the sick bay, along with the cadets."

He released the breath he was holding. The cadets were okay, and together. A fierce rush of pride gave him strength: his fellow cadets had evaded capture.

"What about the Tremist?" he asked. The relief didn't last; there were twelve active Tremist on the ship. The cadets outnumbered them by six, but he'd already seen the enemy up close, in action. Engaging them directly would never work. They needed a plan, something with guile and surprise.

"There are six on the bridge. Five moving through the ship. And one in the bathroom. Plus the one you locked in the engineers' tunnel."

The lift stopped and they got out. The way was clear, so they stepped onto the moving track and were propelled toward crewside, port. Elizabeth would have to be their edge; he knew where the Tremist were, but they didn't know where he was. It was a start.

"Can you isolate them?" he asked. "Can you lock the one in the bathroom?"

"Done," Elizabeth replied.

Now there were eleven to worry about. "Brilliant. What about the others?" he said.

"The five are not near your position, but can move through certain areas. I cannot stop the six on the bridge from accessing the Egypt's controls, and I cannot stop them from leaving. They are trying to gain entrance to my mainframe, and I will not be able to hold them off much longer."

Losing Elizabeth would be game over. Not only would the Tremist have complete control of the Egypt, they would be able to find the cadets without having to do a room by room search. They'd be able to eject the escape shuttles before the cadets could use them to escape.

"How much time do we have?" They reached a faster section of the track. Mason kept his balance, wind roaring in his ears.

"I suspect I will be loyal to the ESC for another hour, perhaps sixty-eight minutes."

Mason and Merrin almost fell sideways as the Egypt began to accelerate. The cube had to be clear now, towed along by the Hawk's tractor beams. He imagined it floating in space.

And now the ship was moving. Not a good thing.

"Tell me about the weapon," Mason demanded.

"Please narrow your query."

"The big cube thing in the storage bay!"

"That is classified."

"Tell me *something*. Who made it?"

A pause. "I have no information about its creation. I could not tell you even if ordered to."

"Can you tell me anything?"

"Stand by. I will try to gather information for a more complete report."

The walkway dumped them at the elevator on the left side of the ship. Sick bay would be four levels up, a couple hundred feet aft. The other cadets wouldn't be far. They *seemed* safe, but the moment the Tremist took control of Elizabeth, they'd be sitting ducks. Or, more accurately, fleeing ducks that would be easy to find. Not to mention the Tremist could leave the bridge and begin a manual sweep at any time.

Mason and Merrin rode the crewside elevator up, then jogged down the hushed hallway.

"Are we still clear?" he asked Elizabeth.

"Two Tremist are making a sweep toward crewside. The earliest they could be at your position is three minutes. I will inform you as they get closer. It's likely they will enter crewside, but not stray too far from the bridge."

Mason broke out in sweat again. Elizabeth telling him was one thing, but he wanted eyes on the enemy, to know exactly how they were moving and where. Parts of the Egypt were still unfamiliar to him. He half expected the enemy to be around every corner, behind every door.

The ship was quiet save for the constant background hum. Not quiet in a good way. It was a tomb now. Nearly lifeless. The crew numbered in the hundreds when it left space dock two weeks ago—there was usually never an empty hallway; someone was always walking somewhere. Now the crew was either dead, or worse, on the Hawk.

They rounded the corner into sick bay, and Mason saw how alone they truly were.

Chapter Thirteen

The room held eighteen cadets counting Mason, Merrin, Stellan, Jeremy, and Tom. Ages seven to thirteen. All of them bunched on one side of the bay, doing their best to stand at attention but fidgeting for the most part. The younger ones were wide-eyed; the older ones sweated through their suits. They saw Mason in his armor and a few of them gasped, even though he'd removed the helmet. He thought about immediately tearing the rest off but decided losing the protection it offered would be foolish.

Commander Lockwood, bald head shiny with sweat, lay on his back in a bed, burns covering his neck and the side of his face. His ESC uniform was singed in places, but burned away completely under his right ribs. There the skin was black and red. He was going to die if they didn't get him to a real hospital soon, that much was clear. Mason felt hollow, because he knew Lockwood, who was the unofficial cadet herder sometimes. He also felt heavy, because when Lockwood died, they would truly be alone. Just Elizabeth to keep them company on a ship controlled by the enemy.

The cadets waited quietly at a safe distance while Stellan administered fluids through the IV. Jeremy's eyes were red with tears. Tom was silent and sullen. Mason approached the bed slowly. He didn't want to see the wounds up close, but couldn't appear unnerved in front of the others.

Lockwood barely moved, just rolled his eyes toward Mason. "Cadet Stark," he said in a hoarse voice. "Report."

"Yes, sir," Mason said. "We're the only ones left, sir. There are six Tremist on the bridge and five roaming the halls, and I had Elizabeth lock one in the bathroom."

"A damn shame, that is," he said. "Were you on the Hawk?"

"Yes, sir."

"Impressive." He coughed, wet and deep. "You see our crew?"

"Yes, sir. They're alive. Prisoners, sir."

Mason felt pressure behind his eyes, and a lump in his throat. *I will not cry.* He had to be strong. If they were the only ones left, someone had to be strong. If Susan were here, it'd be her, but she wasn't. *A Stark leads,* she told him, many times. *Our parents were leaders. Leading is a responsibility, not an honor. A duty.*

Duty. He hated the taste of the word now.

"You listening, Mason?" Lockwood asked. The hair on the right side of his head had been burned away. His voice was shaky and weak.

"Sir," Mason said.

"I understand your sister was acting captain before she left the Egypt."

"Yes, sir."

"I'm hurt, son. Bad."

Mason looked over the wounds. "It doesn't look so bad. Not for a commander in the ESC."

Lockwood cracked a smile, but it turned into a grimace.

"Jeremy, another ten units," Stellan said.

"No! No . . ." Lockwood said. "I need to be lucid. The pain is fine, boys. Pain can be a soldier's friend, if one uses it to stay sharp."

"Sir," Mason said. "What was in the storage bay? The cube."

His eyes cleared, free of pain for a moment. "They took it, yes?"

"Yes, sir."

"You know what it is?"

"No, sir."

"It's the end of the world, son. We got greedy. The whole ESC, the whole united worlds, this is our doing. We got greedy."

The sweat under Mason's armor turned cold. If it truly was a weapon, the Tremist had it now, and there was no one to take it back.

"What is it?"

"It's a cross gate. The biggest ever built."

At first, Mason thought he misspoke. A cross gate was exactly that: a gate. A ship would deploy it, usually from the engineering side. It looked like a chunk of metal that would unfurl in space, pieces moving until there was a circle with rims no thicker than Mason's wrist. The circle would be big enough to fly a ship through. The gate would fold space until whatever distant location you wanted was right inside the gate. It allowed for instant travel throughout the galaxy, if you knew where you were going.

But what Mason had seen wasn't a gate. It was a chunk of metal from which thousands of gates could've been made.

"Sir?"

"It's one gate, Cadet. One gate."

Mason remembered the size again, the length and width. Imagined it unfolding in space. His brain simply couldn't process it, the same way it was hard to imagine the distance between stars.

"We came out here . . ." Lockwood's voice rasped and gurgled until he coughed. ". . . to negotiate a treaty with the Tremist. To share Nori-Blue."

The idea of a treaty with the Tremist rocked him. The war would be over, and both species would have enough of the planet to thrive on. It seemed too good to be true, even though the idea seemed so easy.

Lockwood's eyes said it *was* too good to be true.

He continued. "That's what we were here for on paper. But it was never going to happen. The ESC will not surrender even partial control of Nori-Blue. This is all classified, by the way."

Mason just nodded. He felt Merrin grab his hand and squeeze. Across the bed, Tom watched the commander gravely. And still the other fifteen cadets remained quiet, listening, as they were trained to.

"Instead we were going to unleash the biggest cross gate ever created. The cube unfolds. It's really made up of hundreds of thousands of poles that will . . . telescope. Extend."

Mason began to see the truth, the intent, before the commander finished, but he had to hear it. He had to hear it to believe.

"Big enough to pass a planet through . . ." Lockwood said.

"Sir . . ."

"We were going to cross Nori-Blue into Earth's orbit. It would share the same orbit as Earth, just on the other side of the sun. After Nori-Blue adjusted, we'd have an inhabitable planet right next door. With the planet that close to the ESC's main bases, the Tremist would have no chance. No chance to win."

It was brilliant, yet horrifying. To steal a planet from its natural orbit and add it to our solar system. Mason couldn't understand how the ESC could've come up with this plan and put it into action. Nori-Blue didn't *belong* in our solar system; it wasn't natural. Could they even know for sure what effect it would have? The balance of gravity in the solar system would be thrown off. Unless they had some way to compensate.

Lockwood seemed to read his mind. "It's better than the first plan. We were going to destroy Nori-Blue, so the Tremist couldn't have it if we lost. But none of that matters now. None of it. What matters is they have this gate we created, and they know what we intended. I don't know what they're going to do with it, but it won't be good. It won't be . . . you understand? *Do you?*"

Mason felt his heart thud, and pause, and thud again. His insides were as cold as space. It wasn't hard to imagine what the

Tremist would do with the gate. If the ESC had planned to steal Nori-Blue, the Tremist would want to steal it first.

Lockwood reached up and squeezed Mason's arm so hard he felt it through the armor. The commander was shaking now.

Mason's words came out in a tumble. "Sir, we'll be okay. I had Elizabeth lock a Tremist in the bathroom. And Tom locked one in a tunnel. There are only eleven left. And I made it off the Hawk with Merrin. We can take the ship back and rally a hunting party to track the gate down." He was speaking for Lockwood's benefit, trying to offer the man some comfort. He knew this was the worst way to die, leaving eighteen cadets alone to fend for themselves. But maybe he was strong enough; maybe he would hang on a little longer.

"Can you do that?" Lockwood seemed to really be asking.

"I promise, sir."

Lockwood nodded gravely.

"Cadet Stark. I name you captain of the SS Egypt. Take her back . . . and stop those bastards from using the gate."

Chapter Fourteen

Commander Lockwood sank back into the bed when Stellan administered more of the painkiller. His eyes fluttered before closing. "He needs to rest," Stellan said. "There's hope for him if we get to a base with a proper hospital."

Mason's mind was still, like a stalled fossil-fuel engine. He tried to get it running again by replaying Lockwood's words. He'd just been named captain. He was captain of the Egypt, responsible for the cadets, and responsible for recovering the ship from Tremist hands.

Mason wanted to turn off his emotions but didn't know how. He wanted to be cool and calculating like the captains who made it into the lore books, like Captain Renner certainly would. That was impossible, though, so he decided to fake it. He'd read in a textbook once a quote by the famous Captain Reynolds: *I am not a brave man. But bravery, like most things, can be faked. And sometimes, in rare instances, it will lead to the real thing.*

"I need you with me if we're going to take back the ship," Mason said to Stellan. Someone else would have to watch over the commander. Lockwood's condition was awful, yes, but the man had given him an order. It was time to stop thinking about his health and start thinking about the mission.

"I'm sorry," Tom said, wrinkling his nose. "Did he just name you captain?"

"You heard him," Merrin said.

Tom looked at Merrin for what seemed like the first time, as if he was just now remembering the unmasked Tremist on the engineering deck. Thankfully, he didn't bring it up and make a huge deal in front of the other cadets.

"And we're just going to follow your orders?" Tom said.

"If you want to remain in the ESC, yes." Mason didn't want it to be like that, not right away. Pulling rank was not something he admired. But it was something Susan had once talked to him about, when Mason took his *Future Commanders* course in fourth year. How if you didn't put someone in line it could show weakness. Which would spread. Being in command meant sometimes you had to sacrifice a friendship. Not that Tom was his friend or anything. Or at least a good friend. Mason didn't really know.

"Then what's your plan, Captain?" Tom said.

Mason addressed the room now, the waiting cadets. He knew most of their names, but not all, which shamed him. He had spent two weeks in the same room and hadn't bothered to remember each of them. Once their shared spacetime was up, it was likely they would never see each other again. It was always easier to say goodbye when you didn't know someone.

"None of you asked for this," Mason said, "but Earth is relying on us now. We have a mission. Some of you have been training for a year, some of you have been training for six. Either way, this is what we signed up for. We're going to take back this ship, and then I'm going to need each of you on the bridge. If you specialized in something at school, go to that station. We'll be learning on the fly, but we have a basic idea of how a starship works, right? That's first year stuff."

A few of them smiled.

"That's great, Captain," Tom said, "but what about the part where we take back the ship? You know, from the Tremist that are currently flying it."

Mason's eye twitched; he hoped no one saw. Tom wanted a

plan right this second, but Mason didn't have one. Not even close. They had to immobilize each Tremist, one at a time if possible. All it would take was a few sweeping talon beams to cut them all down. A methodical attack would win out over blunt force. Mason's training was still there, and he was glad for it. But it was one thing to use your skills in a training exercise, and another to use them in a hostile situation.

The odds were against them, maybe stacked too high. The escape shuttles were still under their control, for now. They could save themselves and leave the Egypt in Tremist hands. *Not an option,* Mason reminded himself. They had orders, and the king had the planet gate. If they didn't warn the rest of the fleet, no one would.

So for bravery, Mason would have to fake it.

Mason touched the space under his ear. "Elizabeth, where are the Tremist now?"

When she spoke, her voice filled the room, not his ear. "The six Tremist are still on the bridge, now joined by two more. That leaves one locked in the bathroom, one in the engineers' tunnel, and three roaming the ship. Those three are heading for the gravity-free bay on the starboard side, sir."

Mason tried to remember the functions of the gravity-free bay. It was smaller than storage but could still act as storage. The doors could open to space, with a force field to hold the air in. And every surface had the ability to become magnetic. The magnets could be toggled on and off instantly, the way Mason had done to make Tom lose his race. And magnetic fields often didn't get along with energy weapons, depending on what kind they were. . . .

Mason asked, "If the magnetic field is in place, will their talons work?"

A pause. "No. But photon cannons will be operational."

"Perfect," Mason said, smiling. To the cadets, he said, "I hope you remember your zero G training."

. . . .

➤ Two cadets—a smaller first year boy and a girl trained in medicine—stayed behind with Commander Lockwood. Merrin sealed them inside, in case the Tremist won, but the two cadets would have the ability to use an escape shuttle before the Tremist gained total control of the ship. Tom gave them access to the ship's cameras, so it would be up to them to decide when to leave.

The remaining sixteen marched through the ship on silent feet, to the sub-armory located two levels down. There Tom and Jeremy stood grim-faced, passing out handheld P-cannons to the cadets, the same kind Ensign Michael had given to them earlier. These barrels glowed with the same swirling colors as before, shifting weirdly like Mason's Tremist armor. He wondered where Ensign Michael was now, whether he was dead or alive.

Jeremy was sweating. So was Mason, but he stood off to the side, giving a nod to any cadet that looked his way. A few nodded back. One boy's lower lip was quivering, and Mason was again reminded of who they were. Not true soldiers. Mason almost pulled the boy aside to have him join the two in sick bay, but the boy took a breath and set his jaw. It inspired Mason. Gave him a burst of hope that they weren't truly doomed, no matter what actions they took.

Merrin came up to him at one point. "I know you're being strong for all of us." She could always see right through him. "Just know you don't have to be strong for me." She touched the back of his hand with her fingers, then turned away before Mason could say anything. He felt a rush of warmth for Merrin, and a cold, poisonous anger for the way he'd acted toward her.

Down the hallway, he saw Tom accessing a computer terminal in the wall. Just far enough away to be outside the main group.

"Elizabeth," Mason whispered. "Give the audio to Tom's terminal."

"I told Cadet Renner he had a message from Captain Renner, in the event of her death."

"Wait—" Mason began.

There was a click, and then Captain Renner speaking all at once, mid-sentence. "—seeing this, then something happened to me. I'm really sorry about that. I knew when I got pregnant with you things were going to be rough. I wanted to give you that home life you deserved. You know, with Grandma's money we could've afforded to get one of those big Earth houses with a huge sprawling lawn and all that."

Cut the audio, Mason thought but did not say. He felt the shame of listening in on a private moment, but couldn't stop himself. From far away, he saw Captain Renner's face on Tom's screen.

"I wanted that for us. But the threat our species faces is too grave, and I hoped you would understand why me and your father chose this life for us. And I think you do understand. So I'm here to say I'm sorry I couldn't give you that normal life. I'm sorry we pushed you so hard and demanded so much of you. I'm sorry we seemed cold at times. But I wanted you to be hard, my darling. *A hard soldier is a strong soldier is a living soldier.* Grandpa told me that when I was a little girl, and he said that's how he was able to stay alive during those cold nights on Titan. I hoped I would live long enough to see the end of the war with you, but that's not the case now. When it was over, I wanted to give you that life I dreamed about. A safe life. Your father will have to give that to you now, and if he's not around, I know you will find it yourself. Because you're strong. You have me and your dad in you, and I know that will be more than the Tremist can handle. I'm sorry, baby. I hope you never have to see this."

Tom stood at the terminal, frozen, his head bowed.

Mason felt pressure behind his eyes, and he wished he was still wearing the helmet. He thought of his own mother, the day of the First Attack. His parents were rushing out the door, late for the meeting. His mother gave him a quick peck on the cheek, then left. She popped back in a moment later and said, "I love you," and smiled.

Mason had said, "I love you, too." And then the door had shut and he never saw his parents again.

Don't think about this now. Lead. Lead your soldiers.

They need you.

He banished the memory, feeling hollow.

At the terminal, Tom pushed the heels of his hands into his eyes, and when he turned back to the group, his eyes were free of tears. It was like the message had freed something inside of him. He didn't look devastated; he seemed lighter.

Mason looked away quickly, and ordered everyone to set their P-cannons to paralyze. He wanted the Tremist alive. It was unlikely the Tremist King would accept hostages as trade for some of the captured ESC crew, but maybe the cadets could learn something about the weapon, and the king's intent, by questioning them.

The cadets followed his order, and the barrels of their P-cannons hummed and shifted to a milky green and white.

"Captain," Elizabeth said in his ear while the cadets messed with their newly acquired weapons. A few practiced firing stances; Tom showed a group how to run a diagnostic to make sure the weapon was performing at peak capacity; Merrin led stretches with everyone else.

"What is it?"

"I'm afraid I miscalculated about the number of Tremist on the ship."

His throat clenched. There were really fifty on board. Or a hundred. Or five hundred. More Tremist ships were incoming. *Stop*, he thought. *Wait for the analysis.*

"Yeah?" he said.

"There is one more Tremist on the ship than my previous report, but he's been hiding from me." No relief. One Tremist was okay, but not one that was somehow hiding from *Elizabeth*.

"How—how is that possible?"

The computer hesitated. Never a good sign. "It's a Rhadgast, sir."

She was talking directly into his aural nerve, so no one else heard. "Say again?"

"A Rhadgast."

Now Mason really wanted to flee. The word froze his blood.

"They're real?" The Rhadgast were a myth, something soldiers talked about seeing but could never confirm. They were Tremist, it was thought, but a different kind. Some people claimed they could control magic. Rhadgast supposedly meant wizard in the Tremist tongue, although *that* was never confirmed either. What Mason knew is that they were dark, and moved like spiders, and could control lightning with their hands. A dangerous thing on a starship.

"They're real?" Mason said again. Jeremy was watching him now, but pretended to study his P-cannon when Mason noticed.

"I believe so, sir. He matches all reports."

"Where is he now?"

"I can't get a good read. He's interfering with my sensors. I think he's near the gravity-free bay, two levels up, maybe three."

An idea came to him then, about how to possibly deal with the Rhadgast. *If* he could lure it. He turned to Tom, who was demonstrating the proper grip on a P-cannon to a first year. "Can you turn the gravity on and off in the gravity-free bay? On my command?" He pointed at the dataslate hanging from Tom's belt. "With that thing."

Tom looked at him in annoyance for two full seconds, and Mason was about to ask again. Then he said, "It would take a second after the command, but sure. I'll use *that thing*. It's called a dataslate, by the way."

Merrin held up her own. "I'm actually faster on this thing than Thomas."

Tom raised an eyebrow.

Merrin smiled a close-lipped smile and wiggled the dataslate back and forth. "*Be prideful of the uniform, but not of your abilitie*s. ESC handbook page thirty-seven, under the title *Cadet Guidelines*."

"She . . . might be faster," Tom said. "That conclusion is not verified."

Mason couldn't smile, not with so many lives at stake. But it was there, under the surface. "Perfect. Back each other up. Just wait for my command." It was amazing how the seed of a plan could occupy his mind, even if he only saw the edges of it right now. To Elizabeth, he said, "What are the Tremist doing now?"

"They're moving the fallen ESC members into the bay. I anticipate they'll send the casualties into space."

The sudden anger, hotter than the Egypt's main engine, burned away the fear. He was grateful for it, hoped it would last.

The cadets were armed and waiting. He debated telling them about the Rhadgast, but knew the fear it would bring might unravel them on the spot. It wouldn't prepare them, either, since no one was trained in how to deal with one. It felt like lying, but was still the best course.

"We're ready, Captain," Stellan said softly. He gave a small nod, and Mason realized it wasn't Stellan calling him captain, so much as it was Stellan trying to present a kind of unified atmosphere under Mason's command. He appreciated it more than he could show.

Mason told them a very basic outline of the plan, hoping to come up with the rest on the way.

"Just listen for my voice," he said. "Do what I say, when I say it, and we will make it home. Understood?"

"Yes, sir," many of them replied in unison. Merrin smiled slyly and Tom gave a nod of approval.

Then they broke as one and moved to the crossbar, to meet the enemy head-on.

Chapter Fifteen

Mason led the fifteen cadets (ten boys, five girls) in two loose lines, following the perimeter of the now-empty storage bay. The bay was enormous in its emptiness, and Mason tried to imagine every square inch filled with the cube. With it gone, all of the perimeter levels were exposed above and below him, full of sharp shadows and dark places.

Easy places for a Rhadgast to hide.

His eyes darted from space to space, searching for a ghost, but seeing sleeping Fox fighters instead. The Fox fighters were one-man spacecraft with thrusters on every surface, which allowed for insanely quick maneuvering. They were shaped like arrow-heads, the weapon units clustered underneath, almost like the Hawk. He made a note of their location, in case they were needed later. He'd never flown one before, but had studied the basics in the *Starships of the Earth Space Command II* course.

During the transit from port to starboard, Elizabeth couldn't find the Rhadgast again. Then she refused to confirm she'd seen it in the first place. Her systems might be compromised, she said, and she might not even be aware of it. Which meant Mason would have to fully rely on Tom and Merrin to change things in the computer, if he wanted to be sure. For now, the ship was haunted, and Mason was the only one who knew.

Once they reached the outer door to the gravity-free bay,

Mason called a full stop. To their credit, the cadets appeared solid. None of them whimpered in fear or let their lips quiver, even if they had to be terrified on the inside. Mason was. An instructor once said if you didn't call it fear, then it couldn't be fear. That sounded completely untrue. Still, they were hiding it well, which Mason hoped would translate to steady aim and quick reaction times.

Mason figured he should say something here. So he tried: "Aim true. Take a second, rather than firing wildly. Don't hit each other." He paused.

Jeremy stepped next to him. "If one of the Tremist is taking multiple hits from a cannon, switch to another. Don't be slow, but don't get crazy."

Then Merrin. "Quick reminder," she said, giving her best smile, which Mason had to admit was the best he'd ever seen. "We take these guys out, all that's left are the Tremist on the bridge. And then we're in the lore books."

Mason fought the smile he wanted to make. Captains didn't smile before combat. But he let approval show through, approval of his men. "Let's show them what ESC cadets are made of."

A cheer would've gone up then, under normal circumstances. But this was battle. Instead the cadets who were friends clapped each other on the back and nodded and a few even smiled. They had their P-cannons. They were as ready as they ever would be.

Without warning, the ship accelerated. Hard. It had already been moving, but now the speed had them all bracing their legs for balance. Where were they going? Mason said, "Elizabeth? Location."

"We're in the Coffey system, Captain Stark," she said in his ear.

Nori-Blue's system. Three hundred and two light years from Earth. The Tremist had the gate, and they were going to use it. Things were happening too fast. Mason had to retake the bridge *now*. "Is the king's Hawk still nearby?"

Another pause. "Captain, they've deactivated my long-range scanners. I'm blind."

The Tremist on the bridge were taking Elizabeth apart piece by piece, it seemed. Soon she'd be under their control completely.

Time to move.

"Any questions?" he asked the group.

"What about the Rhadgast?" Jeremy said.

Mason clenched his teeth.

"What?" Jeremy said, glancing around. "I heard Elizabeth talk about it."

The cadets instantly appeared shaken, shifting from foot to foot, whispering the word like bad gossip.

"Sorry," Elizabeth said.

Mason held up his hands; the cadets fell silent. "If there is a Rhadgast, we deal with it together. It's still made out of the same stuff as us."

"We don't know that," Stellan said helpfully.

"Everything is made of atoms," Merrin countered.

"I heard they steal your soul," one cadet, a skinny brown-haired boy, said.

"Yeah! I heard they drink blood, like a vampyre," said a second year, by the look of her.

"Space vampyre," said another.

"Enough," Mason said. "If you want to run to an escape shuttle and take your chances in the cold black, I won't stop you." He held their gazes one by one, until he was as sure as possible that they'd hold it together. "Are you ESC?"

"We are, sir," Merrin said. She winked, because they both knew it was a joke for her to call him *sir* after all they'd been through together.

"Then let's do it," Mason said. Four buttons were next to the door, three green and one red. He pressed all three green simultaneously, and the door slid open with a blast of air. It took a certain amount of faith to jump out into a room that was nearly as large as the main storage bay. The door opened on nothing but air, and a drop many, many levels down. So high up that the magnetic forklifts at the bottom were tiny, like toys. And where he stood, the gravity was a very real thing. He couldn't see the upper levels without leaning too far into the bay: there was an overhang above the door that blocked his view.

But a captain had to go first. Taking a deep breath, Mason grabbed both sides of the door and flung himself into the open space.

Chapter Sixteen

As he shot into the bay, Mason's heart stopped pounding so hard—partly because it no longer had to work against the forces of gravity, and partly from relief. He did not fall: he flew.

The level the cadets were on was halfway up the side of the bay, which was twenty levels tall like the storage bay. But this bay was narrower, like a rectangle stood on end, and instead of open levels, there were just doors in the walls, and handholds between them for maneuvering. The handholds looked like hundreds of scars in the wall, and they were all a person had to hold on to if gravity was suddenly returned to the bay. A number on the wall across from Mason read 11, so he was eleven levels up from the bottom.

Mason was flying faster than he'd anticipated, but that wouldn't be a problem; he simply rotated so his feet would land on the wall he was rushing toward. He bent his knees and absorbed the impact, reaching out for the nearest handhold. There he held on across from the doorway the cadets huddled in, ten levels of empty space below him, nine above him.

Secured to the wall, he looked straight up.

At the top of the bay, the three Tremist were assembling the dead crew members in a line, next to a vertical access door built into the ceiling. They hadn't noticed his entrance. He swallowed, feeling disoriented, because the Tremist were *standing* on the ceiling like it was the floor. Their heads were closest to him. It made Mason feel, for an instant, like he was hanging upside down. Like the floor with the magnetic forklifts below him was really the ceiling. He shook the illusion as best he could, tried to remember he could make any surface the floor, depending on how he considered it in his mind.

The dead soldiers were stuck to the ceiling, the black ESC body bags secured somehow. Mason touched the space under his ear. "Elizabeth?"

"Yes, Captain."

Mason waved at the cadets, and they began to pour through the doorway, launching themselves into the room one after another. "Do they have the gravity turned on up top or are they using magnets?" The Tremist still had their feet on the ceiling. One was staring at him, and as he watched, the other two took notice of the cadets flying into the room and rebounding off walls. This was it. The Tremist wouldn't leave a bunch of flying ESC cadets to roam free.

"Pick targets!" Tom called out.

The three Tremist were pulling the talons off their backs, in what felt like slow motion. Mason prayed they wouldn't work. He had to trust they wouldn't work. If they did, it would only take seconds for them to bisect the cadets, who continued to move, bounding from wall to wall between levels nine and thirteen, appearing like flies caught in a glass cylinder.

"They're using gravity to hold themselves to the ceiling, and magnets for the body bags," Elizabeth said. "Sir! Talons are cycling. If they find an open frequency their weapons will be able to fire in the bay!"

"I thought you said—" He stopped himself. *Adjust, adapt . . . don't dwell.* "Tom! Merrin!"

Tom and Merrin were across the bay. Merrin nodded at Tom, who pushed off in Mason's direction. Mason stole a quick look above: the Tremist were trying to figure out why their weapons weren't firing.

"Cycling!" Elizabeth said. "They'll have weapons in six to nine seconds!"

Tom hit the wall next to Mason, dataslate in one hand. "What?"

"Turn off the ceiling's gravity!"

"Handholds!" Jeremy shouted to everyone. The cadets stopped their wild circular dash from wall to wall and clung to the nearest handhold. They spaced themselves evenly so as not to cluster targets.

Tom had already pulled up the gravity-free bay controls on his slate, and thumbed a few icons. Two seconds later, the Tremist were floating free but the body bags remained in place, held fast by the magnets.

"Fire!" Merrin shouted.

As they surely realized that floating in the open would make them easy to burn, the three Tremist jumped off the ceiling in unison, flying *down* in a dive, right toward the cadets below them.

The cadets, all of them clinging to the handholds with one hand and both feet, opened fire with their P-cannons. The balls of light the P-cannons produced were greenish-white now. They sped across the room, angled toward the ceiling, and splashed on the walls, leaving behind smoking patches the size of fists. But the Tremist were diving too fast, heading right for them. Mason watched as a few of the braver and bigger cadets collided with two of them in midair, trading punches and kicks. He tracked the third with his gun but didn't want to risk hitting one of the cadets; the Tremist were fully mixed among them now, sharing levels nine through thirteen halfway up the walls.

It was no good. They'd blown their chance, when the Tremist had been at a safe distance. And Mason would not accept any casualties. There was another play.

"No!" he screamed. "Break away! Break away! Head for the walls! Stop firing!"

They didn't hesitate. Any cadet not already on the wall pushed off the Tremist they were engaged with and grabbed a handhold. One cadet slammed into Tom by accident, and his dataslate went spinning upward, Tom making panicked grabs for it.

The Tremist were tumbling in space now, drifting. Two looked unharmed, but the third's mirror-mask was cracked along the jaw.

And all of them still had their talons.

"Talon cycle complete!" Elizabeth said. "They can fire!"

Mason watched as all three talons crackled to life, bristling with green energy.

"Hang on!" Mason screamed. Once he saw each of the cadets secured to the wall, some above him and some below, he said, "Merrin! Gravity!"

Merrin operated her slate, tongue between her teeth, as a green talon beam began to etch the wall next to Mason's head. Mason flinched away, holding on, not daring to try for another handhold.

"Any time would be good!" His whole body was tense, expecting to feel the hot, deadly bite in the next second.

Instead, gravity resumed.

The once-weightless blood in his body sank, and he was hanging on the wall now, as were the other cadets.

But the Tremist had nothing to hold on to. They fell ten levels to the floor far below, never crying out or waving their arms, just dropping like stones. Mason watched as they hit the ground among the forklifts, felt each thump reverberate through the walls. A ragged cheer went up, as the cadets held on for dear life.

"Take gravity away," Mason said, "but secure the Tremist with magnets." He kept his eyes on the Tremist, expecting them to move, but they didn't. No one could survive a fall from over ten levels. Not even space vampyres.

Merrin nodded. "Done."

A second later Mason pushed off the wall. The others did the same, spinning around, tumbling, doing backflips or frontflips. They still had a bridge to retake, currently held by eight other Tremist, but the victory felt good. He counted quickly: all the cadets were accounted for.

After a few seconds, the cheers turned to gasps. Mason pushed off diagonal from the wall, not crossing the bay, but landing on the adjacent wall, where Merrin and Tom clung. They had their heads tilted back, eyes on the ceiling.

Mason followed their gaze.

And saw the Rhadgast dive through the ceiling door and into the bay.

Chapter Seventeen

"Grab the wall!" Mason shouted, and heard it echo among the recruits: *Grab the wall grabthewall!* They scrambled through space, reaching out for the nearest hand-hold. Mason only barely registered the movement around him. His eyes were on the Rhadgast descending toward them.

The Tremist wizard seemed to slow under his own power, drifting down, righting himself in the air so he came feet first. He was cloaked in a billowing black robe that flowed away from his body, expanding like wings. The mask was typical Tremist, but instead of a mirror, his blank oval face throbbed with violet light. Looking directly into the mask burned Mason to his core. It was like staring into the face of a demon. Mason was no longer captain of the SS Egypt; he was just another cadet out of his league.

The Rhadgast wore purple gloves up to his elbows. Gloves that crackled with violet electricity. Bright tendrils of it crawled up and down the sleeves. As the Rhadgast flowed down in a controlled descent, a sudden burst of light filled the room, emanating from the gloves. The electricity lanced out, snapping through space, and shocked the nearest cadet, sending him into spasms. Someone screamed; Mason hoped it wasn't him. It only lasted a second, but when he blinked the zapped cadet was crying, his uniform smoking. It knocked Mason back to reality, the injury of one of his soldiers sharpening his senses and turning the anger into something he could use.

"Release your weapons!" the Rhadgast hissed, sounding part machine and part snake.

"Yeah, right," Merrin muttered.

"Fire!" Mason screamed in response.

All at once, P-cannon fire lit up the bay. The Rhadgast flew around impossibly, turning tight loops and diving and rising again, like a shark that swam through air, avoiding the photon balls that seemed slow in comparison.

The Rhadgast zapped another cadet. This one's leg caught fire. Mason didn't stop shooting, but saw in the corner of his eye as the boy beat at his leg. Luckily Stellan was right there to help smother it. He tried to anticipate the Rhadgast's movements, but none of the photon balls came close. It was useless, and soon their weapons would be overheated, and they would be at the monster's mercy.

Mason knew what he had to do. The Rhadgast would either kill them or disarm them, and neither of those was an option.

What would Susan do? What did she do for us already?

"Be ready, Tom!" he said. He couldn't say more, lest the Rhadgast know Mason's plan. He just had to hope Tom was as quick as everyone thought. He didn't ask Merrin, because he knew she wouldn't do it. Not a chance.

Tom understood. There was new respect in his eyes, for Mason and the sacrifice he had to make. "Aye, Captain . . ." Tom said back.

"Hey!" Mason shouted.

The Rhadgast spun in space. Mason wondered if he had some kind of propulsion system layered into his robe, maybe a belt that allowed him to control gravity when there was none. Or maybe it was dark magic; maybe he was a ghost. The way his faceplate glowed like a supernova, the way his robe seemed alive, lashing like a tapestry of snakes, Mason feared it was the latter possibilities.

The Rhadgast's gloves buzzed with electricity, the same sound they made seconds before firing. Mason tucked, then pushed off hard with both legs, rising a level and avoiding a blast on the wall where he'd just been. He felt static wash over him from behind, tickling the skin under his armor.

His heart sang with the near miss, but he still had to keep the Rhadgast's attention. "Nice shot!" he yelled from his new spot on the opposite wall. Hey, there wasn't time to think of a proper comeback.

Mason was buying time, because it was too soon to do what he had to do. It hurt him, because he didn't want to leave anyone behind. But at the same time, maybe he would see Mom and Dad again, and they would remember him. Maybe he would see his sister. And no matter what, he would never have to be afraid again.

By now most of the cadets had found handholds on the wall. Only a few stragglers remained, but they'd be on the wall in a few seconds. His heart pounded so hard it hurt. If he could take out the Rhadgast, Tom and Merrin would be able to retake the bridge. He knew they would. They were brave, and they knew what was at stake. His death would be worth it.

The Rhadgast studied him now, like he was impressed Mason dodged one of his lightning attacks. Which was good. But Mason had to move *now*. He could only hope everyone had a good grip.

"What are you doing?" Merrin said. "Mason, no!"

He coiled his legs, then launched himself straight off the wall horizontally.

The Rhadgast was about to blast him, but had to raise his hands instead to catch Mason as they collided.

"Now, Tom!"

Tom knew what to do. The gravity came back, and they were no longer tumbling sideways, but falling, the same way the three Tremist had fallen. The Rhadgast growled and tried to peel Mason off, but Mason held on, squeezing his eyes shut. He hoped the ground wouldn't hurt much.

The air roared in his ears and he heard Merrin shout "Mason!" at the top of her lungs.

The Rhadgast began to shock him with both hands, and the current made Mason's jaw slam shut. His skin was alive, crawling with hot bees that buzzed in his skin and stung every inch of him. His tongue got in the way of his teeth, and his mouth filled with hot blood. Mustering all his strength, he rotated in the Rhadgast's grip until he could tuck his knees up against the Rhadgast's chest. The numbers on each level rushed by. He saw 6, then 5. Moments to live. Almost two seconds had passed, maybe more, but it felt like his whole life. The calm came over him as level 4 blurred past, and Mason rejected it. He didn't want to feel calm, in that instant. He didn't want to accept anything, and he didn't want to die in the enemy's grasp.

Mason screamed, pistoning off with his hands and knees, trying to leap off the Rhadgast's chest. He tore free, kicking at the same time, the way he would kick off the bottom of a pool to reach the surface. He was falling too fast to see numbers now, but level four seemed so long ago.

In the next instant, he heard the Rhadgast slam into the ground—

And gravity disappeared.

The ground still rushed at him, but Mason's legs were already pointed down. He fell to his knees hard and tumbled across the floor until his back banged into one of the magnetic forklifts. He drifted upward again, shaken and bruised, but the impact was only a fraction of if he'd hit full force.

"You're welcome!" someone called from high, high above.

Mason blinked rapidly, clearing his head, and looked up. Tom clung to the wall still, holding his dataslate high. He'd removed gravity as soon as the Rhadgast hit. A window of less than a second. Tom had saved him.

Mason was torn between wanting to cry and laugh. He was

alive. He was still here, still able to fight. And so were the other cadets.

The pain from the drop was fading but left behind aches. He double-checked to make sure no bones had snapped. "Report . . ." he said groggily. This close to the bottom, Mason looked at the now four fallen Tremist stuck to the floor. Their masks caught the light strangely, but none of them so much as twitched. His plans for questioning one would have to wait. Hopefully they could retake the bridge without killing the rest. Mason found he had no satisfaction from it, just a grim coldness in his chest. A terrible voice that said *It was you or them.*

"The starboard side is now secure," Elizabeth said, not seeming to notice how close he'd come to dying. "The eight Tremist on the bridge are now aware of your presence, but I predict they won't leave to pursue you, since the bridge is an excellent defensive position."

High above, the cadets began to pull themselves down the wall. They knew better than to cheer and congratulate each other, since a Rhadgast cut their last victory dance short, but they did smile. And Mason smiled back at them. A tiny droplet of blood floated out of his mouth.

Tom reached him first, and actually held out his fist for Mason to hit. "Nice work, Stark," he said. The cadets were on the ground now, so Tom reinstated gravity and removed the magnets under the Tremist. Mason dropped a few inches to his feet. The cadets the Rhadgast had electrified were shaken and upset, but not mortally wounded. It seemed the Rhadgast hadn't been shooting to kill, but to capture.

Merrin stalked over and shoved Mason hard, with both hands. He stumbled back, banging his shoulder on a forklift. "Hey!"

"Don't you *ever* . . ." She didn't need to finish. She was shaking her head, lips pressed together.

"I'm sorry—" Mason began, but Merrin pulled him into a

hug. Mason didn't have a chance to hug back before she pushed him away and joined the cadets crowded around the dead Rhadgast. Now that he wasn't flying around the room, the Rhadgast didn't look so scary. Just another Tremist in a dress. He had landed in the middle of the other Tremist, on his back. Another few fractions of a second, and Mason would've been among them.

"Now what, Captain?" Jeremy asked as he finished checking the talons: all of them appeared busted by the fall.

Mason was about to say, *Now we retake the bridge,* but the four Tremist on the ground began to stir.

Chapter Eighteen

"Uh, Captain?" one cadet said.

The Tremist were groaning, limbs twitching on the floor, as if waking from a particularly long slumber. Their armor scraped softly against the metal.

"Impossible . . ." Tom whispered.

The nearest Tremist grabbed Merrin's leg, and she shrieked, kicking it off.

The deep purple face of the Rhadgast began to glow brighter. They had to move. Now.

Mason lunged for the Rhadgast and grabbed his right arm. The tingle of building static made his hands itch, but Mason worked hard to strip the glove. Tom saw what he was doing and got down beside him, working on the other hand. The Rhadgast tried to pull away, but he was still weak, and Mason and Tom had the strength of fear.

"Can you lock them in here?" Mason said to Tom.

"I can!" Jeremy said.

"Stun them!" Merrin commanded the cadets. A few fired their P-cannons at the Tremist, but it seemed to wake them up *faster*.

"Elizabeth, how are they still alive?" Mason asked, fighting to keep his hands steady. He almost had the glove off. It was thinner than he'd anticipated, soft. He ached all over, and the sudden burst of adrenaline made his bruises burn in new ways.

"I am unable to answer that question. Perhaps their armor has capabilities I am unaware of."

"Perhaps!" Mason replied.

Jeremy was working at one of the terminals on the wall. "I can lock them in here, but once the Tremist gain full control of the bridge they'll be free!"

When both gloves were off, Mason and Tom stood up. The Rhadgast was fully awake now, and he grabbed Mason's ankle.

"*Boy!*" he hissed.

Mason kicked him in the face.

"Let's go!" he shouted.

The gravity disappeared once again, and Mason jumped off the floor as hard as he could. The cadets rose alongside him, drifting toward the ceiling. Mason removed the armor plates from his right hand and arm, then worked the glove on in their place. He felt it shifting the way the Tremist uniform had, shrinking until it was the perfect size for his hand. It covered from his fingertips all the way to the top of his arm, sealing against the armor on his shoulder. In the next second, he felt the glove link to his brain in some way he didn't fully understand. It was like a second layer of skin now. He didn't test it, but the electricity felt just within his reach, waiting for a command.

Tom, rising next to Mason, had handed his own glove to Merrin. She was putting it on her left hand, since Mason had the right.

"She's the warrior," Tom said, grinning.

Below, the Tremist had almost gathered their wits. One had even pushed off in pursuit. Mason could hardly believe it: how had the fall only knocked the Tremist unconscious? The armor must've been more extraordinary than he first thought. Or they really were shapeshifting werewolf space vampyre ghost zombies.

At the top, the cadets flew side by side through the door and into the corridor above, where they promptly fell to the floor.

The dead crew were still in place on the ceiling, and Mason hated to leave them there, but respects could be paid later, once they were finally safe. The crew would've agreed.

Mason locked the door shut behind them and asked Merrin to drop the pursuing Tremist again. She did.

➤ With two Rhadgast gloves, Mason hoped it would be easier to retake the bridge, but knew the odds were still stacked against them. The Tremist had the defensive position, and there was no way the cadets could use gravity against them this time. Not to mention they were up against eight Tremist this time, not three. It seemed hopeless. He should save the others, order them to take escape shuttles, then blow up the ship. If they didn't, and the Tremist gained control, it would not only mean *their* end, but the end of countless others. It would be so easy for the enemy to fly the Egypt into ESC territory, ignore a few hails while they got close enough, then unleash a surprise attack on an unsuspecting base. Or even Olympus.

But the massive cross gate was still in Tremist hands, and no one knew it.

Giving up wasn't an option.

"If we fail . . ." Mason whispered to Tom during the walk. He was hoping Tom would have a similar thought. And he did.

"The Tremist won't have the ship for long," he whispered back, holding up his dataslate. Mason saw a self-destruct countdown on the screen, set for nineteen minutes. By then the Egypt would explode, or they would have control of the ship.

Mason nodded at him, unable to speak. Nineteen minutes, and they might all be particle dust drifting through space. The thought chilled him so much it actually steeled his resolve. That was no way for a soldier to die, vaporized by his own ship. So his mind turned to getting the job done.

It still amazed him that the electricity came from the gloves, and not the Rhadgast themselves. They weren't wizards after all, just a different kind of Tremist, with different weapons. Mason suspected there was more to them, though, otherwise their legend wouldn't be so terrifying and widespread. They would be men, not myths. He wondered what would've happened had the Rhadgast chanced across them on solid ground, where the cadets would've had nowhere to run and no tricks to pull.

Along the way, Merrin and Mason went over a plan. They stopped in the brig and picked up locking bracelets, to immobilize the Tremist after knocking them down.

Mason touched under his ear. "You figure out how the Tremist survived that fall?"

"Uncertain," Elizabeth replied. "The moment before, all vitals were gone. I noticed an energy surge around their armor. Sir, I posit their armor is responsible for bringing them back. The energy field may have restarted their hearts and bolstered their central nervous systems."

Mason shivered. *Hopefully I don't have to test that function on myself.*

"They're still in the gravity-free bay?" Mason asked.

"Affirmative."

"Good. Keep turning gravity on and off in case they get any ideas about crawling out of there."

"Will do, sir."

Mason smiled. "What would I do without you, Liz?"

"You would be at a disadvantage, sir."

"A big one. Is the bridge aware that their friends are neutralized?"

"I put up a communication barrier between starboard and the bridge. No transmissions got through. They may be on alert because of this, but they don't know what happened."

They reached the stairwell that would take them up one level, right outside the bridge. Mason went over the plan one more time. Willa, a wiry fifth year, began rubbing her eyes and yawning to get them to tear up. Her right eye was blue, the other green.

"I'm ready," she said, tangling up her strawberry hair with her fingers.

"The bridge is still locked," Elizabeth said in his ear. "All eight Tremist are accounted for."

"Perfect," Mason said. They walked up the stairs slowly, but their footsteps still rang softly on the metal steps. At the top, Mason opened the door and stuck his head out, just to be sure: it was clear, an equal stretch of hallway to both sides, punctuated by doors and lifts that ran to different places. The hallway was starkly lit in white. Just across the hall was one of the bridge entrances—a wide, automatic door that split down the middle.

Mason stepped out, P-cannon in his left hand, Rhadgast glove on his right. The doorway to the left of the bridge led to someone's office, and it was indented enough to provide cover. He pressed himself there and waved out Merrin and Willa. Merrin squeezed in next to him and said, "Hi," softly.

"Do you forgive me?" Mason whispered.

"Eventually," Merrin replied with a smile. Which was good enough for him.

Mason nodded to Willa, who sat down right in the middle of the hallway, grabbed her ankle . . .

And began to scream at the top of her lungs.

Chapter Nineteen

Long, wailing screams that rattled Mason's eardrums. Real tears welled and spilled from her eyes, and she rocked side to side, shaking her head all around. "My leg!" she screamed. "MY LEG! HEEEELLP!"

It took ten seconds, but the door to the bridge hissed open. Two Tremist marched out with talons. Mason ducked back into the doorway, then peeked around the corner with one eye.

"Quiet!" one shouted. "Quiet or I'll blast you!"

Willa stopped screaming and rolled onto her side. "It hurts! They left me they left me!"

"Where are the others?" one said.

Mason wanted to yell, "Right here!" but they were facing away from him at the moment, and throwing away that advantage would be foolish. So he just stepped out from behind cover, raised his hands, and fired off a volley from both weapons. The glove only required a thought and the P-cannon a squeeze of his finger. Merrin was right beside him, doing the same thing. Violet lightning crackled down the hallway, narrow and precise, until the Tremist were on the ground, convulsing next to Willa.

"Now!" Mason said.

Willa sprang upright, and behind her the thirteen other cadets burst through the doorway, P-cannons at the ready. Mason led the charge into the bridge, where the six Tremist remained. They froze. Mason wanted to laugh. The sight of that many ESC cadets pouring into the room, automatically using the various consoles for cover, had to be startling. In four seconds the cadets were well covered, with sixteen guns pointed at the Tremist, not counting the two Rhadgast gloves.

Not a weapon was fired. The Tremist didn't raise their talons with that much firepower pointed at them, and the cadets didn't want to risk damaging the equipment. Mason could tell the Tremist feared the Rhadgast gloves from the subtle way they shifted and stared. The talons were superior to P-cannons, sure, but the cadets already had line of sight. Outside the dome, space crawled by, the black punctuated with dazzling white pinpricks. The Coffey system's sun glowed like a hot marble millions of miles away, and the large green planet of Nori-Blue dominated the front view. It was so beautiful, Mason had to work hard not to look, to keep his eyes on the targets.

"Hands where I can see them," Mason said, trying to keep the grin out of his voice; it wasn't too difficult when he remembered the hard part was just beginning.

He and Merrin kept their gloved palms pointed toward the Tremist as the cadets slowly circled around from behind. Mason watched carefully, tense, as the cadets slapped locking bracelets on all the Tremist, then forced them into kneeling positions.

Willa and another fifth year, Terrence, went to rip their helmets off, but Mason said, "No," and they stopped. He didn't want the crew to see their purple hair and too-pale skin. Merrin didn't deserve their suspicion, and it would only make their jobs harder. She seemed to recognize the danger of being revealed and bit her lower lip. She mouthed the word *thanks* at Mason, and he nodded discreetly.

"All Tremist neutralized for at least the next three hours," Elizabeth said through external speakers.

A deafening cheer went up on the bridge. The cadets pumped

their weapons in the air, jumping up and down. Mason was glad for it; they would need that feeling to get them through. He wanted them to hold on to it, wear it like armor.

One of the Tremist began to laugh. A long, cackling laugh that Mason knew was forced.

"What you laughing at?" Jeremy said, moving to kick the Tremist in the chest.

Mason stopped him with a hand and stepped forward. He held out his glove and let electricity crawl over it.

"Tell me the joke, so that I might laugh with you," he said.

The Tremist shook his head and got himself under control. "I'm just imagining how the king will peel the flesh from your bones . . . when he finds out you still have his daughter."

Chapter Twenty

Luckily, only Tom and Merrin got it. The other cadets had no idea what the Tremist was talking about. So Mason had Stellan and Jeremy and Tom, and four fifth years, stand the group of Tremist up and march them off the bridge before anyone could ask questions. Merrin went with them, since the threat of her glove would go a long way to keeping the Tremist in line.

"Keep your distance," Mason called after them. Their hands might be bound, but their feet were not.

The fifth years half dragged, half carried the two unconscious Tremist behind them.

Mason approached a curly-haired cadet named Andrew, who was dragging a Tremist by the leg. "After you're done, relieve the two cadets in sick bay and report on Commander Lockwood's condition."

Andrew dropped the Tremist's leg, and was clearly about to complain, but Mason just raised an eyebrow.

"Sir, I'd prefer not to," Andrew said anyway.

Mason lowered his voice. "I can see the burn on your neck. Get it taken care of."

Andrew tried to pull his collar over the burn, which made him wince. "I'm functional," he said.

"I know that. Let's make sure you stay that way."

Andrew nodded somewhere between reluctantly and thankfully. Mason clapped him on the arm, then reentered the bridge.

He was left with seven cadets staring up at him. He stood on top of the slightly raised platform in the middle, where the captain's chair was, but had not yet taken the seat. It felt wrong. The bridge was shaped like a circle with an X in the middle. In the center of the X was the captain's chair. Forward and to the left was the pilot console. Forward and to the right, weapons. In rear left was communications. Rear right was the link to engineering, where Susan usually sat.

Surrounding the perimeter of the circle were long, low consoles that monitored every other function on the ship. A station for life support, for the synthetic gravity, for controlling cross gates.

"I'll be back," he said. "Find a station you think you can handle. No fighting. If you don't feel comfortable on the bridge, I could use someone in the engine room, and in life support. There are enough of us to fill all the spots."

They stared at him.

"Get to it," he said.

They did.

Mason watched for a moment, then left the bridge and moved down the crossbar until he caught up with the others.

"She's one of us, you know," the lead Tremist was telling Stellan and Jeremy. "Don't trust her. Just take off my helmet and see for yourself."

Mason brushed him with the glove, letting electricity come to the surface. The Tremist yelped and jumped off the floor. "Stop talking," Mason said.

Once they reached the brig, Mason gave each Tremist a cell and had Tom turn on the audio-dampener so they couldn't talk to each other. Then he sent the fifth years back to the bridge, minus Andrew. Only Stellan and Jeremy, the two who didn't know Merrin's secret, remained.

Mason stepped into the first cell and pulled the leader's helmet off with one smooth motion. His violet hair was plastered flat under his suit, and his violet eyes were narrowed in disgust, studying the cadets before him.

Until they settled on Merrin.

"As you can see, Merrin has some resemblance to the Tremist. We don't know what that means, but we know it doesn't matter. Merrin is one of us. For right now, it doesn't leave this room. If that is a problem, let me know and I'll put you in one of the cells." Since there were only six cells, all full, Mason hoped that didn't seem like a fun option.

"Understood," Stellan and Jeremy said together.

Merrin was staring at the Tremist with her lips parted, shaking her head so slightly it seemed like a tremor. "No . . ."

"We don't know what it means," Mason was quick to say. *And it doesn't matter anyway.*

"But the resemblance is there," Tom added.

"It's hair and eye color, so what?" Jeremy said.

"It could be a trick," Stellan said. "They're rumored to be shapeshifters. Remember how they just *reanimated* in the gravity-free bay? There is not enough data to make a conclusion." Mason appreciated Stellan's logical take at the moment. Thank Zeus no one was making a big fuss.

Merrin was looking at the floor now; the Tremist was staring her down, sneering really, like, *Ha ha, got you in trouble.* Mason was tempted to black out the cell, so no one could see in or out, but he didn't want to make it seem like Merrin couldn't handle it.

"You okay?" Mason asked, because he had to.

Merrin nodded after a moment. "Thanks. I just . . . I want to know what it means."

"We'll find out," Tom said plainly, as if it would be the easiest thing in the galaxy.

"The girl isn't just one of us," the lead Tremist said. "She's a princess. Stolen from her parents by human scum." Merrin stood tall now under his gaze. "Remember your old life, princess? Your father misses you."

Mason didn't want to believe it, but then he remembered the cold recognition the king had on the bridge. If Merrin truly was a princess, Mason had a feeling they would see the king and his Hawk again. Which might work in their favor, if they were smart about it. He tried to imagine his best friend as alien royalty and just . . . couldn't. Not that she wasn't regal—there was definitely something about her, something he hadn't quite figured out yet. But it was just too crazy of an idea.

Merrin clenched her jaw. "I just saw my father two weeks ago. Save your lies." With that, she turned on the full audio-dampener. Behind the plastic, the Tremist laughed silently. Almost as an afterthought, Mason blacked out the cells. *Let them sit in the dark.*

The five of them walked to the bridge in silence. Mason was ready for a hot meal and bed, but those seemed further away than ever. He passed the corridor that would take them to sick bay: Mason wanted desperately to talk to Commander Lockwood, to relay all that had happened, but that would be wasted time. They needed to cross to Earth, to make sure it was safe, then cross to Olympus, where the call would be put out to every ship in the galaxy. No planet was safe as long as the Tremist possessed the gate. It was as simple as that. They were finally in a position to sound the alarm. And maybe, if things were safe, they could pursue the king's Hawk and recover the crew.

And his sister.

Mason returned to the bridge to find it . . . running.

The perimeter positions were filled, and the cadets were communicating with each other, updating the status of the ship, sending information to scroll along the clear dome, bright numbers and letters against black space.

Tom took weapons control in the front right, and Stellan drifted to the engineering station in the rear right. Jeremy took communications behind Mason's left. Merrin sat down in the pilot's chair to the front left, disengaging autopilot and letting the Egypt drift through space under her residual momentum. Mason knew each of them had specialized in these stations during battle simulations. Now they would be put to the test.

"Ready for systems check, Captain," Elizabeth said.

One by one the stations sounded off. Each seated cadet turned, announced their station—gravity, atmosphere, life support, scanners, shields, radiation—and said, "Ready." He listened, but didn't see. His eyes were for Nori-Blue straight ahead, a world so similar to his own, green and alive against the night. It was outlined on the dome's heads-up display, in case he missed it.

He took a slow breath. In, then out.

It was either too late to warn his people, or it wasn't. His hunch was correct, or it wasn't. They would win the day, or they wouldn't. Mason was prepared, he thought. In a place he didn't belong, afraid in ways he didn't know he could be afraid, but ready to do his duty the best he could. Susan would expect nothing less. So would his parents.

Tom was the last to turn in his chair. He smirked. "We are fully armed, Captain, and ready."

Mason looked at the captain's chair. It was large, meant for a full-grown man or woman. The armrests had two panels with various controls on them. They could flip open and produce twin control sticks, if the captain ever wanted to pilot the vessel himself.

The whole crew was watching as he stepped onto the platform and sat down in the chair. The cushion hugged him comfortably, and he fit better than expected. Merrin gave him a small smile and spun back to the pilot console. Tom nodded and did the same.

"Cross gate," Mason said.

A bulky second year to Mason's left turned in his chair. "Ready, sir."

"Release a gate," Mason said. "Open a course to Earth."

Chapter Twenty-one

The second year turned back to his console and punched in a series of commands. Two seconds later, the bridge glowed with a soft green light, briefly, then faded back to white.

"Gate away, sir," the second year said.

From the front of the engineering side, starboard, Mason could see a ring of silvery metal drift out in front of the Egypt. Slowly, it began to expand as the curved metal tubes within the hoop telescoped. What started as a small hoop no bigger than a shuttle grew until it was large enough to swallow the whole front right wing. It drifted farther, expanding, until it was a big silvery circle in space, big enough for the Egypt to pass through.

"Charge the gate," Mason said. His hands were sweaty, mouth dry. If the cadet had done the math correctly, the gate would fold the fabric of space just outside of Earth, and they'd have a perfect view of their home planet. The bridge was very quiet, very still, as if all the cadets were holding their breath. Mason certainly was.

It would only take a few seconds to charge the gate . . . and then what? What was he supposed to do? It would depend on what they saw on the other side of the gate, but even then Mason had no idea. If the way was clear, and the Egypt went through, he still didn't know who he was supposed to report to. He imagined sending out a fleet-wide broadcast—something reserved only for the highest ranks, and only in the direst of emergencies—and wanted to throw up. *Stop*, he told himself. This *was* an emergency, a dire one. He wouldn't get in trouble. The fact that they'd retaken the ship should overshadow everything else.

Mason hoped the Olympus would somehow be waiting right there, so he could just open a channel and relay what he knew and then get his crew to safety. He wished it so hard he was almost dizzy with the fantasy, and he realized instantly it was just that—a dream. *Let me get us back to the Academy, that's all.* He had never looked forward to studying more than he did at that moment.

"Charged," the second year said.

Outside the Egypt, the cross gate was spinning lazily, clockwise.

The space inside the ring began to ripple, the white dots of stars swimming drunkenly, and then in an instant they were all gone, replaced by a perfect, steady view of Earth. The cloudy blue planet hung in space, appearing the size of a large orange held at arm's length.

"What is that . . . ?" one cadet breathed.

"Zeus!" cursed another.

The space around Earth was not empty.

It was filled with too many Tremist ships to count.

But that wasn't what made Mason's head swim dangerously, what made him unable to get out of the chair. It was the gigantic cross gate unfolding in space, right before their eyes. While the stolen gate was still mostly a cube, the process was definitely underway.

Mason wasn't going to get his crew back to the Academy. He wasn't going to open a simple com channel and then go back to being a student. The sweet dream he'd had only moments ago turned sour, and he wanted to scream at the unfairness of it all.

Because things were worse than what he had dared to imagine.

The Tremist were going to steal Earth.

Chapter Twenty-two

The cadets seemed to realize it as he did. The bridge erupted in exchanges of information as the cadets checked and double-checked their systems, preparing for engagement. Mason barely heard them. His ears were ringing for some reason, and he felt a little faint, his eyes a little swimmy.

The Egypt hadn't yet gone through the gate; it wasn't too late to stay on this side, near Nori-Blue. He imagined a quick end—the cloud of Tremist ships zipping across space to focus fire on the Egypt. If the Tremist scanners were half as good as the ESC's (and why wouldn't they be?), the Tremist would be aware of the Egypt almost immediately.

Mason could press a few buttons, and the Egypt's gate would power down, stop its spin, and begin the contraction process. They could still run away.

But they could still try to save the world.

With icy clarity, he saw now what the worst part of command was. The glory came by chance, after you made the hard calls. After you made choices about people's *lives* in an instant.

He had to make a choice, even though it was the last thing he wanted to do.

"How many ships?" Mason whispered to Elizabeth.

"Ninety-seven," Elizabeth replied without emotion. He felt a sudden, hard spike of jealousy then. Elizabeth didn't feel a thing. Ninety-seven ships was just information to her, not a sign of certain doom. Or if she understood what it meant, she probably wasn't able to care about it.

"The king's Hawk is among them," Elizabeth added, which let loose a cloud of butterflies through Mason's stomach.

Tom spoke over the cacophony. "How many ESC in the area, Elizabeth? How many friendly ships?"

Merrin waited patiently at the pilot console, hands on the controls, ready to move forward or back at Mason's command. She didn't ask for an order, just waited. Mason almost hoped she'd decide for him.

"Stand by," Elizabeth said.

The gate, once an enormous cube, resembled a spider waking up from a nap. The bridge magnified the view of it, and Mason could see thin spears branching off, extending, and reconnecting with other pieces. It was like a cloud of metal, growing larger in all directions, blue slivers of Earth suddenly becoming visible through the latticework.

"Three ESC ships in the area," Elizabeth said. "None are engaging. One is a pleasure barge, and two are ESC personnel-carrier shuttles. All three are on trajectories to take them out of the system. We are effectively alone."

The bridge hushed at the words.

Tom spun his chair around. "We can't go," he said. "They'll destroy us."

They still hovered outside the gate, with ninety-seven black specks in front of Earth, like the screen was just dirty—like Mason could just wipe the enemy ships away with his hand. The bridge, helpfully and automatically, zoomed in on the various Tremist vessels stationed around the ever-unfolding cube. There were the enormously long and tall Isolators, which dwarfed even the Egypt. They didn't resemble animals, but rather a bulky rectangle on its side, thinnest in the middle, with bright red twin engines in the rear, one stacked on top of the other.

Also present were vessels Mason didn't have a name for, of

various sizes. Some had purple engines, some blue like the Egypt. The big guns on the moon should've made short work of them. It was supposed to be classified, but Susan had once told him there was a gun on the moon that could create a particle beam as thick as Mason's forearm. A beam of pure matter designed to impale ships and core them like an apple.

But the moon was dark and silent, as if all ESC had evacuated.

"Are you listening?" Tom demanded. "Captain?" he added.

"I'm listening," Mason replied. "But we still have to go."

A few of the cadets—Mason didn't look away from Tom, so he didn't know which—muttered their displeasure. One even said, "He can't be serious."

Another said, "Shut up, he's acting captain."

Mason wanted to power down the gate, but could they really leave Earth at the mercy of the Tremist? Even if the chances they could help were slim, they might be able to slow the process down and buy time for reinforcements. And that was enough.

Tom bolted upright out of his chair. "You're an *idiot*. They'll destroy us immediately. We have to warn the fleet."

"I'm sure the fleet has already been warned," Mason said. "You think Earth didn't send out a transmission or two when these guys showed up?"

Kellan, the second year running the cross station (Mason only just then recalled his name), said, "Sir, the gate is getting hot. We need a decision."

"One second," Mason replied with a nod. He wished he had a thousand seconds to decide. Ten thousand.

"Elizabeth," Merrin said, "where is the rest of the fleet located?"

Elizabeth didn't speak for five whole seconds. Then: "The ESC main forces are amassing behind Saturn. Right now there are twelve ships present. By the end of this universal hour, there are expected to be forty-seven. In seventy-eight minutes those ships will cross into Earthspace to engage the Tremist."

"What about Olympus?" Tom said. "Where is Olympus?"

Elizabeth was quiet for ten seconds, presumably while she gathered data from the system-wide information net. "Olympus is unavailable for another two hours. Her cross system is jammed."

Convenient the cross gate for the space station would go down *now*.

This is a coordinated attack, Mason thought.

Elizabeth spoke again. "Update—it appears the ESC may wait for Olympus's firepower before moving. I will receive another orders update in nine minutes. We are commanded to cross into battle formation behind Saturn at once."

There it was: a clear command.

Seventy-eight minutes were left, maybe more, if the ESC decided to go without Olympus. The gate was already triple the size it was before, a giant sphere of crisscrossed tubes, fine as spider silk from this far away. Now there was only one question to ask. It was the question that would determine if Mason and his crew could join the relative safety of the fleet, or if he would have to ignore orders once again. This time the order wouldn't be petty, though. Ignoring the command might destroy them all. Looking at the amount of Tremist in system, maybe *might* was the wrong word.

So he took a breath and prepared to ask the question, trying to numb himself against the impending answer.

"Liz," Mason said. He swallowed, throat dry. "At its current rate, how long until the gate unfolds and is operational?"

Elizabeth waited three more seconds. When she spoke, her voice sounded sad, even though Mason knew that should be impossible. "Thirty-two minutes," she said.

The air seemed to go out of the bridge. No one spoke. Mason fought not to scream. "Don't they *know*?" he said. "It'll be too late, don't they know?"

"I'm telling them," Elizabeth said. "They are very busy. They are ignoring my Primary One channel. They are—"

"What is it?" Mason said.

"Tremist have entered Saturnspace. The fleet is trying to cross out, but the Tremist have sent nimble fighters. The Sparrows are destroying cross gates as they deploy." Mason imagined the needlelike ships zipping through space, attacking cross gates like a swarm of bees.

He felt cold all over. The world was ending right in front of him. How they recaptured the bridge seemed to mean nothing now. Absolutely nothing. Still their cross gate floated just in front of the Egypt, waiting for them to pass through. First the moon's defenses had been knocked out somehow, and now Saturn—the Tremist had thought of everything to ensure their victory.

Had they thought of eighteen cadets aboard the SS Egypt?

"The fleet is where we have a chance!" Tom said. "We'll never get close by ourselves."

"If we leave here, Earth is gone," Mason reasoned.

Tom took a step forward. "I won't let you kill us all in some insane act you think is bravery."

Merrin spoke very quietly. "The fleet won't come in time. It's us or nothing."

"It's suicide," Tom said.

Mason stood up on watery legs. "Arm everything we've got, Renner. That's an order." He tried to use the voice of a captain. He had to sound sure of his decision, so the others didn't detect his uncertainty.

"Arm the weapons yourself," Tom said, preparing to stalk off the bridge.

He made it three steps before Mason grabbed his upper arm and held him fast. "Get back to your station."

Tom's eyes were wet and bloodshot. "Make me."

Mason was about to shove him back toward the weapons console, but Tom flung his arm off and swept Mason's legs out from under him. A fast, brutal move Mason hadn't expected. He landed hard on his back, and Merrin let out a yelp of surprise.

"Thomas!" Jeremy shouted.

"I'm taking over this—" Tom began shouting to the bridge, until Mason spun on his back and kicked Tom's legs out from under him. Tom fell hard next to Mason and the two rolled together, trading punches and elbows, too close to do much damage. Mason's glove tingled against his skin, and it felt like the thing *wanted* to pour electricity into Tom, but Mason thought *no!* and the tingle faded into the background.

"*Stop it!*" Merrin said. "This isn't the time."

"I won't let him take us on a suicide mission!" Tom said through gritted teeth. He was trying to shove Mason off.

Mason's face was hurting from several blows; the armor protected the rest of him. It was a good kind of pain, though, it made him sharp, woke him up a little from the stupor of seeing so many Tremist ships in one area, so very close to home.

Mason bounced Tom's head off the floor, harder than he wanted to. Tom's eyes swam for a moment, then cleared. "Listen to me!" Mason pleaded. "We're the only hope Earth has!" Tom stilled in his grasp; Mason had gotten on top of him and was pinning his arms in place. "There is no one else."

Nobody spoke. The gate was still there, waiting. Through it, a tiny yellow dot blossomed next to Earth. It took a second to register as an explosion seen from very far away.

"There is now one ship in the area," Elizabeth said. "The pleasure barge is all that remains."

"Let me up," Tom said.

"Are you going—" Mason began.

"I said *let me up.*"

Slowly, Mason climbed off of Tom Renner.

Tom stood up and dragged his hand under his split lower lip, smearing blood. He straightened his uniform, snapped it tight around his waist. Then walked to the weapons console and sat down.

"Let's do this," Tom said.

Merrin looked to Mason: her luminous purple eyes were wide, but not quite from fear. Mason was momentarily struck by how beautiful she was. *And you've thought so all along.* Now that he knew she wasn't human, Mason wondered how he ever thought she was in the first place. She was something more.

She looked away when Mason kept staring at her, cheeks turning a light shade of purple. Suddenly, reality came crashing down around his shoulders. He had to sit back down. He made himself look at each one of the cadets, realizing their lives were in his hands. This was what it felt like to be captain. It was the worst feeling ever, and Mason couldn't wait to give up the job.

A plan came to him then, one that would make him *and* Tom happy.

"Are we ready?" Merrin said, hand on the throttle lever.

Were they?

Mason didn't know.

But it didn't matter, because it was time to fight back.

"Take us through," he said.

Chapter Twenty-three

They all felt the weird tingly static as they passed through the gate. In one second they were 302 light years away, and in the next, they were in Earthspace. A very crowded space, at the moment.

So it was best not to dawdle.

"We are fully armed," Tom said, hunched over his display. "At maximum range for particle beams."

"Target the bulk of the cube," Mason said. More than half of it had deployed into superlong tendrils, but the other half was still solid, closer to cube form. It was a metallic ball of yarn with hundreds of strings pulled off it, all knitted together to resemble layers of spiderwebs.

"Targeted!" Tom said.

"Fire all standard particle beams."

Four thin beams of white light shot out from the Egypt, two from the front of each forward prong. They reached the cube instantly, four parallel lines that stretched thousands of miles. In the distance, the cube seemed to drink in the light, glowing a soft bluish-green.

"It's shielded," one cadet replied behind him.

"Ineffective," Tom said, voice dropping.

"Add electron beams!" Mason said. Two more superthin lines of light shot out, these a yellowish color, not truly lasers since they were comprised of matter, not light. The cube glowed brighter for a moment.

"The Tremist are now aware of us," Elizabeth said calmly, as if this was news. "Moving to intercept."

Tom spun in his chair again. "We don't have the power to get through the cube's shields. It's time to go."

"Wait," Mason said.

"I *gave* you your *shot*," Tom said.

"Just *wait*," Mason barked. The bridge quieted. In the far distance, a few of the ships began to glow with bright blues and violets and reds, as their engines engaged and they began heading toward the Egypt.

"Stellan," Mason said.

"Yes, Captain," he replied, behind Mason's right side. Stellan had taken a special course in ESC shielding tactics, since his major field of study was going to be engineering.

"Can you scan the shield and tell me if slow-moving objects can get through? Objects of higher mass, but very slow moving." *Like a person*, he didn't say, not yet.

A moment passed. "Yes . . . yes, they will."

Mason breathed a sigh of relief, which he almost found funny, considering how many enemy ships were flying toward them at that exact moment.

"Good," Mason said. "I need volunteers."

Chapter Twenty-four

"Jeremy, you're in command," Mason said.

Mason had been thinking about it in the back of his mind, and Jeremy would be the one to make the hard decisions. Better than Mason could, probably. Stellan was on the Academy path to becoming a captain, but there was still fear in him that just wasn't present in Jeremy. Mason thought of the time Jeremy had knocked his head against Tom's just to get them to stop acting like idiots. Jeremy was the one, even though Mason knew without a doubt that Jer would rather be fighting alongside them instead of giving orders.

Jeremy seemed to turn a shade of pale green, but he nodded. "Aye."

If Stellan felt slighted, he didn't show it. Mason figured Stellan knew his own limitations, and therefore knew he wasn't ready for the job yet. He wouldn't let his ego get in the way.

Mason addressed the bridge: "I have a mind to land on that cube and destroy it before it steals our home. If anyone wants to—"

"I do," Merrin said, raising her hand.

"I'm going," Tom said. He gave the ghost of a grin. "If only because I don't trust you to get the job done yourself."

Mason nodded at both of them. He hoped they knew it was highly unlikely they'd return from the mission. They had to know that.

Jeremy stepped up to the captain's chair. "Three orders," Mason said to him. "Drop us on the cube, then get out of here before the Tremist destroy you."

"What's the third?" Jeremy said.

"If you can come back and get us, that'd be great." Mason almost grinned.

Jeremy nodded. "Consider it done."

"Not yet, Mr. Optimism," Tom said. "There are klicks to go before we sleep."

"Drop another gate for an in-system jump," Mason told the bridge. "When the Tremist get too close, fly through. Once we're clear, move out."

Then Mason left with Merrin and Tom at his side.

⋗ The three donned spacesuits in a room on the two lowest levels of the crossbar, directly under the bridge, where the shuttle bays were all in a row. It was a room specifically designed to allow easy access to outer space. Behind clear walls to the left and right, the Egypt's small collection of shuttles waited in their separate bays, shiny under the overhead lights.

The spacesuits they wore were similar to the Tremist armor, in a way, close to the same color—jet-black, so as to blend in with space. They were the same size and shape as his stolen armor, too, but with ultralight jetpacks on the back to allow easy maneuvering through space. Mason and the others had logged a hundred hours with them during their second and fifth years at Academy I. Mason was loath to take off the Tremist suit, but there was no time to try and rig a jetpack to it. He left it buried under some clothes in one of the lockers.

He was very hot inside the suit, until the internal atmosphere kicked in and began to regulate his temperature. He worked the Rhadgast gauntlet over his already-gloved hand and felt it reestablish the connection. *Good.* Mason had been worried the gauntlet needed direct contact with skin to operate.

Beside him, Merrin and Tom finished suiting up. They put their helmets on at the same time. The helmets were snug, with clear faceplates from their foreheads to their chins. The suits hissed as they sealed. Merrin gave a thumbs-up, and so did Tom.

All that was left was the bomb. It was located in the sub-armory in the wall, behind a panel. Elizabeth had to unlock it for them. It looked like two short cylinders glued together and was magnetic, so Mason could stick it to his suit. They played rock-paper-scissors to see who would hold it, and Mason won, partly because he threw his hand a tenth of a second late, and knew they were both going for scissors. His rock meant he would carry the bomb. He stuck it to the side of his leg. It ran from his hip to his knee.

Mason studied the seam under his feet, where the floor would split apart on outer space, and the two halves would curl up into the clear walls.

"Remove gravity," he said.

The lightness returned to his stomach, and he pushed off gingerly and floated toward the ceiling.

"Why did I sign up for this?" Tom muttered, coming through clearly in Mason's helmet speakers.

"Because you're brave," Mason replied.

"Oh, right, that."

"We've done this before," Merrin said. "No big deal at all. Just this time it's . . ."

"Real space," Tom said. "Which is infinite, most likely. That means forever."

"Thanks, Thomas," Merrin said. They were holding on to handles in the ceiling, appearing to hang from them.

Jeremy came through the com: "Prepare to drop. We're moving through the gate now."

Twenty seconds passed where all Mason could hear was his breath.

"What's the plan?" Tom finally asked.

"We blow up the gate," Mason said.

"Ten seconds," Jeremy said. "It's hot out there, guys!"

Mason's heart began to pound. His heart monitor buzzed against his arm, helpfully asking him to calm down. It almost made him laugh. He shared a look with Merrin and Tom, and they nodded at him.

"Five, four . . ." Jeremy said.

In the floor, the locking mechanism *clunked* as it opened. Mason felt his jetpack humming against him, softly, a gentle vibration.

"Three, two . . ."

Mason tucked his legs under him so he was effectively standing on the ceiling, coiled into a ball, ready to spring out; Merrin and Tom did the same.

Then the seam zipped open, the two halves retracting into the walls too fast to follow, and for the briefest moment, before they were ejected from the Egypt, Mason could see everything. The vast inky space around him, so huge it was hard to think about. Impossibly huge, beyond comprehension. And there in the middle glowed the blue-white ball of Earth, and in front of that, the machine humans had created, which could now be their undoing. The size of it was incomprehensible, the time and effort required to create it incalcuable.

The Tremist ships were so close. Silent hulks in space. The clouds on Earth were full of soundless explosions, as shuttles were destroyed before they could leave the atmosphere. It was beautiful and horrifying at the same time. In that moment, Mason knew that everything was counting on them, and at that point, there was nothing he could do but try his best.

The atmosphere in the room exploded into space, and the three cadets launched themselves off the ceiling and out of the ship.

Chapter Twenty-five

Space opened up around them as they cleared the Egypt, and Mason realized how wrong it was. Humans didn't belong in outer space, inside little people-shaped suits that held in some air and heat. The sensation was like nothing else. There was literally light years of nothingness in almost every direction.

But none of that mattered, because the gate was in front of him. It blocked out most of the Earth now, still growing. The three of them were heading right for it. Mason risked a look behind and saw the Egypt powering through the black, its blue engine glowing bright, with Tremist in pursuit. The pursuers were too far away, though, and the Egypt was already heading for the gate that would take it to Saturn.

In his helmet, Merrin gasped as they got closer, and Tom said, quite calmly, "I can't believe we're doing this. . . ."

More limbs unfolded from the gate; it was not really a shape, but a geometric pattern. They flew toward it, and their reverse thrusters began to compensate, to prevent them from turning into paste upon the gate's surface.

The Tremist ships all around didn't seem to notice them. They floated lazily, like boats in a harbor, waiting for anyone foolish enough to mess with their stolen gate. They glowed in the yellow-orange light of the sun, which was a hot, too-bright ball ninety-three million miles away. Mason grinned behind his faceplate; the Tremist were in for a surprise.

"WHOOOOOOOOO!" Tom screamed suddenly, and Mason felt giddiness rising up inside him, too. They were on target, the gate still growing so that Mason had to turn his head 180 degrees to take in the whole thing from left to right. What remained of the cube was just ahead, a few kilometers out now. They were going to land on the side: the top part was a tangle of telescoping limbs and unfolding metal, slowly whittling down to the bottom. Mason tried to judge how much time they'd have once on the cube, but it was impossible—he was too amped up with adrenaline. His breath rasped loudly in his ears, and he realized that, despite the intense speed with which he was moving, it felt completely normal. He could've been floating in the gravity-free bay, or drifting in a pool. The suits seemed to compensate for any g-forces he'd be feeling.

They were going to do it.

They were going to land on the cube, easy as pie, and plant the explosives. Then they'd take off and wait for a pickup. The ruined gate would surely scatter the Tremist from Earthspace. Mason was already grinning, his fear forgotten.

Until he realized the jetpacks weren't slowing them enough. The gate was growing much too fast now.

"Manual override!" Mason screamed. "Slow down!" He squeezed his fists and pumped his arms back, like he was elbowing someone behind him, and felt himself slow a little more. The gate was just in front of them, the surface shimmering weirdly. He felt the shield as they passed through: there was resistance, like stepping into a vertical wall of water, and then they were inside. Stellan had been right.

"I can't slow down!" Merrin yelled. She was pumping her arms back, but the jetpack wasn't responding, not like Mason's and Tom's.

Mason was still a hundred feet from the cube when Merrin hit the surface. Her pack gave a bright burst of reddish light, and she spun sideways, cartwheeling off the cube and into space.

Chapter Twenty-six

"No!" Tom screamed.

"Hold on, Merrin!" Mason said as he touched down feetfirst. He felt the power in the cube under his feet, the deep vibrations as the thousands of moving parts did what they were designed to do.

Merrin didn't cry out, didn't scream, she just tumbled, her thrusters firing wildly, pushing her up the side of the cube, into the moving forest of metal. At any moment, a piece could swing up and bat her into space, or split her suit wide open, or just kill her through blunt force trauma.

Mason pushed off the cube vertically, following her.

Tom called after him, "Let me! You have to plant the bomb!"

But there was no time. Mason saw how fast she was moving, and knew he could catch her, but only now, only if he went at this exact moment. Tom groaned in frustration, and Mason knew he was following hard on his heels.

"Just get it done!" Merrin told them both. A piece of the gate sprouted under her, tossing her sideways, and she bounced across the top of the cube, where so many parts were extending and flipping upward.

Mason flew around the top corner of the cube, controlling his thrusters with as much focus as he could muster. It was a nightmare: thin poles swung back and forth, shooting out, making connections. Merrin bounced off many of them, but none could catch her, or slow her down much. Mason gave another burst of speed by extending his hands, and skimmed over the top, praying the moving ground under him wouldn't suddenly spring up and out. It was like swimming above a thousand sharks, waiting for one to bite you in half at any moment. He reached Merrin halfway across the top, grabbing her wrist, where her suit was thinnest and easiest to hold on to.

"Gotcha!" he cried, then felt a little silly. Merrin was giggling, though. The girl was laughing with the maze of flying metal all around them, like it was some kind of game, or just training.

"Well, you took your time," she said flatly.

"I got held up," Mason replied.

Tom zoomed up behind them and eased to a stop, ducking his head under a moving piece of gate. Mason couldn't see the circumference of the gate now. It curved up and out of sight in both directions, hundreds of miles across now, maybe thousands. But the dozens of Tremist ships around them were plainly visible, close enough to see lights behind their windows; if the three cadets had been noticed, Mason figured they were safe here: firing upon them now would risk damage to the gate, assuming Tremist weapons could even get through the shield.

Tom grabbed on to Merrin so Mason could set the bomb. He pulled it off his thigh and knelt on the gate. Up here he'd have to work fast: the pieces were moving so quickly it'd be hard to arm the bomb before it moved away. Even now, as Mason stood atop the cube, he felt himself dropping inches, as pieces slid out from under his feet. The cube was shrinking rapidly.

"Hurry!" Tom urged. His voice was giddy with the same thing Mason felt: the nearness of victory. They could plant the bomb and the *entire* Earth would be saved. Yeah, they'd be getting medals for this mission.

Mason was on his knees, about to secure the bomb, but movement caught his eye. Above them, a Hawk was coasting toward them, just one hundred meters away, now fifty. It came to a stop, blocking out half the sun. It was the king's Hawk, no doubt. Mason's blood would've frozen if not for the temperature regulator inside his suit.

"Um, how much longer?" Tom said.

"Don't mean to rush you!" Merrin added with a shaky laugh.

Mason gave a snarl of frustration and prepared to remagnetize the bomb.

But then a door opened in the bottom of the Hawk, and four Rhadgast dropped through the bottom like falling stars.

Chapter Twenty-seven

The three cadets were now deer in an earthen forest, running from wolves. Mason held Merrin's hand tightly, too tightly maybe, but he couldn't risk letting her go, not with her ruined thrusters.

"I'm dead weight, let me go!" Merrin said, voice harsh in his helmet. "They won't hurt me!"

"Yeah, *that's* gonna happen," Tom replied.

"They do seem friendly," Mason added.

All around them, purple bolts of lightning crackled across the surface of the cube, chasing them. For a brief moment, Mason hoped they would short out the gate, but then realized the ESC engineers would've accounted for something as simple as an electrical strike.

The bolts hit Mason too, but his suit was insulated. He still felt the heat from each blast, and the hairs on his body standing up. A temperature warning in his helmet began to beep, and sweat dripped onto his faceplate. He swam left and right, over and under poles, as the floor shrank away beneath them. They had two gloves themselves, but what chance did they have against four Rhadgast?

Merrin tugged at Mason's arm, her ruined thrusters making it harder to pull her along.

"I'm sorry," she said quietly. "I can't control it!"

Mason risked a glance behind and was rewarded: as he

watched, a Rhadgast was batted into space by a pole across the back of the legs. It sent him spinning away, executing backflip after backflip. Then another was pinned between two moving poles. It was perfectly silent, but Mason could imagine the scream as the Rhadgast arched its back unnaturally, arms flying out. The poles separated, and the Rhadgast floated like dead space junk.

That left two, which was two too many.

They were nearing the end of the cube now, on the other side. Nowhere else to go. "Just plant it!" Merrin said. "I'll try to hold them off."

"She's right," Tom said, zipping past them over a tangle of metal and under a rising arm. "We have—" Tom was cut off as a pole swung up suddenly, batting him into space much like the first Rhadgast. The blow to his chest knocked the wind out of him, the explosion of breath making Mason's ears ring. Tom spun through space, thrusters trying to compensate for his crazy trajectory. "Just do it!" Tom gasped. "Plant them, Stark! I can regain control!"

So Mason did. He slowed himself, and spun hard, extending his hand and firing his glove at the two pursuing Rhadgast. The Tremist wizards were ready, though, and met him with their own volley, as Merrin joined in. Purple lightning danced over the surface of the cube, rising and falling, curling, thick violet veins that writhed in silence. The tendrils met and wound against each other and built a kind of wall between them, blocking the Rhadgast from view behind a web of bright light.

Mason slammed the bomb down and pressed the button to make it stick, all while keeping his glove up. Heat began to build in his hand, and he saw Merrin next to him, half-crouched, braced against the lightning. Mason reached down to arm the bomb—it was only a single button he had to press, helpfully labeled ARM—but as he did, the piece of cube he'd adhered it to shot away into the darkness, taking the bomb with it.

It was gone.

Chapter Twenty-eight

There was nothing to do now but fight. Mason and
Merrin continued to trade lightning with the two
Rhadgast, who were coming closer all the while. The floor continued to sink, until it was thin enough to see over the edge, to
see how flat it had become. Soon there'd be nothing to stand on,
and the cube would be a circle.

The forest of metal was nearly gone, too, as the poles found
the places they were supposed to go, and went there. The gate
stretched and curved up to either side of them; many of the
Tremist ships were now inside the enormous hoop.

Mason sweated inside his suit, not wanting to give up. But there
wasn't much time left. Soon the Rhadgast would overpower them,
and the fight would be done. The pieces slid under his feet, again
and again, until they were standing on a thin, flat square. Soon that
broke apart too before the Rhadgast could reach them; it split in
half, throwing the combatants in opposite directions. The wall
of lightning sputtered and broke, the remnants crawling over
Mason's suit. He tumbled away, grabbing for Merrin's arm, the
big blue Earth flipping again and again past his vision.

"Gotcha!" Merrin said this time, grabbing on to Mason's arm
with both hands. The Rhadgast floated in the distance. Halfway
between them, the gate finished sliding together, becoming thinner and thinner as the pieces telescoped out. Now it was just a
flat line, much too large to even see the curve to it, though

Mason knew it was there. The gate was now a hoop as big as a planet. Mason watched it complete itself and finally stop moving.

They drifted in space; the Rhadgast didn't seem interested in them now that the gate was safe. The two wizards swooped away to collect their fallen comrades. Mason and Merrin passed through the shield again—that stepping through a wall of water feeling—and into open space.

"It's okay," Merrin said, tears in her voice. "We tried."

Mason couldn't look at her. Trying wasn't enough. Nobody rewarded you for trying, only winning. They had failed, and now billions would pay.

"It's okay . . ." Merrin said again, more to herself, it seemed.

Tom jetted over from above, having regained control. Together, the three of them held on to each other and didn't speak. After a minute or so, the Hawk returned, hovering over them, and Mason knew they would soon be captured—they would become the prisoners of war he once meant to free. Maybe Susan was still on the Hawk, alive and waiting for him.

The gate began to spin, slowly at first, almost too thin to see, as if someone had drawn it with an ancient graphite pencil. It gave off a faint, white-blue glow. And it wasn't just spinning, Mason noticed; it was moving, drifting almost, toward Earth.

The Hawk was going to pick them up, but Mason wondered if running out of air was preferable. Then he saw that neither thing was likely to happen, at least not right away.

As he watched the moon, it suddenly took on a strange texture—black specks against the ashy gray surface. A moment later he realized what he was looking at.

The ESC had crossed into Earthspace simultaneously. Half a hundred ships, with engines and weapons bristling bright.

The whole fleet was here, and ready for battle.

Chapter Twenty-nine

The blackness of space lit up with the sizzling light of hundreds of particle beams, all of them centered on the bottom of the spinning cross gate. But the ESC had created it well—they'd clearly learned from the last time the Tremist blew up a gate, so many years ago. It was the most powerful shield Mason had ever seen, or heard of. Yet the ships were manned by soldiers, and soldiers didn't give up—they kept their beams burning, probably well past the point hundreds of alarms would be screaming inside the ships. *Warning, warning, overheating may lead to a hull breach, which could result in loss of life.*

Long seconds passed, and the shield sputtered and sparked, but held. It was so bright Mason had to look away. Whatever failsafes the ESC had built into the shield had been stripped; they *should've* been able to turn it off with a command, but the gate seemed to fully belong to the Tremist now.

And as the three stranded cadets watched, the first of the ESC ships was destroyed in a puff of blue-white light. It was a country-class vessel like the Egypt. Then another ship was destroyed, this one a spark of orange-yellow light, with a fireball that lingered despite the lack of oxygen. Still the ESC focused their particle beams on the gate, ignoring the Tremist ships that swarmed around them like bees. No, like sharks—with pairs of giant jaws clamping shut from top and bottom.

Mason watched it dispassionately, the weight of the outcome

crushing his feelings until he was just . . . switched off. The ESC would either win out, or they wouldn't, and there was not a Zeus-banished thing he could do about it.

From the cluster of ESC ships, he saw the SS Egypt break away and swoop toward them. Jeremy must've locked on to their signal; he'd come back for them.

Tom gave a victory cry, but it sounded halfhearted. The gate still held. There would be no victory until it floated in pieces, spiraling apart in random trajectories.

"Will they break through?" Merrin asked. Though she wasn't really asking.

"I don't know," Mason replied automatically.

The Egypt dodged a few Hawks that gave up their pursuit when they realized the Egypt wasn't a direct threat to the gate. Soon the ship that had been their home the last two weeks hovered above them. The same door opened in the bottom, and they used their remaining thrusters to fly inside. Once gravity and atmosphere returned, Mason hurried to the bridge with Tom and Merrin, putting on his stolen armor along the way.

When they entered the bridge again, the gate was still whole.

Chapter Thirty

Mason retook command of the Egypt in time to see the end of the world.

He stood on the bridge with what was probably the first crew of cadets to ever see battle, to ever run their own ship. If it happened before, it wasn't in any of the lore books at Academy I.

The spinning gate wasn't just drifting now, it was moving with purpose.

Toward Earth.

The com station was a constant crackle of chatter—orders given, orders received. They were mandatory, so they filled the Egypt's bridge with their noise. Most of the ESC particle beams had overheated, and the gate was no longer under assault, aside from the occasional blast from a ship that had played their beams smart.

"What do we do, Captain?" more than one cadet asked him.

Watch, he wanted to say. *Watch our failure. Watch the end.* Because what did it really matter?

The gate would not be destroyed, that much was clear. So there was nothing to do but watch.

The warrior in him balked at that—the part of him he wanted to grow as he got older. You weren't supposed to just watch, you were supposed to fight. To the bitter end, like the soldiers in the old stories. That was what a real soldier *did*.

Sad, then, that Mason only felt like lying down. Maybe falling asleep, right there on the bridge.

"Mason," Jeremy whispered. He was right beside him. Tom was watching him too, and Merrin. They were probably watching him so they didn't have to watch the gate.

Mason shook himself from his trance, only because the others were still counting on him. He wouldn't have done it for himself.

Still the gate moved: a spinning hoop they only saw because the Egypt so helpfully highlighted it for them. The nonsentient computer on the bridge painted the gate a brilliant red color, not unlike fresh blood. According to the numbers scrolling on the dome, the gate was thinner than a strand of hair.

Engage, engage, voices on the com yelled. *Do something, fire, fire everything, fire what you have:* the orders from the com had devolved into pleas. Please help us, they said.

"Orders?" Tom finally said.

Merrin had been waiting at the pilot station the whole time, hands wrapped around both control sticks. She was half turned in her chair, waiting for an order, eyes narrowed. Fierce in a way Mason envied.

She gave him the smallest nod. He knew it meant *I'm with you.*

"Wait," Mason said. He felt pressure behind his eyes, and not for the first time. The words came automatically. "We're separate from the fleet. If we attack the gate, we'll be destroyed. Wait."

No one argued.

Maybe it was a coward's move, but it was smart. The gate would not be destroyed, and as captain, Mason would not turn his crew over to certain doom unless there was a chance, however small. That was his responsibility.

He told himself that.

. . .

➤ When the gate finally reached Earth, their view of the blue planet disappeared from one instant to the next. The gate spun faster, the computer told them, faster and faster, and then it folded space, and through the hoop they saw new stars. Stars the computer didn't recognize. There was a sun blazing inside the hoop now, a smallish yellow thing that didn't look too different from the sun in the center of Mason's solar system.

The gate moved over the Earth faster than he thought possible. Absurdly, it made him think of something he saw once, something terrible, when he was watching an Earth lore video about the twentieth century. It was about a phenomenon called bullfighting. Men would taunt bulls with colorful blankets. The bulls would run at the blankets instead of the men, and the men would sweep them over their faces, quickly, and then reset as the bulls turned around. It was quick. That's how quick the gate was now. The gate swept over the Earth, spinning faster than ever, and then it powered down, and the stars he knew returned, but the Earth was gone.

Chapter Thirty-one

The com was silent now. No more chatter. And the Tremist had even stopped their attack. Both fleets hung separately in the black that was no longer Earthspace. It was just regular old outer space, plain and featureless.

"There was a sun . . ." Tom said slowly. "Through the gate."

No one said anything. Merrin took her hands off the control sticks and let them fall to her sides.

"There was a sun," Tom said again. "Wherever they took Earth, there was a sun. They didn't just drop them into the cold black."

"Doesn't matter," Stellan said, sniffling. "The calculations needed are too precise. They could never position a planet in the exact right space to keep conditions on the surface the same."

"That's exactly what we wanted to do," Jeremy said, "with Nori-Blue."

"It's different," Merrin said. "Nori-Blue isn't full of sentient beings. If the ESC messed up, they could reposition it. Even if there were adverse weather changes on the surface, it would've been worth the price of stealing it."

Mason felt weary, hearing them talk. What did it matter if there was a sun? It was almost like they were in shock, or hadn't truly registered what had happened yet. *Earth was no longer in the solar system, and they had no idea where it was.*

The gate began to contract, a slow reversal of the unfolding process they'd tried so desperately to stop.

The fighting resumed. One moment, space was dead and still with the stationary hulks of hundreds of spacecraft, some whole, some in pieces, some scored black. The next, the void was alive with fire of all colors. Beams and balls of light exchanging in space that was no longer Earth's.

The ESC ships were named with little transparent tags the computer pasted onto the dome. Mason and the others were able to watch as the SS Kenya exploded in the middle of two other ships—the SS Paraguay and New Zealand, which both drifted away, wounded, venting white geysers of atmosphere. From this far away, Mason couldn't see the bodies tumble into space from the torn-apart crafts, but he knew they were there.

But the Tremist were taking hits too. An Isolator's side thrusters malfunctioned, and the gigantic ship veered sideways into two diving Hawks, which promptly exploded with puffs of green fire, impaling the Isolator at the same time.

"Captain," a cadet breathed behind him. Mason didn't know who. He needed to make a choice, or they'd be next. He needed to get his crew to safety. There was no honor in suicide, and no honor lost in living to fight another day.

In the next second, he learned he wouldn't have to run against orders after all, because the command to retreat was given. The message came as a scrolling green text along the bottom of the dome:

ALL SHIPS REPORT TO OLYMPUS.

Followed by:

GUARD YOUR GATES. DO NOT ENGAGE THE TREMIST.

"Finally," Tom said, but he sounded stunned, or slowed. Like he was very cold, or had just woken up from a deep sleep. "We should definitely go to Olympus. Olympus will protect us." It was very possible he was in shock. Was Mason in shock? He might've been. He wasn't sure how to tell. Nothing felt real, that's all he knew. His hands were a little numb.

In unison, the remnants of the ESC fleet began to drop cross gates. But the technology was too slow. The Tremist were able to laser the gates into spiraling pieces that glowed like embers, leaving the ships stranded until they could deploy another. As Mason watched (that seemed like all he had been doing for the last thousand years—watching), a huge Isolator flew in tight above the SS Japan and sucked the whole ship up into its open cargo area, leaving the Japan's cross gate to spin unattended.

"Captain," Merrin said calmly, jarring him back to reality.

Mason nodded; the fight was lost here, and they had their orders. "Drop another gate," he said. "Rendezvous with the fleet at Olympus."

A few of the cadets let out grateful sighs and focused again on their stations.

Until the dome's surface blurred slightly, and Tom's dad, Vice Admiral Bruce Renner, appeared on the screen.

Chapter Thirty-two

The vice admiral didn't look well. "Thank God you're all right," he said immediately. He had the same features as Tom—dark hair and eyes—with a short silvery beard. A beard that was gelled with drying blood from a gash above his right eyebrow. His nose was broken too, purple and crooked. Behind him, something showered orange-white sparks in a brilliant arc.

"Where's your mother?" he said, looking down at Tom, who sat behind the weapons console. "What are you . . . ?"

It didn't take long for him to realize. Bruce Renner's lower lip quivered, and then his jaw clenched. And then he nodded.

Tom's head hung, and he was completely still.

The vice admiral looked at Mason now. "Are you in charge?" Voice like steel, just like Tom's mother's had been.

"Yes, sir," Mason replied.

"And there are no ranking officers on the craft?"

"Just Commander Lockwood," Tom said suddenly, in a normal voice, "but he's injured. Gravely."

The vice admiral took two seconds to consider this, blank-faced. Through the dome, Mason watched the battle rage on. Silent explosions, in every color imaginable. But more and more of the ESC craft were escaping. It wouldn't be long before the Tremist recognized the Egypt on the fringes of the battlefield.

"We were boarded, Dad," Tom said. "The Tremist took every-one, or killed them, and we hid."

"We took back the ship, sir," Merrin said.

"I see that," the vice admiral replied. "Well done. But I don't want you to rendezvous with the fleet at Olympus. You are ordered to cross to a remote base and settle down there. Some-where small enough the Tremist won't know where you are. Understood?"

The huge gate was halfway back to its cube form, curling inward like a dying spider. It wouldn't be long before it was ready for transport.

"Negative, sir," Mason said without thinking. A few cadets gasped, but what was the vice admiral going to do, throw Mason in the brig? "Regrouping at Olympus is a mistake. The Tremist will just take the gate to Nori-Blue and steal it too. We have to stop them."

Instead of reprimanding him, the vice admiral went blank-faced again. He looked very tired. His eyes were slick with tears that weren't quite ready to fall.

After what seemed like an eternity, the vice admiral nodded. "The order to regroup came from Grand Admiral Shahbazian himself. I can't ignore it."

"We can't let them take both planets," Mason said, suddenly lightheaded. A cadet did not disobey an order. A cadet *did not* disobey an order from the grand admiral.

The Egypt's crew gave up a murmur of agreement; the other cadets were on board. It was strange: seeing Earth disappear should've crippled their resolve, but it seemed to make them stronger. They had nothing to lose. Mason was ready to fight for what was left of humanity, for the billions out there who were lost, possibly freezing to death at this very moment. Mason was ready.

"Are you aware of the Egypt's mission?" the vice admiral said, using his admiral voice again.

"Not completely, sir," Mason said.

"The Egypt held the gate, but it also held the Lock." Behind the vice admiral, the sparks still showered. Mason heard footsteps, and an alarm blared. The vice admiral was on the SS Russia, which was currently evacuating. "The Lock was the experimental counterpart to the gate. If the gate was ever stolen, the Lock could be used on a planet to freeze it in place. Who is your ship's AI?"

"Elizabeth, sir," Elizabeth said.

"Greetings, Elizabeth," the vice admiral said coolly. "Give these cadets access to the Lock."

"Done."

"Plant the Lock on Nori-Blue's surface," he said. He was looking at his son now. "The Tremist will be able to home in on its signal eventually, but it will buy the time we need to move our entire fleet into the system." He suddenly appeared doubtful. "Can you do this? Son?"

"We can do it," Mason and Tom said together.

"You do your mother proud," Bruce Renner said. "You do me proud. I am proud of all of you. You are no longer cadets, but among the ESC's finest. Now go, before it's too late—"

His signal was suddenly cut off.

"Elizabeth!" Tom shouted. "Where is the Russia?"

She highlighted the vice admiral's ship on the dome. "Intact, Ensign Renner, the broadcast was interrupted by—"

Then *she* was cut off.

The dome fuzzed once more, and then the Tremist King was onscreen, holding Susan Stark next to him with a handheld talon pressed against her temple.

Chapter Thirty-three

"Susan!" Mason cried out. He couldn't help himself. Susan's eyes were deep purple, and one was swollen shut. But she managed to smile at Mason. A normal smile, like she wasn't currently held hostage by what was presumed to be the deadliest being in the galaxy.

"Hey, little brother," she said. And they were the sweetest words Mason ever heard. He promised himself to later promise to Susan he would never play a stupid mean trick again, not ever. Or against her, at least.

The king's dark oval of a face seemed to float next to hers, ready to suck her in like a black hole.

"Mason Stark," the king said, voice rasping through his mask, clear but metallic.

"Yes," Mason replied. He clasped his hands behind his back and squeezed them together; they were the only things that were shaking, for now. Susan was in danger, but Susan was *alive*, still breathing, her heart still pumping. At the moment, the crushing defeat was insignificant; Mason knew he shouldn't feel that way, since an ESC soldier's first duty was to the ESC, but he didn't care.

"I will make this simple and easy for you," the king said. "You will deliver the girl Merrin Solace to me, or this will be the last time you see your sister alive." He spoke like Merrin wasn't sitting five feet in front of the screen, right where he could see her.

Mason was about to answer—he wasn't sure exactly what he would say, but he was going to say something—when Merrin turned slowly in her chair, away from the screen, and mouthed a word at Mason, slowly, so he could read her lips. . . .

The word was *hostage*.

"Please, don't make me," she said immediately after, out loud, creating a fake scared voice. It didn't sound very fake, though.

Hostage, she had mouthed. The king was going to great lengths to get his daughter back, so she obviously still meant something to him.

"Where's *Earth*?" Tom demanded.

Mason felt a flush of embarrassment. Here he was worried about his sister's life, when the whole planet was at stake. But he knew demanding the return of Earth wasn't going to happen, so why bother demanding it? Even if the king was willing to return the planet for his daughter's life, the giant cross gate was still contracting, and nowhere near wherever Earth had gone.

Mason had to act fast, though, or the ruse would fail. He put a grim look on his face and marched to the pilot station, then grabbed Merrin by the neck and lifted her out of the chair. She went along with him, pretending to struggle in his grasp, but not really fighting it. Then, against all instinct, he put his P-cannon against Merrin's head, and made himself a mirror of the king. His stomach flipped then flopped, and sweat broke all over him. He was *definitely* going to throw up this time.

The crew was murmuring quietly now, clearly confused but not sure what to do about it. Tom was staring at Mason out of the corner of his eye, but didn't seem surprised; he'd probably seen Merrin mouth the word from his angle.

The king's faceplate meant Mason had no idea what his reaction was. Susan had the same expression as before, mainly because her face was too swollen to change—only her lips parted slightly.

Mason spoke first: "No one will lay a hand on Captain Stark

again," he said. It was strange to call her that; he supposed he was also Captain Stark, kind of. "As you can see, I have something to trade for her life." The words sounded funny in his mouth, like he was trying too hard to sound like a grown-up. But he needed to show the king he was serious.

"You would threaten one of your own?" the king said, after what felt like a minute.

"I believe I just did," Mason replied.

"Please . . ." Merrin half whispered, writhing a little in Mason's grasp. He wanted to say he was sorry, even though it was her idea. It felt so wrong. He had to press the P-cannon to her temple to keep it from visibly shaking. He would apologize after. It was an act, but all it would take was a simple press of a button to end Merrin's life. Mason wanted to throw the cannon across the room. He'd rather hold a burning coal.

"A trade, then," the king said.

Susan shook her head, just slightly. Of course she'd be against the cadets coming in contact with the king or any of his crew. But Mason wouldn't just leave her behind. He wouldn't just say goodbye and turn the dome screen off.

"On neutral ground," Mason added quickly. He wasn't about to step onto the king's Hawk and just hope they'd let him leave. Not a chance.

The king cocked his head, just slightly, like he was studying Mason through the screen. Mason held his posture, ignoring the sweat. The wait for his answer felt like forever. No one on the bridge made a sound.

"On the surface of Nori-Blue," Mason said.

The only neutral ground that ever existed, Mason figured.

The exchange would be their cover: if the Egypt was going there for a prisoner trade, no one would suspect the Lock. They'd just have to plant it before the Hawk arrived.

"Agreed," the king said.

Susan's head drooped. "Mason, don't go," she said.

The king ignored her and said, "If you betray me, young captain, I will make her death a million times worse. I will make it take years."

Mason tasted metal at the back of his throat.

"I won't," he said.

Chapter Thirty-four

The dome screen snapped off, revealing the black of space again, and the drifting hulks of charred and twisted metal, some of which still smoldered despite the absence of oxygen. The Tremist fleet was disappearing, making the jumps to light speed and beyond, using a technology the ESC engineers were still trying to replicate. They looked like shooting stars, bright white lines that faded as quickly as they came. In the distance, the computer tagged the king's Hawk; it was banking away and powering up for faster-than-light travel.

The cross gate would buy them some time on Nori-Blue, but the Hawk wouldn't be far behind.

Mason took his hand off Merrin's neck and she rubbed it. He felt his cheeks burn, feeling ashamed even though it was an act. She only punched him lightly on the shoulder. "Well done. I was hoping you weren't going to muck that up."

Mason cracked a smile, then gave a full-on laugh. It exploded out of him, made of equal parts stress and relief.

He stopped laughing when a third year at the perimeter console to his right asked, "What in Zeus's good mountain was that all about?" He was a boy named Kale, if Mason remembered right. His mind was a little mushy at the moment.

And another said, "Yeah, seriously. What's going on?"

Mason wasn't about to tell them, *Oh, yeah, the girl piloting our ship? She's not just a Tremist, but the king's daughter. But you should still trust her!* Instead he said, "It's need to know, crew. Stay focused."

"What about Earth?" Kale asked.

The answer came to him then.

"The Tremist are smart," Mason said. "Smarter than us, supposedly. Which means they wouldn't just destroy our planet. That would guarantee we retaliate with everything we've got. If we ever found the Tremist homeworld, they know we could contaminate it with just a few cores from our ships' engines. So what would they do?"

It was Tom who answered, his voice clear and strong. "They would hold it hostage. They would use it, not destroy it. There isn't a greater bargaining chip in the entire galaxy, I'd bet."

"So would I," Mason said, smiling at him.

He had to believe it. Earth was safe. Or else what were they fighting for?

"Stay focused," Mason said again, putting all the authority he could muster into his voice.

The cadets were ESC after all, so after some grumbling, they got back to work.

> Merrin moved the ship farther away from what used to be Earthspace, then Mason asked for a cross gate. Only a few were left on board, since there had been no time to collect the ones they had used. Which meant they had to make each jump count. One to get to Nori-Blue, and one to hopefully get out. Plus a few extras in case they had to do some jumping around to avoid the Tremist.

While the gate was expanding, Mason asked Elizabeth where the Lock was located. It was housed in a small storage area on crewside. Tricky. Mason would've expected it to be starboard, on the engineering side, where stuff like that was kept. Had the cadets failed in taking back the ship, it would've taken the Tremist much longer to find the Lock.

Mason took Tom, Stellan, and Jeremy with him, after Elizabeth recommended four cadets to carry the Lock.

"Take a right here, Captain," Elizabeth said, as the four of them marched down a corridor. Mason was once again struck by how empty the ship felt. They took an elevator two levels down, then Elizabeth had them stop at what appeared to be a regular old door to a regular old room—an office maybe, or an officer's personal quarters.

The door was locked, though, and Elizabeth took ten full seconds to open it.

"There have to be several locks stacked on top of each other," Tom said quietly, more to himself.

When the door finally slid open, Mason could see it was nearly a foot thick. Not your regular office door.

The room was small and cubelike. Mason had had enough of cubes. To the left and right, the walls were lined with heavy-duty personal lockers, eight to each side. On the opposite wall, four large hunter-green backpacks hung on hooks. And in the very middle of the floor was the Lock.

Now Mason understood why four were needed to carry it. The Lock was four separate pieces. Four cylinders stood on their ends, forming the corners of an imaginary square. Like the points on an ancient compass. They were each two feet tall, and just thick enough that one could easily carry it like a football, hugging it to their chest. Each was just the right size for the backpacks.

"Let's pack it up," Mason said, and the four of them did, picking up the cylinders and zipping them safely into backpacks. Each cylinder was very heavy, very dense, and Mason knew carrying them for long would be a problem. His back seemed to groan when he slung the pack over his shoulders.

"How do we turn it on, Elizabeth?" Tom asked.

"Arrange the cylinders in the same position," Elizabeth replied. "It should activate on its own, once the Lock senses it's on Nori-Blue."

"*Should?*" Stellan said. He was visibly nervous, sweaty and pale. Probably because he was smart enough to know that Mason would choose him for the ground team, to help plant the Lock.

"As you know," Elizabeth replied airily, "the Lock is highly classified, and I am only vaguely aware of its operational details."

"Brilliant," Mason muttered, and the four of them carried their heavy packs back to the bridge.

Once there, Mason gave command back to Jeremy.

Jeremy almost made a pouty face with his lips—almost. Mason knew he'd rather be on the ground with them, in the thick of it, but if everything went right, there wouldn't be much action. Mason needed him on the ship, even though he would've been glad to have Jeremy watching his back.

"I get it," Jeremy said quietly. "I'll take care of things."

Mason nodded to Merrin, and she joined the group, making it four again, counting Tom and Stellan.

Merrin made a sound as she shouldered the backpack. "Ugh. What's in this thing, osmium?"

She didn't seem all that upset by the turn of events. Or she was terrific at faking calm. Of course Mason wouldn't trade her back to her father, and of course she knew that, but she'd still be close to the king and his Rhadgast again.

While Tom and Stellan made sure their stations were covered, Mason pulled Merrin aside.

"Are you okay?" he said.

She raised a violet eyebrow, then shrugged. "Don't I look okay?"

"You look great. I mean, you seem fine. But I just want to make sure. I can't imagine how . . . so if you want to talk . . . or you need to talk . . ."

"I don't really care about my past right now." He might've imagined it, but Mason thought her voice quavered.

"I just want to make sure you're okay," he said. "That's it. We can talk about whatever you want to."

"You know me," she said. "I'm a good soldier."

Which wasn't really an answer, but Mason knew she would keep it together. The part of him that was just Merrin's friend, not her captain, ached. *Her father is the king of our enemy.* He thought the words in his head and still found them hard to believe. *Her father is why your parents are dead.*

Mason would die before he let that become an issue between them. She was not responsible. Not even a little bit.

Merrin squeezed his shoulder before he could say more, then checked on Willa, who was taking over the pilot console.

Twenty seconds later, the four were jogging as quickly as they could back to the shuttle bays. They stopped briefly in one of the smaller galleys, to rehydrate and cram a few protein bars down their throats. There wasn't time for a nap, but the food would give them a bit of energy. It felt like they'd been fighting for weeks, when really not even a full day had passed.

"I wish the cook was still here," Stellan grumbled.

"You don't like cardboard?" Tom said. "Hundreds of years of human engineering, and these things still taste awful."

"At least they get the water right," Mason added, cracking open the last bottle.

Then they were off again.

Mason was glad the bays were close, because carrying his portion of the Lock made his shoulders feel like they were crawling with fire ants. No one spoke along the way, saving their breath. Mason and Tom chewed on an extra bar and split the last bottle of water.

It wasn't until they reached the outer door to the nearest shuttle bay that Mason turned around and said, "I need all of you. You're the best. But if you'd rather stay here, this is your last chance. I don't know how things will go down on the surface, or if the Egypt will be able to stick around long enough to pick us up."

Mason imagined them living out their years on the surface, building tree houses and learning to hunt the game that populated the forests. Finding an abandoned Tremist or ESC base they could use for shelter, if they were lucky.

Stellan raised his hand. "I would like to . . ." he trailed off.

"Please," Merrin said, tossing her hair over her shoulder indignantly. "Like I would miss this." Maybe pretending she wasn't afraid was her way of coping, much like how Mason had pretended to be brave.

Tom didn't say anything, but he didn't have to. The order had come from his father, and Mason figured he couldn't stop Tom from going if he tried. Not that he would. Tom had lost his mother, just hours ago, really, but he was standing strong. If Mason had seen Susan fall from that catwalk, would he be as functional? Would he still be doing his duty? *I don't know,* he thought.

Stellan lowered his hand and sighed. "All right . . . I'm in."

Mason typed in the code to open the bay door. Through the clear wall to the left, Mason saw the empty room and remembered the moment right after the floor split apart. Right then he had known that all he could do was try his best. And so he would try again.

The shuttle was a Dragon-class transport model, the Dragon part meaning it was fast. It looked like someone had taken two huge triangles and glued them atop each other, then blown air into them, expanding the triangles into convex shapes, connected at all three corners. Like a semi-inflated balloon. It was waiting for them right in the middle of the bay.

Mason lowered the rear hatch, and the four walked into the small cargo compartment, which was really just two benches that faced each other, with various equipment one might need to traverse a strange new world. Mason went to the pilot chair, which looked out through a narrow strip of window that curved around the entire top half of the shuttle, giving a view of 360 degrees.

Tom fired up the systems, set the engines to warm. Stellan secured the packs holding the Lock. Merrin came into the cockpit, which was open to the aft section, and peeled off her Rhadgast glove.

"I don't want this," she said, handing it back to Mason.

Mason took it from her, accidentally brushing the back of her hand, which was warm and dry. She was chewing on her lower lip. "Why?" he said.

"I prefer a P-cannon. The glove doesn't feel right. It feels like it—" She stopped abruptly.

"Like it what?" Mason said. He could smell a strange perfume in her violet hair, something he'd never noticed before.

Tom was pretending not to listen. The shuttle's engines slowly spooled up, at first a low and throaty *buuuuuuuuurrrrrrrrrrr* rising to a high-pitched *eeeeeeeeeeeeeeeee*.

"Like it wants to be with the other glove," she said.

Mason considered his right hand, and the glove he now held in his left. The one on the left had expanded now that it was off Merrin's hand, but he knew it would shrink again when he put it on, and stop at his shoulder, the perfect fit. The material seemed like some kind of grippy rubber, but thin enough that he could still make precise movements with his fingers.

"You're sure?" Mason said. It felt greedy to wear both gloves, but Tom didn't ask for it, and if Mason was honest, he wanted them both. He wanted the full power of the Rhadgast.

Merrin patted him on the shoulder. "Yep." Then she disappeared into the aft compartment, and Mason heard her strap herself to the bench.

Jeremy's voice broke through on the shuttle's com: "We are now parked in Nori-Bluespace."

"Thanks, Jer," Tom replied, entering their current location on the computer. It would calculate the precise path to enter the planet's atmosphere, the path that would provide the least atmospheric resistance. Coming in too hot would turn them into a collection of cinders like *that*.

"You ready for this?" Mason asked Tom.

"Of course not," Tom said. He pulled up the navigation page from the copilot seat.

Mason removed the armor plates from his left hand and arm, then tugged on the other Rhadgast glove. A moment later, it shrank to a second skin, sealing at the shoulder. He was bone-tired throughout his body, but his hands and forearms felt . . . strong. Wearing both gloves felt right in a way he couldn't explain. He looked at his palms, wiggled his fingers, felt the electricity dwelling within. It was waiting for his call. "Me neither," he replied quietly.

"But let's do it anyway. Pad clear," Tom said.

"Ready," Mason said.

"Ready," Stellan and Merrin echoed from the rear.

Mason punched the big red button on the ceiling, and the floor broke open in an instant—one second there was solid starship-grade flex-metal under them, the next the inky black of space, with the big green sphere that was Nori-Blue right in front of them.

The atmosphere rushed out of the room, taking the shuttle with it, and the four cadets dropped toward the planet, toward humanity's last hope.

Chapter Thirty-five

The gravity compensators reduced the stress on their bodies, but Mason definitely felt how fast they were moving. As soon as they were clear of the Egypt, Mason pushed the throttle near his left wrist to max. In a matter of seconds, they were traveling at two percent of the speed of light. The Dragon's twin engines were screaming, yet the vibrations were minimal. The big green planet grew larger, and larger still. There were barely any clouds, just an expanse of endless green.

And then they were in the atmosphere. The windows were suddenly opaque—red and orange with flames. Mason eased the throttle back and the air conditioners kicked on with fierce buzzing sounds. Cold air blasted him in the face, but he was roasting from the chest down.

He pulled back on the control stick to level out, maybe glide forward for a few thousand klicks, but the stick suddenly yanked out of his hand. He grabbed it again, heart in his throat, but couldn't pull it back. The shuttle dropped into a steep dive, and then the fire was gone, and Mason could see trees. A forest spread out in all directions for as far as he could see.

"Pull up!" Tom shouted.

"I'm trying!" He heaved on the stick with all his might, but the ship continued its dive. "Elizabeth, control this thing!"

No reply. The ship leveled out suddenly, pressing Mason into his seat, and then banked hard to the right, pulling with enough force that if the compensators hadn't been on, they would've been crushed to death in their seats.

"Elizabeth!" Mason shouted again.

The shuttle finished its turn until it was heading the complete opposite way, for the southern hemisphere—what had been named, unoriginally, the Southern Forest. It was a place the ESC had not even begun to map out. The Wildlands, some soldiers called it. The throttle pushed forward on its own, until they were screaming over the trees at fourteen times the speed of sound.

"What are you *doing*?" Merrin called from the back, followed by, "Stellan just threw up."

Mason glanced over his shoulder: Merrin was wide-eyed, and behind her, through the strip of transparent hardglass, the forest was flayed open from their passing, like the wake from a boat.

"I'm not doing anything," Mason replied, as calmly as he could. For a second, he considered shocking the shuttle's controls with his gloves, but decided that was the worst idea ever. A power failure would send them tumbling into the trees at just, oh, somewhere around sixteen thousand miles per hour.

Five seconds later the engines began to wind down, and the speed readout plummeted. The trees became less of a green blur and more distinct. Two seconds later, they were cruising at a comfortable 200 miles per hour. It was clear the shuttle wasn't just malfunctioning, but being controlled by someone remotely.

Tom saw the building first. "Look!"

In the distance still ahead, a tall narrow building was visible. At first Mason thought it might've been an ESC installation, but no—ESC bases were low-slung and blended in with the environment, to better hide visually from Tremist scouts. Plus they were already way too far south.

Then suddenly they were hovering next to it, and Mason could see it clearly:

It was some kind of ancient skyscraper. It had broken halfway up, and pieces of it were strewn around a clearing in the forest. Like a giant had punched the building and broken the top half all to bits. Still not responding to Mason's input, the shuttle dropped a few hundred feet to the clearing, between two large crumbling sections of the building. The skyscraper wasn't gigantic, not by Earth standards. If you added up the pieces, it looked more like something from the twenty-first or twenty-second century of Earth, before the new cities were built atop the old. The building was constructed from some kind of silvery metal that looked totally out of place in the lush forest. The metal surface was cut into a brick pattern that caught light from the blue sun. Lightly, the shuttle touched down on the grass.

The com readout on the dashboard flickered with an incoming transmission from an ESC base to the north, but Mason couldn't answer it. The system wouldn't respond. With a hot sigh, the shuttle powered down, leaving them with the sound of ticking metal. The trees were enormous from ground level, challenging the skyscraper for height and blocking much of the light. It felt like dusk down there.

"What just happened?" Tom asked flatly.

"No idea," Mason said.

Tom tried to pull up a map of the area, but right then the ship powered down *completely,* leaving them in near darkness save for some red backup lights embedded in the floor and ceiling.

Mason hit the ignition, but the shuttle was dead.

"I have a bad feeling about this," Merrin said.

"Uh, seconded," Stellan added.

"I guess it's time to get out," Mason said. They didn't have a real plan yet. He needed to trick the king into giving his sister back, while keeping Merrin . . . that was all he knew. Maybe bringing Merrin had been a bad idea; if they failed, she was captured. But if they failed without her on Nori-Blue's surface, she still had a chance. *Too late now,* Mason thought.

Mason felt lighter as he walked to the shuttle's exit ramp, a

side effect of Nori-Blue having less mass, and thus less gravity than Earth. He lowered the ramp, and air thick with the smell of jungle rolled in. It was sweet and heavy and humid, a little tangy, and coated the back of his throat. He stepped down the ramp and came out next to one of the fallen pieces of skyscraper. The metal looked ancient, clumped with dirt and worn by time. A lot of time.

It went against everything Mason knew: Nori-Blue wasn't supposed to have a sentient species, but the skyscraper didn't build itself, and he highly doubted it was the ESC—or the Tremist, for that matter, unless they'd been aware of Nori-Blue's presence for that much longer.

Nori-Blue's equivalent of birds and insects made strange sounds in the trees around them, a kind of layered warble from which he couldn't distinguish any one sound. It put his teeth on edge. He remembered a lesson from his class *Wildlife of the ESC Colonies*. He and his fellow fourth years had seen video of chittering bat-like creatures hopping from branch to branch, roosting in trees that could swing their branches down at the ground reflexively, to knock aside furry two-legged creatures that liked to gnaw on the tender roots. He remembered a bird that was not a bird at all—it was the size of a fat dragonfly, but looked like a miniature house cat with tiny sets of wings all down its back. The alien animals all looked so cute on the video, until he learned that most of them could kill him.

Now that he was here, Mason was suddenly not a huge fan; Nori-Blue made his skin crawl. He definitely preferred the deck of a ship under his feet.

But they had a job to do.

"Let's assemble the Lock and get out of here," Mason said.

The four went back inside, grabbed their packs, and exited again. They jogged for the woods, keeping the skyscraper on their right side. In the gloom, it appeared gold in color, not silver. Under the built-up crud, it might have even been majestic.

Mason stopped just within the tree line, where the growth above them was so thick it let in almost no light. The trees swayed above him, but Mason didn't know if it was the wind, or if these were the kinds of trees that could move.

Focus. The king's Hawk would be there soon, if it wasn't already, and Mason wanted to make sure his team wasn't anywhere near the Lock by then. He just had to hope the shuttle would power back up.

Mason cleared some dead roots and minor vegetation aside with his feet, and the four of them placed their cylinders down in the dirt, positioning them the same way they had been on the Egypt.

"Yours is too close to Mason's," Stellan told Tom after a moment.

Tom made a minor adjustment.

"Too far now," Stellan said.

"I'm trying—"

SNAP-hiss. The cylinders lit up like they had before, emitting a gentle hum. The Lock was activated.

"That was easy," Merrin said.

"Hey brainiac," Tom said to Stellan. "What's your theory on that tower back there?"

"A long-dead alien race," Stellan replied without hesitation. "There is no other explanation, unless we've traveled through time, which is impossible. So there is no other explanation."

Theories weren't going to keep them safe right now. The skyscraper was a distraction, but Mason couldn't ignore that the shuttle brought them here on its own. Was that even possible? Had Elizabeth predetermined this spot and then not told them?

Mason tapped the skin below his ear to open a channel to the Egypt. "Hey Jeremy, what's it look like up there?"

"Like space. Black mostly."

"Keep me posted," Mason replied. "Is Elizabeth okay?"

". . . Uh, yeah? What do you mean?"

"Can you put her on?"

There was a pause, followed by, "She's not responding. But she's still online, and operating."

That made the hair on Mason's arms stand up against his gloves. But he had to ignore Elizabeth's status, at least until they were offplanet. The Hawk wasn't there yet, so they still had some time. And his curiosity was getting the better of him.

"Start the shuttle," he told Tom.

"Please," Tom prompted.

"Start the shuttle, please," Mason said, even though he was technically Tom's superior. For right now, anyway.

"Whoa, where do you think you're going?" Tom said.

Mason was walking toward the building. From this angle, he could see the doorway in the bottom floor. The skyscraper was huge, but the door was small, and not even a door, just a vertical rectangular opening framing the darkness within.

"I have to know why we were brought here," Mason said.

"On second thought, Stellan can do the shuttle," Tom said. "I'm coming with you."

"I can totally start the shuttle!" Stellan said, hurrying for the ramp.

Mason looked at Merrin, who raised her violet eyebrows. "Let's check it out."

If the inside was structurally stable, maybe they could use it against the king: lure the Tremist inside, and then grab Susan in the darkness or something. They would need an advantage no matter what. If the trade happened on open ground, Mason had a feeling they'd all be taking a ride in the king's Hawk.

The three of them approached the tower, falling into a wedge pattern with Mason in the front, slightly spread out so they didn't make one big target. Mason kept his hands ready; he could feel a charge crawling across his palms, tickling him. The warble of life around them began to fade the closer they got, as if the tower was muting it somehow. It became very quiet within ten steps, then absolutely silent five more later. As if they'd passed through some kind of shield that kept the noise out.

Mason turned around; everything behind them looked okay. Stellan waved at them from the cockpit of the shuttle. Merrin waved back.

"Creepy," Tom said.

The entrance was right in front of them now, shadows within. Mason swallowed and reminded himself he'd gotten this far. Then he stepped inside the tower, and his friends followed.

He was not prepared for what he would find inside.

Chapter Thirty-six

Columns rose up around them, disappearing into darkness above. Everything was filthy and crusted with time. Yet the air smelled fresh, not ancient. As far as Mason could tell, the entire tower was one incredibly tall room.

"There," Tom whispered. "Just ahead."

Tom pointed to a single pillar in the very middle of the room. It was just a few feet taller than Mason. Resting atop it was a pure black sphere, like someone had dipped a basketball in the blackest paint imaginable.

"Come closer," a voice said, filling the entire tower. Filling Mason's *mind*.

He couldn't be sure if he'd imagined it, until Merrin said, "Yeah, right."

But the voice didn't seem hostile; it wasn't dripping with malice. It was more like an invitation.

The sphere on the pillar began to glow. "Closer, please? Don't make me come to you," the voice said again.

"I wonder if Stellan needs help with the ship," Tom said.

Mason wondered that too. Perhaps Stellan needed *all* their help, and maybe they should go try to help him, like right now.

"Oh, for Adams' sake, I won't bite!" the voice said.

In the blink of an eye, the sphere was hovering a foot above the pillar. On the surface was a perfect image of a bright red heart. It beat slowly. "See? I love you."

The voice came from the sphere.

So Mason took yet another chance, and began to walk toward it. Once they got halfway, the heart changed into perfectly clear words that said THANK YOU! in neon yellow. It was like a video screen covered the sphere, like the peel of an orange.

"I have been waiting so long for your arrival that if I told you how long, you would call me a liar," the sphere said. Now it showed various scenes of the forest around them, the sky above, flickering back to the beating heart, and then a smiley face.

"How long?" Mason asked.

"I may have forgotten. But—never mind. You really don't have the time. I have to tell you something, and then I have to send you on your way. Your enemies, they are close."

"What—" Tom began.

"Stop!" the sphere said. "I mean, please stop. My name is Child. I am a creation of the People, who last populated this place you call Nori-Blue. I am what you call intelligence that is artificial. I am more powerful than you can possibly imagine."

A cold finger prodded Mason's lower spine. The way Child had said it . . .

"The People make you humans and your Tremist enemies look like blithering idiots," Child said, and an image appeared on his screen of a man's sneering face.

"You brought us here," Mason said, realizing it as he said it.

"Of course," Child replied. "You are the first sign."

Mason almost asked what he meant, but didn't want to get scolded.

"Thank you for not asking that question," Child said. "I saw your Egypt in orbit, and decided now was the time to reveal the truth. Because you can deliver this truth to both sides equally. You are a human and Tremist united."

He meant Merrin. A Tremist cadet in the ESC.

But what truth . . . ? Mason's stomach turned. He almost

didn't want to know. Or he wanted to know *right now*, to get it over with. The dread soured the taste in his mouth.

"Let me be clear," Child said. "I do not trust the Tremist, and I do not trust the humans. You have both grown self-centered over your years. Both sides would use the truth for their own gain, not for peace. But I have seen into your hearts, young ones, and I know you can end this war."

The heart came back, beating happily on the surface of the sphere.

Just then, the com in Mason's ear clicked.

It was Jeremy. He sounded out of breath. "—gotta bug out. Mason? I gotta bug out. Tremist in the system in a big way. Not just the king's Hawk—*all of them*. I'll try to come back. Hole up tight, buddy."

Before Mason could reply, the com went dead.

The others hadn't heard.

"The Egypt had to leave the system," Mason told them, swallowing. "The Tremist are here."

"*Listen*, then," Child said, before the others could reply. "This is the truth you will bring to your people."

Chapter Thirty-seven

Instead of telling them, Child granted them understanding. In one moment, they knew nothing. Then
the sphere emitted tight beams of light into their eyes. Mason
squeezed his eyes shut and flinched away, but the beams tracked
his eyes, pierced his lids, and fed directly into his brain.

In the next moment, they knew it all.

Humans and Tremist weren't alien to each other. They didn't
evolve on separate planets.

They both came from Nori-Blue.

They were both children of the People.

At the height of the People's civilization, war broke out, as
wars tend to do. By this time, the People had technology that
even the Tremist would not be able to understand. They had
thrived for so long that, over fifty thousand years earlier, they
had actually evolved into two different species. The new species
were known as the Fangborn, beastly creatures that were all
cunning and strength. It was like some of the People had peaked
through evolution, then began reverting back to animal form.
The unaffected People lived on to become the Adams, who were
the same as they'd always been, physically weaker than the
Fangborn, but more intelligent.

As the Fangborn overwhelmed their former brothers, a large
group of Adams escaped Nori-Blue in two ships.

They split up to ensure their survival. One ship went to what was now called Earth, and the other went to the Tremist home-world.

That was a few million years ago, give or take thirty-four thousand.

But the Fangborn, they're very much alive.

Waiting under the surface of Nori-Blue.

Waiting for the Adams to come home, so that they might have something new to feast upon.

➤ To Mason, the Fangborn sounded more like monsters than people.

But Child's story made sense. Or at least it explained how the Tremist and humans appeared so similar. Take away the violet eyes and hair, the nearly translucent skin, and Merrin was a human. And their similarities weren't just physical, either. Both races had ruined their planets. Both were greedy for another to ruin. That's what this whole mess was about.

"Are there any Adams left?" Mason asked, breaking the silence.

"Only their children. Only you. The pure bloodline is gone. But listen carefully." An exclamation point, glowing in green, appeared on the sphere. "As last sentinel of the People, I have been tasked with preserving their history, so that whoever might return to Nori-Blue would know the truth, and be able to share it. I've created a book that contains everything."

The sphere was now an image of gnashing teeth and frantic, violent images too quick for Mason to process. "The Fangborn have been waiting impatiently, trapped underground in an extremely powerful stasis field created by the Adams. They've built their cities in enormous caves, hidden from both Tremist and human. And they've been watching. They know you're here. And while they can't hurt me directly, they know you three are in a position to bring this truth to both sides. If the Fangborn are revealed before the planet is colonized by either side, they will be at a disadvantage. They're counting on people becoming comfortable before they attack. They will eat this truth, if they can."

Mason shivered. *Eat.*

"Wait," Merrin said. "Why don't you just keep them underground?"

"Ahhh," Child said. The sphere began spinning lazily.

"What is it?" Mason said. "Tell us!"

"Well. I brought you three here because I believe in you. But also because I'm running out of energy and will no longer be able to maintain the field. I've been doing it for a very long time, you know."

"How much time do we have?" Mason said, his heart beating faster.

"Nineteen minutes. Actually, eighteen minutes and forty-seven seconds."

Mason didn't know whether to laugh or cry. He just stood there, feeling like he'd been slapped.

"You idiot!" Tom said. "You brought us here and now you're saying they're after *us,* when they weren't just . . . what, a half hour ago? *And* they're about to be freed for the first time in millions of years?"

"Exactly," Child replied, with no hint of remorse.

"Oh," Tom said. "Well, you shouldn't have done that."

"I did not say it would be easy," Child said, pulsing with a heart again. "But I know bravery is strong in all of you. You wouldn't be here otherwise. Dig deep and find it."

Easier said than done, Mason thought.

"Now come," Child said. "Before it's too late."

Chapter Thirty-eight

Child floated off his pillar and began to drift away.

Merrin started forward, but Tom said, "I don't know about this. And I'm not saying that because I'm scared. I mean, I am, because I'm smart, but that's not why."

Mason didn't know about this either, but he knew when there was a choice, and when there wasn't. This time there was no choice. It was too incredible to be a trick, and he couldn't figure out the angle if it was one. Which meant it was probably the truth, and both races were counting on them.

So they followed Child at a distance. The sphere floated to the back of the tower, and a hand appeared on the surface every so often, beckoning them forward. At the back was a winding tunnel that curled to the left, descending in a helix. The way was lit, but Mason couldn't see how—the lighting was ambient, with no obvious source.

"A little quicker, please," Child urged, picking up his pace. The cadets broke into a jog, spinning down and down, first ten complete spirals, then twenty. Mason had no idea how far underground they were.

After somewhere between thirty and forty spirals, the tunnel ended in a huge cavern. It reminded Mason of an indoor stadium on Earth, but with rough rock walls. In the center of the cavern was a pillar similar to Child's.

But on this one rested a book.

"Go to it!" Child said.

Mason ran toward the pillar, and out of the gloom at the other end of the cavern, he saw something. An opening to another tunnel.

He slowed.

"They can't get in!" Child said. "Hur—"

A deep roar cut the sphere off. Two more followed, louder than before. Then Mason heard the scraping sounds of claws on rock and the gnashing and grinding of teeth. All coming from the darkness at the other end of the tunnel.

Tom stopped completely, and Merrin slowed. Mason sped up, because he knew getting to the book sooner meant leaving sooner.

"The Fangborn try, but they can't," Child said. "I promise. They just like to try. The People made sure I could protect their knowledge, and I do. For another few minutes, at least!"

Mason was at the book. It rested open, flat on its spine. It was huge, bigger than any book Mason had ever seen. In fact, carrying it out of there was going to be a problem. It looked as if it was bound in gold.

"Touch it," Child said.

Mason did.

And then everything changed.

Chapter Thirty-nine

In the span of a few seconds, the book transferred the entire history of the People to Mason. He could feel it in his brain like a weight. Right now it was a locked box, near to bursting, so heavy his head swam and his eyes blurred with tears. He felt a strange buzz inside his skull, similar to the electricity he felt in his gloves, but more distracting.

"Easy, easy," Child said. "Don't try to look."

There was simply too much knowledge. Mason didn't want to open the door to that knowledge, because it felt like it would all collapse on him.

"Just carry it. You can share it with others. But don't try to look until you're somewhere safe. Somewhere you can sleep."

Mason nodded.

"What did you do to him?" Merrin demanded.

From the tunnel, the howls increased. Howls and roars and strange chuffing sounds. Mason could hear the Fangborn breathing.

"Mason Stark is now the living conduit of the book, the messenger who will bring peace to the Adams' children."

"Oh," Tom said. "Is that all?"

"The book must remain here in case you fail."

By now Mason's head was clearing, but he felt the knowledge dwelling inside him. He understood what Child meant by *fail*. He meant if Mason died, and another conduit was needed.

"Go now," Child said. "Back up the tunnel, back to your ship, back to your fleet. Make the truth known before there is nothing left to save. Go!"

They went.

Up the tunnel, as fast as they could. As the cries of the Fang-born dwindled, Mason could hear the blood pounding in his ears. The return trip went too fast—he didn't want to be topside just yet, where they would have to keep running and fighting. All Mason could think about was the wealth of information in his head, the insane truth that could change everything. Suddenly he was afraid for his life for a totally different reason.

They sprinted across the main floor, past Child's pillar, and through the doorway into murky daylight. Just then the com clicked in Mason's ear, and by Merrin's and Tom's reactions, he knew they heard it too.

"This is Vice Admiral Renner broadcasting across all frequencies. The Tremist force is in system now. Do not fire heavy weapons. The Tremist have stationed themselves low in the atmosphere, betting we won't use heavies against them at the risk of contaminating the planet below. The gate—"

There was a bright spark in the sky, and the vice admiral's voice crackled briefly with static, then he coughed wetly. The word *gate* sent a chill across Mason's shoulders.

He could see the gate now, unfolding low in the atmosphere. It was just a tiny speck at this distance, a shiny dust mote. The Tremist were already in the process of stealing their second planet of the day.

"We need to stop the gate," the vice admiral said, sounding defeated already, with just a hint of steel left in his voice. "The Olympus is on its way. We hope it will scatter them like—" He cut out again.

The gate was growing, looking again like a spider with a thousand unfurling legs. If the Tremist took Nori-Blue, that was it. There would be no home for humans. And the Tremist would definitely be at risk if they settled down on Nori-Blue: the Fang-born would devour them, and possibly use their technology to spread throughout the galaxy.

His ear clicked twice more, which Mason knew meant the speaker was only speaking to him. "Stark," the vice admiral said. "Did you get the Lock in place?"

"It's done, sir," Mason replied. Tom looked at him quizzically.

"Good." That was all he said.

"We have to stop this," Mason said, hearing the frustration in his voice. Frustration he saw on Merrin's face and in Tom's eyes.

But it wasn't enough that the odds were already impossible. Right as they were about to run for the shuttle, the king's Hawk crested the trees behind it, its weapon clusters bristling with green light.

Chapter Forty

They ran anyway. Mason ran as fast as he ever had before, ignoring the way the soft ground sucked at his feet with each step, how the tall grasses tangled around his ankles, threatening to trip him, as if the whole planet was aligned with the Fangborn. As if it too was saying, *You don't belong here. Be gone.* Or more likely: *You don't belong here, but you're never going to leave.*

They never had a chance. Mason screamed when he saw the Hawk fire the first thick green laser from under its belly. He could see Stellan in the window, waving them forward. He could hear the shuttle itself powering up, now that Child wanted them to flee. But the Hawk didn't shoot to kill, only maim. The rear engines on the shuttle exploded in a geyser of blue and silver flames. One of the underside engines gave a high-pitched whine—*errrrreiiiiiiii*—and then it exploded too, shoving the rear of the shuttle upward and almost sending it into a somersault. The shuttle slammed back down, smoking and crackling, completely useless. Stellan popped up in the window a few seconds later, seemingly okay.

They were stranded now, on a planet full of monsters that wanted to kill them. Monsters underground and now monsters in the air. Mason wanted to scream again, in frustration this time. The heroes in the stories always had something go right for them, there was always a bit of luck. No matter what the odds were, they found a way. He wondered how many would-be heroes didn't get that sliver of luck, and were never mentioned again.

Not only were they stranded, with the king's Hawk closing in, but the Lock was only a few hundred feet away in the shallow woods. If the Tremist had any way to track the Lock, it would be destroyed sooner than Mason had hoped.

The Hawk hovered over the clearing, taking its time like a slow predator stalking its prey. This close to the ground, Mason saw it was truly massive, taking up over half of the clearing, casting a long, wide shadow on the ground.

"C'mon, we have to make a stand," Mason said. The others nodded—no question, because they were the best the ESC had to offer—and they took off again for the shuttle. The wiser plan would've been to try to lose them in the forest, to try and force a pursuit, since Merrin was what the king was really after, but none of them were about to leave Stellan behind. That option had only crossed Mason's mind for a single instant, and the very idea disgusted him.

When they got there, Tremist were rappelling down from the sides of the Hawk, enough to kill all of them. Mason reminded himself he had the Rhadgast gloves and was not completely helpless just yet.

Stellan was waiting for them at the rear door, which was smoking and barely wedged open. Mason held his breath as they wiggled through, not wanting to inhale the sharp and hot gases coming off the wrecked engines. Together, Mason and Tom wedged the door shut, not quite sealing them in. If they were about to become POWs, they would make the Tremist earn it. And maybe, if they were a good enough distraction, the Lock would survive a little longer.

Through the front part of the curved windshield, they watched

the Hawk settle into the clearing, touching down on the pieces of broken skyscraper. The segments collapsed like rotten tree trunks, crumbling into puffs of silvery dust.

Help us, Child, Mason thought. But there was no answer.

At the edge of his hearing, Mason heard a low rumble coming from somewhere. Underneath his feet, maybe. It was probably just vibrations from the Hawk traveling through the ground. How much time had passed since Child had warned them about the stasis field? Ten minutes? Fifteen? Mason had no idea.

"We have to do something!" Tom said.

"What defenses does the shuttle have?" Merrin said coolly. Stellan was sweating over the controls, hands shaking.

Tom opened a panel in the floor and pulled out fresh hand-held P-cannons. He pressed one into Stellan's hand and held it there until Stellan took a breath and closed his fingers around it.

Suddenly, Mason heard a voice:

You are a Rhadgast now.

It was *Child's* voice. In his head.

You are a Rhadgast, so clap your hands.

Clap your hands?

Whatever. Mason was ready to try anything at this point.

So he clapped his hands.

And the gloves sparked with purple light. In the next instant, Mason was holding a crackling sword forged entirely from lightning the color of Merrin's eyes.

Chapter Forty-one

The others froze.

The blade felt solid under his hands. If he closed his eyes, it would've felt like he was holding some kind of ultra-light pole. But Mason could smell the heated air and hear the buzzing. He swung the blade sideways and it still felt solid.

He took his left hand away, and the blade remained. He opened his right hand, and the blade snapped out of existence, just a wisp of smoke to prove it ever existed in the first place.

"*Cool,*" Tom said.

"How—" Stellan said.

Merrin was just smiling at him, a slight upward curve to her lips. The sword wouldn't get them out of trouble, Mason knew, but it might be that sliver of luck he thought about before. It might make the odds tip in their favor.

He was trembling with the new possibilities. Through the windshield they could see the king walking toward them, flanked by a small guard of mirror-mask Tremist. The king's black oval of a mask seemed to eat the light around him, making shadows from nothing.

"Make it come back," Tom said.

Mason clapped his hands again, and the blade returned. He could feel the power coursing up and down his arms, as if the gloves gave him some kind of new strength that didn't fully belong to him.

The rumbling sound under them increased, which didn't make sense. The Hawk should have been powering down, not up. Maybe they thought it wouldn't take too long to recover Merrin, and weren't planning to stay on the surface.

"Here they come," Stellan said, helpfully.

Through the 360-degree view, Mason watched way too many Tremist line up at the rear door. He had a brief vision of cutting through all of them with his lightning sword, but knew it would never happen. It was the fantasy of a kid, not a soldier. Still, if someone tried to take Merrin, they'd be losing an arm one way or another.

The breach was quick. Four Tremist cut a hole through the door with their talon beams, reducing it to saggy, melted metal in a matter of seconds. Before the smoke cleared, the king stepped inside, boots the color of dried blood stamping down the smoldering metal. Smoke curled around his passing, rising from him as if he was some demon just come out of hell.

Mason held his sword high.

"Impressive," the king said.

Then reached out, grabbed the sword, and squeezed.

The sword extinguished, snapping out of existence.

"But not impressive enough," the king said.

Tom fired his P-cannon next, but the king only absorbed the blow with his impossible armor, and then kicked Tom's legs out from under him. He hit the deck hard, breath gone.

Mason clapped his hands together, but just as the blade sprang back to life, the king punched him hard in the chest, and Mason fell next to Tom. The king put his boot on Mason's chest, and that was it. Mason couldn't breathe, not an atom of air, and he knew he was going to suffocate. There was no way around it. He could feel the blood thumping behind his eyes, felt his lungs spasm as there was absolutely no room to inflate.

Then the king let up, and Mason gasped along with Tom as the king kneeled in front of Merrin.

"My princess," he said. "I never meant for this to happen. Let me explain."

"You murdered an entire planet, Your Grace," Stellan said as calmly as Mason had ever heard him say anything. "There will be no explaining that." He still held his P-cannon, but was wisely holding it with the point down, away from the king.

The king's face was as empty as ever. "I did no such thing."

"I don't *want* your explanation," Merrin said. "I don't care where I came from."

"You must know," the king said.

"I said I don't want to know. Whatever side I started on, I'm on the right one now." Her words were forceful, but her eyes looked slightly wet, like she was holding back tears.

The rumbling grew, enough so that the king looked around the shuttle, as if trying to figure out where the noise was coming from. Two Tremist stepped back outside to investigate.

Mason felt something strange—hope, maybe—when the king had said he did no such thing, that he hadn't murdered an entire planet. It could've been a simple denial or it could've meant something more, that Earth was not truly lost.

Mason thought about springing up again, clapping his hands and swinging down at the king, but the king took a hand and pressed his torso to the floor again, not too hard, just enough to keep him pinned.

Abruptly, the king scooped Merrin off the floor. "I will help you understand," he said. He held her against his chest like a father would do with his child. Then he stalked out of the shuttle, leaving the three boys behind.

They weren't alone for long.

Mason had just gotten to his feet, and was helping Tom stand up, when four Rhadgast stepped into the shuttle.

Chapter Forty-two

It was over. Mason knew that now.

Maybe it had always been over, and their efforts had only been delaying the inevitable. Maybe in some parallel timeline, a Mason Stark won the day and beat back the Tremist and then showed them the truth in time. He wished he were that Mason Stark.

"You don't deserve to wear that," one Rhadgast hissed.

Mason looked down; he was still wearing his stolen Tremist armor, the oily surface shifting between purple and black. It was so natural to wear it, so easy, that Mason couldn't even feel it when he closed his eyes.

"Or those," said another, stepping forward to strip Mason of his gloves.

But just because it was over didn't mean Mason couldn't fight. He clapped his hands with no warning, and the blade returned instantly, crackling and hot, spitting violet. The Rhadgast didn't step back like he thought they would; instead, the four of them clapped their hands in unison and there were now five rods of lightning in the cramped space. But clapping their hands had taken time—a half second, sure, but enough for Mason to swing his lightning blade horizontally, from right to left. The Rhadgast bowed backward from the swing, and Mason changed direction, from left to right, just as fast, a whipping motion. This time he met resistance from two of the other swords, and the heat in his gloves seemed to triple, but he gritted his teeth and put all of his strength behind it.

Which wasn't enough.

The two Rhadgast in the middle shoved hard, and Mason fell back, landing on his shoulders, the blade sparking out of existence. He swung his hands up to clap again, but they were already on him. They had his arms pinned. He thought about lashing out with a couple of knees, but didn't. There was no point, except to vent his own frustration. The first thing they did was pull the gloves off his hands. They broke the seals at his shoulders and peeled them off.

Even a soldier knew the difference between impossible odds, and near-impossible. The odds were only near-impossible when he'd been on his feet. He remembered a phrase from a second year class called *Battlefield Logistics*: live to fight another day. It was supposed to be an ancient saying, but he saw why it had lasted this long. *Live to fight another day,* he told himself.

The four Rhadgast marched the three boys off the ship and back into the dimness of the clearing. The trees swayed back and forth in the wind, bringing alien smells to his nose. Mason looked skyward but couldn't see the gate now. Maybe it had moved, or maybe it had expanded enough, and was now too thin to see.

At least they haven't found the Lock yet.

Ahead of them, the king was carrying Merrin under the Hawk's left wing, back toward the rear entrance. He desperately hoped Susan was still on the ship. Mason wasn't about to tell anybody, but he could definitely use a hug.

"Look," Tom said, head craned back. There was the barest hint of hope in his voice.

Mason followed his gaze to the sky, where Olympus had crossed into view. It appeared half the size of Earth's moon from this distance. In actuality, the space station was a giant ring twenty miles across. It resembled a bicycle tire, with dozens of spokes running to a central hub. The spokes contained hyper-fast shuttles, which took ESC members from one side of the ring to the other in a few minutes. It was said that at any given time the population was around a million. There was no grander thing made by man, or so it was said. It was certainly the most effective weapon they had.

"There's hope," Stellan said behind him.

Sure, there was hope—hope for humanity. Not for them on the ground, though. The Olympus might turn the tide with the Lock's help, but just as Mason thought it, he saw two mirror-masks jog out of the woods from the direction of the Lock.

"Master Gast," one mirror-mask said to the Rhadgast holding Mason's arm. "We've found the device. We're destroying it now."

Chapter Forty-three

Mason had already accepted their failure, so the news felt like a cold slap on the back of his neck, nothing more.

And still the ground vibrated under him.

"I do not like this," a Rhadgast said, and got no response. He lifted a boot off the ground, then set it down gingerly.

The four Rhadgast led them around the Hawk and up a ramp and through a series of hallways, to a door big enough to fly their ruined shuttle through. The door had a smaller door built into it, one that opened at their approach.

"Wait," Mason's Rhadgast said. He kneeled and began pulling pieces of Mason's stolen armor off. It sloughed off like snakeskin, the pieces thumping to the deck around him. Underneath he was still wearing his black formfitting ESC uniform, tall boots and all. It felt good to have the symbol showing again.

"Now go," the Rhadgast said, the oval of his faceplate pulsing a soft violet.

The three boys stepped through the doorway into the huge storage bay Mason had first seen with Susan, the one holding the Egypt's captured crew. Immediately he searched for his sister among the faces. Most of the crew was sitting or lying down, backs against the walls or on their sides. Mirror-masks patrolled up and down the rows, holding talons tight against their chests.

Everyone looked so *tired*. The fight was gone from them, as it was from Mason. He wanted to lie down next to them. The three of them walked forward, past crew that recognized them and gave a nod or a sad look.

"It was a good chase you gave them," said one ensign with a fat lip. "They were complaining about you."

Tom smiled, and Mason wanted to but didn't have it in him.

"A good chase," said a woman's voice behind him. "By the bravest the ESC has ever known."

Mason spun around and threw himself into Susan, almost knocking her over. Tears pricked his eyes, but he kept them in, swallowing against them again and again. She hugged him close and held her tears in too; he felt her breath hitch once, then twice. And he could feel a hole in her uniform, right next to her spine. She flinched when his fingertip brushed bare skin that was badly burned and swollen.

"Sorry," Mason said, moving his hand. He wondered where else she was injured, but knew she wouldn't tell him. Not until the danger was over.

"Report," she said, pulling back to look into his face, unable to hide her big white smile. Somehow, despite its radiance, it was sad, and Mason knew why. They were reunited, but only because Mason had gotten captured. Their fate was more uncertain than ever.

Mason told her everything he could, in the clipped shorthand the ESC learned when information had to be relayed quickly, but completely.

Her face never changed, even when he told her about the truth of their joint ancestry with the Tremist. Halfway through, a Tremist patrol forced them out of the aisle, so they sat against the wall, like the other prisoners.

Mason was just finishing up when the high ceiling went from opaque to transparent, turning into a skylight that spanned the entire room. It showed Nori-Blue's sky, and the Olympus wheeling overhead, firing pinpricks of nearly invisible light. The war was happening up there, all of the ESC's resources on hand.

Humanity's last stand.

But why would the Tremist let them see now?

All at once, Mason knew, and the realization made his head swim. The Tremist wanted them to see.

Because the ESC was about to lose.

The other prisoners watched in silence, like Mason was doing. They watched as another space station warped into view, right next to the Olympus. It was double the size, which meant it had to be at least forty miles across. The level of detail was identical, so Mason assumed they were the same distance away. It was similar to the Olympus—ring-shaped—but this one was a ring within a ring within a ring within a ring. Four concentric circles. It was a Tremist space station, one they had kept hidden since the war started.

"Oh, *come on*," Tom said. "Can we get a break?"

"Seriously," Stellan muttered.

Mason was almost overcome with the urge to laugh crazily: the day had started out with a prank gone wrong and had escalated to *this*.

In the next second, the two space stations began to trade fire. It lit up the sky. The prisoners began to talk in hushed tones, which turned louder, and louder still, until someone was shouting, and then a Tremist was bashing an ensign in the face, and then a sergeant was running, then diving under a talon beam, and the mirror-masks were barking harsh orders at each other.

The ceiling became opaque again. Mason could feel the energy in the room—the prisoners were turning defeat into a nothing-to-lose mentality. The energy was infecting him, vaporizing his fear and replacing it with anger. So what if the enemy had talons: it was time to fight. The Tremist were never going to see the truth about their shared history; they would never understand. There would never be peace.

Both races loved war too much.

So Mason decided to start the fire.

He told Susan the one thing he'd held back from his report. One thing he didn't want to tell her, because he didn't know enough. He didn't know the ultimate fate of Earth, where it was or how many had survived the trip.

But he decided to tell her anyway. "Susan."

When she turned her head, tears were streaming down her face, but her expression was perfectly clear.

"The Tremist took Earth," Mason said, nearly choking on the words. "They used the gate. They stole it."

Her lips parted audibly, but she said nothing.

The group of prisoners to Mason's left overheard, as he knew they would:

What did he say? What did he say? He's just a boy. No, I believe it. I helped load the gate. It's real. He's just a boy. What did he say? Those bastards! Tremist scum. What did he say?

They repeated Mason's words, and repeated them again.

And the fire started.

Chapter Forty-four

Mason had used the truth to rally the soldiers, and it felt like the most evil thing he'd ever done. On one hand, it would give them strength. Their anger would crush their fear. On the other, some of the crew would die. That's just how it would be. He realized this as a massive weight on his shoulders, and instant regret. He wanted to pull back his words, whisper them this time.

No, he thought, *if we stay here, we die. This needs to happen.*

He was just comforting himself now. He knew he was rationalizing.

The word spread. The soldiers were standing now. The mirror-masks tried to beat them back, but the soldiers' hearts were pumping flames.

The vibration was back; Mason could feel it through the deck. Maybe the Hawk was just preparing to take off.

Which meant they needed to overtake the Tremist *now.*

Apparently his fellow soldiers had the same mindset. They rose as one—a wave starting at the walls and rolling inward. The mirror-masks fired random beams of green light, but as Mason watched the Tremist were swept underfoot, their weapons stripped away, their armor barely protecting them from stomping feet. Mason watched as a soldier kicked a mirror-mask in the side of the neck, popping the helmet off. If the ESC were startled by their human-like appearance, they didn't show it. The fire was burning too hot now, the wave of soldiers crushing the remaining guards, stripping their weapons, firing the talons into their owners' bodies.

Susan held the boys against the wall, to keep them from being trampled as the wave moved toward the big door. Someone found the controls, the door zipped into the ceiling, and the wave moved into the corridors, screaming a battle cry the whole time. Mason saw what would happen next in his mind, and it was a beautiful thing. The ESC would break free from the ship, and enter the forests of Nori-Blue, where the footing would be even: the soldiers were trained for forest warfare, weapons or not.

But it never happened.

The stasis is over, Child whispered in his head. *Be brave.*

The vibration underneath Mason ceased, and with a final, crunching release, the ground dissolved under them, and the Hawk fell into the hole.

Chapter Forty-five

Mason floated for two whole seconds, until the Hawk's landing thrusters kicked in and his boots thumped back to the deck. The thrusters cushioned him with a side-to-side motion, making him bend his knees and stumble. Deep thumps echoed through the ship as it was pummeled by huge chunks of rock. The ship landed hard, knocking Mason and everyone else off their feet. His shoulder throbbed hot and red and he tasted the now-familiar tang of blood on his lips.

The corridor was layered thick with people trying to stand upright. A few were groaning, but most were stoic, doing their best not to step on anyone. Bluish smoke curled from a power port in the wall.

"You okay?" Susan said. She was next to him, holding his arm.

"I'm fine," he said, a little dizzy but not about to admit it.

"What the hell happened?" someone asked.

Through the hull, Mason heard a rhythmic low buzzing. Probably the engines trying to restart.

"Keep moving!" someone shouted, and the ragged stream of men and women began to shuffle forward, picking people up along the way.

Stellan helped Tom to his feet, then pressed a hand to a cut on his forehead. "You *had* to go in the creepy alien tower," he said to Mason.

"Kinda wish I'd stayed there," Mason replied.

"You're all with me," Susan said, herding them into a loose square shape. She kept one hand on Mason and the other on Stellan, guiding Tom forward with the group. They marched for a hundred feet or so. A Tremist appeared at one point, firing a short burst from a talon, but was stopped. Mason didn't see how.

Then all power was cut to the ship, and the blackness around them was complete. Mason could only rely on his ears: the sound of heavy breathing, the scraping of boots.

"Maintain order!" a soldier shouted.

"Stay calm," said another.

Susan's grip on him tightened, but then someone plowed into him from the left, pushing him down a side corridor.

"Mason!" Susan's fingers brushed him in the darkness.

"Thomas!" Stellan cried out in the same tone.

A rogue elbow cracked Mason hard in the ribs, and he bent over, wondering how many times he would get his breath knocked out before the day was over.

Somewhere up ahead, metal screeched, and then faint light appeared, turning people into dark shapes rather than a uniform black. The former POWs stormed out of the ship, hooting and hollering, until someone shouted, "Knock it off! Form up in defensive ranks!" Which the soldiers did in record time.

Susan found him again, and together they found Tom and Stellan, who were smart enough not to run outside. While Mason caught his breath, Susan dragged them along, following the soldiers toward the exit. But they were fifty feet behind the group now, the door to freedom so far away, and Mason heard bootsteps thumping in the side corridors around them.

"Hurry," Susan urged.

Mason saw his dim reflection in a small oval mirror about six feet off the ground; the Tremist were coming out now that the huge group had passed. A talon tip glowed green in the gloom of the ship's interior, then fired over Mason's shoulder, a few inches away but still hot enough to burn his neck. The four put on a final burst of speed, sprinting out the back hatch and almost running headlong into the stalled group of soldiers outside. Many of them were looking up, so Mason did too.

Above them was a ragged hole the size of his fist held at arm's length. It was very, very high up. Someone laughed, and the laugh came back to Mason's ears two seconds later. They were obviously in some kind of enormous cavern, but it wasn't the one with the book, unless the Hawk had fallen directly on it. Through the hole, some daylight filtered down, making people distinguishable but still cloaking the area around them. With the dust thrown up from the Hawk's landing, the air resembled a misty fog.

Mason remembered the sounds the Fangborn had made. The terrible, inhuman sounds. The sounds had come from an adjacent cavern, and if this wasn't the one with the book . . .

"We need to get everyone back on the ship," Mason said.

"What?" Susan stared down at him, one eyebrow raised.

"He's right," Tom said, and Stellan nodded rapidly.

Some commander was shouting commands, and the soldiers were fanning out in groups to check the area around them.

"The Fangborn . . ." Susan said.

Mason nodded. The cavern hadn't collapsed on its own. The vibration he'd been feeling made sense now. The Fangborn must've felt the Hawk land, and then went to work on the underside, digging away until the ground collapsed. If there was any sign of their digging up above, it was now mixed in with the tumble of rocks strewn around the tilted Hawk. *And now the Fangborn are free*, Mason thought.

Then he heard the first scream.

Chapter Forty-six

It cut off instantly, no longer than a second, and everyone hushed, listening for more, crouching slightly as the misty dirt drifted around them. Through the murkiness, Mason saw a shape glide by. It was almost a man shape. But it was twice the height and twice the width of any man, of the biggest men he'd seen. It was not a man.

Then another shape appeared to his right, perfectly silent and still. The same inhuman size.

"Back to the ship," Susan whispered, almost too quiet to hear, all breath.

Mason took a step backward, his heel grinding a bit of rock and sounding like a gunshot to his ears. He could hear his blood pumping, which made it hard to listen to his surroundings. *Thump thump, thump thump.* The helpful warning buzzed against his forearm again.

"Good idea," Tom whispered back.

The Tremist were out of the ship now, but they weren't fighting. They were mixed in with the ESC. Everyone was looking outward, and quiet. To Mason's left, an ESC soldier was messing with his stolen talon. Suddenly the tip burst into a sizzling green spark, like a torch, and it illuminated the shape of an arm right next to him. A huge arm, thick and veiny, with a pan-sized hand tipped in claws. It curled around the soldier's waist and pulled him into the shadows without a sound.

. . .

➤ *"Everyone on the ship,"* Mason commanded, using his captain voice.

The four began to back up slowly. There was still danger on the Hawk: if they came across any Tremist, who knew what would happen. But staying outside wasn't an option. A mirrormask fired his talon into the darkness, and the beam lit up two hulking shapes. The beam sliced into the nearest Fangborn's arm, and everyone froze as its roar filled the cavern. The sound echoed off the walls until it sounded like a dozen or more.

After that, it was just blind firing. Talon beams crisscrossed through the cavern, a layered buzz of hornets lighting the darkness in sizzling green. Under that, Mason heard a few strangled screams. The sound of boots kicking dirt made him look to his right, and he saw a pair of legs dragged into the darkness. Susan was pulling on him, but he didn't want to run. He wondered if there was some knowledge from the book inside him—something he could use to beat them, but he remembered Child's words. He couldn't peek at it yet, not until he was somewhere safe. The rush of information could cripple him.

"I'm not going to ask you again, soldier," Susan said. Apparently she had been asking him something. It was hard to hear over the cacophony of weapons and roars. Tom and Stellan were already on the ramp, guiding a few injured soldiers inside.

His sister was still a little stronger than he was, and she pulled him backward, into the relative safety of the Hawk. It didn't make him feel safe, more like trapped. The Hawk was humming with power now, but none of the weapons were firing. The Hawk schematics he'd studied so long ago flooded his mind, and he realized the ship had the capability to push the Fangborn back on its own. Yet no one was operating the topside turrets. Had their posts been abandoned when it was clear the ESC were making a break for it?

Mason tore free of Susan's grasp and ran. He ran as fast as he could, past his friends, ignoring the pain in his body, ignoring Susan's voice calling him back. He could imagine what was happening outside. Eventually the Fangborn would slip past the panicked defenders and get aboard. It was inevitable. So unless the big guns started firing, and soon, Mason figured none of them would be seeing the sky again. Any kind of sky.

So he ran. Straight down the corridor that led from the back to the front of the Hawk. He ran past two mirror-masks who pulled up short and leveled their talons. Mason was already around the curve before he heard the weapons firing.

He reached the bridge with burning lungs and found the door wide open. His pulse was thumping twice each second. The bridge was empty, so he stepped inside. It was more a cockpit than anything—just two large seats side by side, in front of a wide, curving instruments console. Through the window in front of him, he saw only darkness. But the thermal cameras on the console showed everything: tiny humanoid shapes dancing around, swinging weapons left and right.

Bigger shapes huddled farther out, some on all fours, slinking back and forth like a video he'd once seen of a cloned tiger at a zoo. He watched as one of the bigger shapes lunged out from the perimeter, enveloped a smaller shape, and pulled it back to the others.

He couldn't watch.

But he could fight.

He sat down in the right-side chair, the copilot/gunner chair, and looked at the controls. They weren't so different from ESC, and Mason figured that had something to do with their joint ancestry. But he still hadn't given them much thought since first learning them back at Academy I.

Luckily, the top turret was operated by a single control stick. Mason grabbed it, and it came online, a new screen rising out of the console as the turret on top of the Hawk did the same.

Then it was just like his practice sessions on an ESC gun. He moved the control stick around, targeted the bigger shapes, and fired. Blazing heat lit the screen up in white, and when the heat dissipated, the Fangborn were scattered. They were running like a pack of wolves back to a tunnel entrance where even more were gathered. Their heat lit up the screen like his weapons had. He fired again, sending a Fangborn tumbling, and breaking up another group. He could feel the turret fire through the hull, a vibration up his spine that wasn't unpleasant. It was working. The Fangborn were fleeing.

On another camera, he saw the ESC and Tremist pouring back into the Hawk. They weren't fighting each other anymore, instead running side by side.

But it would all be for nothing if the engines didn't start. Having power didn't mean they could fly out of here, not if there was too much damage. And the turret was getting hot. The Fangborn were still running around, dodging his fire, and he knew that in twenty to thirty seconds the turret would need time to cool down. Mason didn't know how long that would take. His fingers sweated on the controls. He couldn't close the rear door yet, because people were still staggering aboard, some carrying injured comrades.

Mason spied the big purple button near the top of the console, a place not easily reached. The ESC engineers had claimed it turned on the engines, but were never sure. This was a good time to find out, Mason figured. So he hit it.

The hull throbbed around him, and fell silent.

The Fangborn were coming out of the tunnel entrance again, so he fired two more white-hot beams of light. Shadows danced on his retinas.

He pressed the button again.

The engines groaned this time, higher pitched than before. Was that good? Were they heating up? The turret control stick glowed red in his hand, and an alarm began to squeal. The turret was overheated. A display showed Tremist symbols that appeared to be counting down—from what number, he didn't know. He pressed the trigger but there was no response.

The Fangborn seemed to sense this, because the hulking shapes began to crawl out from the entrance. One burst forward from the pack, galloping toward the Hawk, where the last few soldiers waited to board. It was going to catch them—there wasn't enough time. Mason would have to close the door or risk a Fangborn getting onboard.

"You're doing it wrong."

Mason jumped in his chair and turned sideways, fists up, as the Tremist King sat down in the pilot seat next to him.

Chapter Forty-seven

Mason froze.

The king ignored him and pressed the big purple button again. He held it for ten whole seconds.

The Hawk sputtered to life.

Another screen showed a top-down outline of the Hawk; it was glowing violet, and pulsing, which Mason figured was a good thing.

The Fangborn was just a few seconds from the Hawk now, but the king pressed a button and the door closed and the Fangborn slammed into it. Everyone alive had made it onboard. With the thermal vision, Mason could see cooling bodies lying around outside of the Hawk.

"Hull integrity?" the king said.

Mason realized he was talking to him. He looked at a display his body was blocking from the king's sight. The hull had been breached in two places, but those areas were sealed automatically. They were ready for space.

"Good to go," Mason said.

The king nodded. The Fangborn must have sensed their prey was escaping, because they broke from the tunnel entrance all at once, like water from a burst dam. If they were as smart as they seemed, then they knew the Hawk escaping would mean the end of their plan. The Fangborn would be revealed to both races, and no one would come back to Nori-Blue, at least not until they were prepared to deal with the beasts. Mason could see the desperation in their movement—it was frenzied. Dozens of Fangborn were about to leap onto the Hawk. In his mind, Mason could already see them latching on to the delicate parts of the ship and shredding everything with their claws.

"We need to hurry," Mason said, feeling stupid for saying something so obvious.

"Indeed."

Here they were, working together to save their people, and yet Mason felt itchy. It was an itch in his brain, and not from the knowledge that was stored there. The being next to him had *stolen* Earth. Had ripped the planet from her solar system. And he might even be responsible for the First Attack that killed his parents. He may have ordered it himself. Mason couldn't forget that. He didn't want to work with the king, even if it was to save the people he cared about.

In the corner of his eye, Mason saw the king's talon on the ground, where he must have set it down. Mason wouldn't need it yet, not until the king got them into the safety of space.

The king heaved back on the main control wheel, and the Hawk pulled free from the crater with a groan and a series of rattles. The Fangborn were close now, but their thermal shapes were washed out in the white blast of the Hawk's engines. Mason's stomach was pressed into his intestines as they rocketed straight up. The king piloted them expertly through the hole they'd fallen through, and all at once Mason could see the sky again. It was near dusk, and the sky was glowing with alien stars. They were free of the Fangborn, and Mason never had to see them again as long as he lived.

The Hawk sliced through the sky with ease, angled with the nose pointed up as it cut through the middle and then high atmosphere. Mason used the angle and jumped from his seat, falling toward the back of the cockpit. He snatched up the talon and primed it in two seconds, while the king still had his hands on the controls.

Make him pay, Mason thought.

Make him pay for everyone on Earth. Make him pay for Mom and Dad.

If the king noticed, or cared, he didn't show it.

Then he said, "Earth is fine."

Mason didn't move.

"I said Earth is fine."

"Okay." It was all he could say. The Hawk thrummed in the atmosphere, and Mason almost lost his footing. Slowly, he walked back to his seat and sat down, holding the talon back far enough so the king couldn't grab it without Mason pulling the trigger. Then Mason said, "Explain."

"We crossed Earth into our solar system, much like what you had planned to do with Nori-Blue. Earth has a new sun now, our sun. Our star burns a little cooler, but your planet is at the exact right distance to maintain current weather conditions. Its inhabitants are alive and well, assuming the ESC agrees to our terms of surrender."

He was holding Earth hostage. The entire planet.

"They're okay?" Mason asked.

"Yes. The year is a little shorter now, and so is the day, and there is some strange tidal activity without the moon, but nothing we can't compensate for. So please stop pointing that talon at me."

Mason kept pointing the talon at him.

They were almost out of the atmosphere now; soon they would be able to see space. Mason hoped there was something to see, that both fleets hadn't destroyed each other while they were fooling around in the cavern.

"Return Earth now," Mason said.

"I'm afraid that's impossible for the time being. I've received word that your Olympus space station destroyed the gate."

Chapter Forty-eight

Mason knew what he had to do at once. The news that Earth would continue to belong to the Tremist didn't matter now. There was nothing he could do to change it, and in truth he had expected it. If it had seemed like the ESC was going to recover the gate, the Tremist would've probably blown it up on purpose. It was too dangerous to exist.

So if the king would control Earth in the coming years, Mason wanted to make sure the king knew what he controlled.

He reached out and touched the king's bloodred shoulder. Just a simple touch. And with a thought, a strange, rolling energy flew down Mason's arm and into the king. He could feel it pouring out of his brain, like liquid electricity. The king gasped softly, tensing in his seat.

In an instant, there were now two people who knew the truth of the humans and the Tremist. Mason was careful to just give him the understanding at first, not the history. The king was still piloting the Hawk, and Mason didn't want to cripple him. Just make him understand.

The king sagged slightly, chin tipping forward, and then he shook his head as if to clear it.

"What did you do . . . ?" he said softly.

"I showed you the truth."

"Impossible . . ."

"You know it's not."

The king said nothing more, and Mason couldn't tell what he was thinking behind his mask.

"Perhaps it is time to negotiate a treaty," the king said.

Then they broke into space, and Mason saw it was too late.

Chapter Forty-nine

Both fleets were ragged and scattered. Ships of every size drifted through space, some of them dark and dead, others with sputtering engines and flickering shields. The smaller ships were still engaging in dogfights, but Olympus and the Tremist space station were both badly damaged. Whole sections of each were on fire, and they seemed to be adrift in space. For a long moment, Mason and the king said nothing.

Then Mason saw the Egypt hanging back from the battle. It was intact.

"First order of a treaty is dropping my crew at the Egypt."

The king said nothing.

So Mason tried again. "You already have Earth. And if I hadn't used the turret, we'd all be dead."

The king was silent for another moment, and then he pushed the engines harder and flew the Hawk underneath most of the battle.

Mason tapped his ear. "Jer?"

Jeremy replied instantly. "Hey."

"Hey."

"What's up?"

"Long story, but I'm coming in on the king's Hawk. Let us dock."

"Okay."

Ninety seconds later, the Hawk sidled up alongside the Egypt and the docking thrusters engaged. The two ships kissed with a muted bang, then locked together. During that time, the king and Mason were busy on two separate com channels. The king was calling off his forces, and Mason was talking to Vice Admiral Renner.

"The planet is no good, sir," Mason said. "There's nothing to fight for. Look where I am." Mason swiveled the console around, and got a good shot of the king.

Vice Admiral Renner actually gasped. "For the love of cake . . ." he exclaimed.

"Sir?"

"Nothing, is the rest of your team safe?"

"There were casualties. But all cadets are accounted for. There's a lot to explain, sir, I know, but you need to call a cease-fire. Now."

The king looked into the camera, breaking from his own com. "You really do, human."

The vice admiral sighed deeply, his eyes calculating as always. "Copy that," he finally said.

The result was instantaneous. Space began to settle. The swarms of dogfights broke apart, and each ship went back to its respective side. The battle was over, with no winners. Mason watched the dead ships drift for a moment, knowing the search and rescue ships would be deployed in minutes. If protocol was followed, each dead ship had inner sections where the crew could gather to await rescue.

Then Mason turned in his seat.

"Next order of a treaty is all ESC personnel will follow me from your ship to mine."

The king nodded.

"That includes Merrin Solace."

"We will ask her what she wants to do."

That surprised Mason, and was more than a little suspicious. Of course Merrin would choose to stay with the ESC . . . right?

Mason only nodded, and together they walked side by side to

the hatch, where not too long ago Mason had watched as his sister stayed behind. Now they'd be together again. That was a kind of victory in itself, but not one he could measure against the destruction he had witnessed since the last time he'd slept.

Susan showed up first, with Tom and Stellan in tow. Merrin was already there; she must've seen the ships were linking up and decided to be near the exit. Which meant she hadn't been locked up, which was a good sign.

When Mason showed up with the king, both groups became stiff. Twenty minutes ago the Tremist and humans had been mortal enemies, and not everyone knew the truth yet.

"There is peace," the king said, and Susan's jaw unclenched, but just slightly. Her little brother standing next to the king was enough proof for now, Mason guessed, but she didn't relax. She took Stellan and Tom by the shoulders and guided them onto the Egypt's deck. Merrin still stood next to her father.

"Come on, Mason. Merrin," Susan said.

"This boy saved our lives," the king told his daughter. "If you stay with me, I will make you one of the human ambassadors. You will still see your friends, and at the same time move both races forward to peace. Stay with me." The king paused, bowing his head a little. "You are my daughter, Merrin. I don't want to lose you again. Let me show you where you came from."

Merrin swallowed.

Before she could answer, Jeremy broke through on the ship-wide com. "Uh, all crew. Get to a monitor."

There was one built into the wall next to the hatch. Everyone watched as a zoomed-in image of Nori-Blue's surface appeared. "Serious seismic activity on the planet's surface," he said. "It appears almost volcanic." Onscreen, a huge section of forest was breaking apart. There was a scale at the bottom that said it showed about one hundred miles. The forest was a green carpet more than anything, the trees too small to distinguish. As they watched, the ground began to disintegrate in the middle, the trees tipping

over and falling into some kind of sinkhole. The circle grew, as more trees were swallowed up, and the diameter kept growing and growing—stretching into an oval shape—until the hole was an enormous black crater.

"What's happening?" Susan asked breathlessly.

She didn't have to wait long for the answer. From the hole emerged a ship larger than anything Mason had ever seen. It was as long as the hole, so nearly one hundred miles. It was too big to have a shape, really, other than the general shape of a rectangle. The ship had to have hundreds and hundreds of levels. It was as black as space. Dirt clods the size of mountains tumbled away and broke apart as the ship passed from the hole and began its ascent.

The Fangborn knew how to fly.

Child, why didn't you tell us . . . Mason thought. He didn't expect an answer so many kilometers away.

But then Child said in a weak voice, *I didn't know.*

The Fangborn ship was still in the atmosphere when it fired a single white laser at two ships flying close together—one a crippled ESC supply ship, the other a Tremist Hawk that was venting purple and green gases. The blast was so bright on the screen, Mason had to squint.

When the light faded, both vessels had vaporized.

Chapter Fifty

Mason had to make a choice. The ESC still in the holding bay would take too long to transfer. There was another flash on the screen, and two more ships just disappeared into dust that glittered in the blue sunlight.

It was time to leave this cursed system. The rest of the ESC would have to wait—there simply wasn't time to transfer them all, not when they could all be vaporized at any moment.

Mason took two steps, grabbed Merrin's arm, and pulled her onto the Egypt's deck.

"Sorry," he told the king, "I need her to fly my ship." He pressed the button that slammed the door down between them. Through the glass window, he saw the king's black mask.

The king said nothing, just stalked away. Perhaps he would've put up a bigger fight if the Fangborn ship wasn't already in the upper atmosphere. Mason studied it for a moment longer. A long and thick horizontal line bisected the front of the ship, almost like lips. The line glowed dull red, like heat was building behind it. It made Mason colder than he already was.

"Let's move!" Susan said, and the five of them sprinted down the crossbar.

They arrived at the bridge to find it fully staffed.

With Commander Lockwood sitting at the nearest console. His burns were healing, but he was still in bad shape. Half his face was pink and shiny with new skin, one eye swollen shut.

Whatever the cadets had done to him, it seemed like it was working.

Jeremy stood up from the captain's chair. "*Finally.* I'm done with this captain stuff."

Lockwood was so weak he just nodded to Mason.

Mason nodded back. "Sir?"

"I am not of sound mind or body," Lockwood said. "The bridge is yours."

Tom joined Susan on the weapons console. "Weapons hot!" he said.

Merrin sat down at the pilot console. "The Hawk has disengaged. We are free."

Mason retook his chair.

The Fangborn ship was in space now. The crew didn't quite gasp, but there were mutterings and astonished sighs. Through the Egypt's dome, Mason saw it eclipse Nori-Blue's sun. Both fleets were plunged into shadow.

On the dome to the right, images of the king and Grand Admiral Shahbazian snapped on side by side.

"All ships in Nori-Bluespace—" the grand admiral said.

"Attack at will," the king and grand admiral said at the same time.

The shadows were banished as hundreds of lasers and particle beams lanced through the darkness . . .

. . . only to bounce off the hull harmlessly. Every beam and bolt fired at the Fangborn ship ricocheted off on some new trajectory, some bouncing back and injuring the ship that fired. White light began to grow under the Fangborn ship, until two parallel beams appeared, brighter than any sun, and danced over both fleets, dissolving any ship they touched.

Then the front of the Fangborn ship *opened*.

The glowing line Mason had seen before now split apart, like a maw. A massive pair of jaws filled with fire inside. The bottom part swung down, like a yawning alligator, then swung up twice as fast, crushing and swallowing two small fighters that had gotten too close. There were small bursts of fire, and then nothing. Like chomping on fireflies. It was eating *ships*, literally eating them, and the maw was big enough to swallow both space stations whole. Somewhere on the bridge, a first year was crying.

The grand admiral broke through the com: "Full evacuation! All ESC retreat on random vectors!" he said, as more and more ships exploded. There were so few left. The cadets were relaying information to each other, but Mason barely heard it. There was something new happening onscreen. The two space stations were trying to flee. But the Fangborn ship held them in place with some kind of force field that enveloped them both. It was a shimmery silver tractor beam that shot out like a laser, split apart, and then folded neatly around the stations. Mason understood why after a few seconds. No reason to destroy that many meals. The smaller ships were pesky and probably not worth the trouble, but if they could isolate both space stations—that would be millions of bodies they could capture and eat.

Someone was asking him something.

"Do we leave? Do we leave?" Merrin said. She was turned around in her seat.

Space was nearly empty now: the ships that were able to flee did exactly that. Wreckage was all that remained. And the Egypt.

And the king's Hawk.

Just then the king broke through on the dome's screen. He didn't waste time. "It seems we have a mutual mission."

"There's no one left," Mason said, then immediately regretted it. Whatever the Fangborn ship was doing to hold the two stations in place, it didn't seem to notice the two remaining ships. Maybe there wasn't enough power to destroy them just yet.

"*We're* left," the king said. "And I won't leave my station behind. Unlike the rest of your ESC. My scientists think the Fangborn ship will deflect all energy weapons, including—"

"We have conventional weapons on board!" Stellan shouted,

cutting the king off. He was more excited than Mason had ever seen him, no hint of fear. "We have a torpedo bay for when core energy has to be diverted to engines! We could fire them!"

Too much risk, was Mason's first thought. The Fangborn ship was simply too enormous to damage, or so it seemed. But could they really sit by and surrender both stations to the Fangborn? All those lives would be lost, and on Mason's head if he gave the order to retreat. They had to try. He looked to Susan but she was already working on the weapons console, bringing the torpedoes online.

"I will provide a distraction," the king said smoothly. "We have no conventional weapons."

"Thank you," Mason said.

The king's image disappeared, and Merrin looked over her shoulder at Mason.

"Take us in," he said.

Chapter Fifty-one

The two ships that started as enemies now swooped in together as fast as their engines would allow. Mason glanced down at his armrest to find the speed meter rising too fast for him to read. The whole crew held its collective breath as the Fangborn ship grew in the dome, until there was nothing else to see.

"Target the source of the tractor beams!" Mason shouted, gripping the arms of his chair. "Prepare to fire all torpedoes on that location."

Tom and Susan worked fast to make sure each torpedo was headed for the right place. They might not be able to harm the ship as a whole, but if they could break the tractor beams the stations would be free to escape.

The maw opened wide, fire curling within. Red and black was all Mason could see. Then a dazzling burst of white that hurt even with his eyes closed. *This is it*, he thought. But the blast was indirect. An alarm screamed as the entire crewside of the Egypt turned into superheated gas. Mason barely felt it, but suddenly the ship was offtrack, the engines failing to compensate for the imbalance. There came a series of thunks as the emergency doors sealed off outer space from the crossbar. They began to spin crazily; stars twisted across the dome, then the two space stations, followed by the Fangborn ship again. Clouds of atomized metal swirled around them—remnants of the entire port side of the Egypt. They were going to die.

But not before they took out the tractor beam.

The Egypt seesawed left and right, but centered back on the Fangborn ship. Merrin's voice pierced the multiple alarms. "Stabilized!"

"Fire!" Mason screamed.

Blue bolts of light sped out from under the bridge, giving off trails of rocket exhaust. They traveled fast and true, exploding on the underside of the maw in great bubbles of orange and red fire that faded as quickly as they came. All at once, the tractor beams were gone.

Mason punched the com: "Olympus, you're clear to go home!"

From under the Fangborn ship, the familiar white light began to grow. Mason instinctively flipped open the cover on his right armrest and slammed his fist down on the big red button. The dome ejected instantly, rocketing away from the bulk of the Egypt. If the cadets hadn't been strapped in, they would've been thrown to the ground. The Egypt ceased to exist a moment later, as the white beam turned it to dust like it had so many other ships in the last ten minutes.

But the angle was wrong. Instead of firing the dome away from the maw, they were headed right for it. Mason saw inside of it, close up for the first and last time. The maw was filled with fire. He could see the smoldering wreckage of ships inside, like pieces of meat stuck between a carnivore's teeth. But they had won: to his right, the part of his vision that wasn't filled with a fiery mouth, he saw the two stations zipping away from the Fangborn ship. The Olympus already had its extra-large gate deployed.

Mason could only hope the king would get his Hawk away safely, and eventually return the ESC crew where they belonged. He looked at Merrin first, then Susan, and wished they had more time. He wanted to say something to them; he wasn't sure what. He wanted to tell Merrin he was sorry—she would've had the rest of her life if he hadn't pulled her onto the Egypt's deck. If he hadn't needed her.

The maw was closing now, swinging upward in a bright orange arc.

Mason shut his eyes.

Chapter Fifty-two

Mason opened his eyes sometime later, after he regained consciousness. Later, he would learn that the dome was not equipped with gravity compensators, so when the dome was suddenly jerked backward at a speed too fast for the human body to handle, everyone on the bridge passed out. They were lucky no one had died. As it was, two cadets had ruptured blood vessels in their eyes, and one had a broken arm.

During the fifteen seconds he was unconscious, Mason saw the history of the People. The book in his brain finally unfolded, and the birth and death of a civilization was in his mind. It was too much to fully understand at once, or maybe ever, but he saw the troubles the People went through. The same things humans had been going through for nine hundred years. It was greed, he figured. The People had wanted more and more, and it took a solar flare to knock some sense into them. The surface of Nori-Blue had once been a city. The whole planet, one giant city. But the flare reduced all of it to just metal mountains. Everything electronic had been destroyed. It was then the Fangborn truly split off and became their own race, and legend said the flare had caused the Fangborn mutation. The People wanted to find a new way to live: though their planet was dead, there were signs it would return to its pure forest state. The Fangborn didn't care about changing, and so they warred.

Before Mason could see the war, he woke up. He woke up

with the content feeling that, no matter what had happened between the two races, Nori-Blue *had* returned to its pure forest state. Only to be warred over by two races who wanted to destroy it all over again, but that seemed to be changing. He had some vague but deep understanding that the universe was cyclical. But maybe that was the human side of him—there could be other aliens out there who were truly wise, who had learned from enough cycles.

Mason's first sight was through the Egypt's dome: he was looking at the much smaller Fangborn ship. Smaller, because they were so far away, he realized. Behind him, the Hawk was at half thrust, engines glowing brighter than the stars. The dome was being towed along.

As the groggy crew regained consciousness, the dome was towed into the storage bay, where the rest of the Egypt's crew was waiting. The dome passed through the force field separating the Hawk from space, and then scraped along the floor to rest in the middle of the bay. The ESC swarmed around it, cheering, beating their fists on the dome. Every one of them was smiling.

Susan stretched and then yawned, tears running down her cheeks. "There were six hundred thousand people on the Olympus today, little brother," she said.

Mason could only nod; he was shaking.

Jeremy opened the doors on the rear of the dome, and the cadets piled out and were lifted onto shoulders and carried around the bay. No one cared that they were all still on a Tremist vessel. It was quite obvious things had changed. How they had changed was still to be determined, but change they had.

The king showed up a few minutes later and beckoned Mason over to the dome. The king boosted him up the side, and then followed with a single leap to the top. The remaining Tremist had gathered in the bay, but their talons were stowed. Mason looked straight down at the captain's chair, wondering if he would ever sit in one again.

"We have a new enemy," the king began, and together he and Mason explained to both races what Mason had learned from the book. While they spoke, mutterings rippled through the crowd and died away.

"What about Earth!" someone shouted. It was echoed many times.

The king held up his hands for quiet. "Earth is safe, and will be returned to your solar system when a new gate has been created. It is now a neighbor to our home planet. A place you will all visit soon, if we're to find a way to stop this new threat."

Mason wanted another cheer to go up, but in truth the wounds between both races were still too raw. There was hope, though. Wounds beginning to heal, maybe. A few people clapped, but that was it.

The ESC stayed in the bay for the rest of the trip. Susan found him later on and squeezed his shoulder and bent down to say something in his ear. "Mom and Dad would be proud," she said, and Mason felt like crying again, but that wasn't what a captain would do. Instead, he nodded.

The trip was long and a little boring, so Mason gathered the others and they went back into the dome and powered Elizabeth up and made her throw battle scenarios at them.

Chapter Fifty-three

Two weeks later it was two days before the start of Academy II. Mason was nowhere near Mars, however—not even in the same solar system. He was aboard the Tremist space station he had helped save. It was called the Will.

The treaty ceremony took place in the central pod, which was a perfect recreation of a park. There was a pond and trees with blue and green leaves, and animals that chittered in the branches. Dark shapes swam under the surface of the pond, which was tinted pinkish gold. There was a clearing in the trees. The inky purple-black of space was visible above them, separated by a dome much like the Egypt's. And through that space Mason could see two planets sharing the same orbit. Earth was the cloudy blue sphere, and the Tremist homeworld, which they called Skars, was a yellowish, slightly smaller orb.

Grand Admiral Shahbazian stood with his entourage on one side, and the king stood with his on the other. The king was not wearing his mask. He was Merrin's father, through and through. Violet hair, pale skin. And kind eyes, somehow. Mason didn't believe it at first. He still wore his armor the color of dried blood. The king was flanked by four Rhadgast. Mason felt like they were watching him the entire time.

In between the two groups was a podium, and on the podium were three pieces of paper and an ancient fountain pen.

Grand Admiral Shahbazian said, "Today I sign this treaty in

the hopes our great races might work together against this common enemy. That we might rediscover our past together and find the link that makes us brothers."

A few photographers snapped pictures. A video feed was being broadcast to both worlds, and every ship in between them.

The king said, "Today I sign this treaty, for those things too."

Tom laughed. Susan nudged him. Mason couldn't help but smile.

"On one condition," the king said.

The manufactured breeze in the park seemed to stall, and there was nothing to hear except the shuffling of branches going still.

"What condition?" Shahbazian said.

Mason thought he knew. Merrin was standing next to him. She was in her ESC uniform, her violet hair tied back in a ponytail. He grabbed her hand, and she squeezed before he could. It felt like a goodbye squeeze. Mason almost opened his mouth to say something. *Wait.* Or, *Don't go.* He never got the chance.

"I would have my daughter returned," the king said.

Merrin tore free of Mason's grasp before the grand admiral had a chance to say no. She stepped forward and said, "I will go."

No one spoke. Merrin walked toward the podium, the halfway point. She turned toward the ESC. "I have to go, but I'll be back." Mason understood her sacrifice then. He knew she probably didn't want to go, even if she was curious about the world she'd been taken from. But by going, she was keeping the treaty alive. By volunteering, she kept the choice for herself. No one was going to make her stay or go. Mason admired her even more then, and wondered if he would be strong enough to do the same, if he was in her position. He hoped so.

Merrin Solace rejoined her father at his side. The news of how she was taken in the first place had made her a celebrity. When she was two years old, an ESC commando named Howerdell had stolen her from the king's previous Hawk during a raid. Rather than reveal who she was and use her, the grand admiral at the time had given her to a couple to raise as their own. The couple—a high-ranking doctor and a junior lieutenant in the ESC—agreed to the task, having waited on an adoption list for eight months. It later came out that Merrin and her new family were watched the entire time, and the ESC had plans to use her when it came down to humanity's last stand against the Tremist. A final bargaining tool. Mason was surprised that news didn't create more Tremist sympathizers. Merrin had tried to reach her family after the battle above Nori-Blue, to hear their side of it, but the ESC had her mother and father locked down somewhere.

There was nothing left to do then but sign the treaty. Afterward, both parties shook hands, but there was no celebration. Too many had been lost, the reason for a treaty too grim.

"I have one more request," the king said after he finished shaking Shahbazian's hand.

"What is it?" the grand admiral replied.

The king looked at Mason and raised an eyebrow. "My Rhadgast have requested this boy come to their school to train. They say he has the gift."

"Out of the question," Shahbazian said in a low voice Mason only heard because he was right next to him. "You've already taken one of my cadets today."

The king nodded. "They will be disappointed. But the offer stands, should you change your mind, young Stark."

Mason was still processing what was said. Invited to train as a Rhadgast? He heard something about a school and a gift, too. He'd be with Merrin at least; she wouldn't be alone on Skars.

"Can I think—" Mason began, but the grand admiral was already guiding him back toward the shuttle.

"Wait!" said a different voice. Mason turned around. One of the Rhadgast was walking toward him, black robes swishing across the floor. He had a pair of violet gloves in his hand. The gloves had shrunk, but Mason knew they would grow. The

Rhadgast kneeled in front of Mason, who stood tall and didn't flinch.

He pressed the gloves into Mason's hand, then leaned forward. Mason could feel the heat coming off his faceplate, could feel heat radiating from under his robes.

"Come and find us," the Rhadgast whispered in his ear, "if you want the truth about your parents."

The Rhadgast stood up and marched away before Mason could formulate a thought. He could barely breathe. The grand admiral was pulling him along again, Mason stumbling after with his gloves held tightly in one hand.

The truth about your parents . . .

Mason would find the Rhadgast, and then the truth. Of that he was certain.

"What did the wizard say to you, son?" Shahbazian asked gruffly. He was staring down at Mason, eyes narrowed.

"I couldn't hear," Mason replied.

The grand admiral grunted but said no more. They walked past the reporters, who took video and shouted questions: "Mason! Mason Stark! Why did the Rhadgast give you gloves? How does it feel to be a hero?" Mason ignored them. He wasn't a hero; he was a soldier.

Over his shoulder, he saw Merrin standing tall and regal next to her royal father. His best friend waved and smiled. Mason forced a smile back. He hoped he would see her again, but couldn't be sure.

He was sure of one thing, though.

It was time to go back to school.

2200: At the turn of the century, global war breaks out.

2210: The Peace Treaty of Athens is signed, dividing the world between East and West, ruled by India and the North American Alliance, respectively.

2379: Mar'ash Kelly, a new energy magnate in the East, unites the crumbling nations of East and West. Earth is under one rule, all resources shared.

2441: With Earth healed and prosperous, man decides to reach for the stars in a big way. The Earth Space Command is founded.

2467: The Warp Gate is developed, allowing man to travel throughout the galaxy instantly.

2470–2639: Man enjoys his newfound freedom and spreads throughout the galaxy, searching for other forms of life. Bases are built on forty-seven terrestrial worlds, none of which are capable of supporting human life. The search for a planet habitable to humans continues.

2640: First Contact with the Tremist (which means "Pale Ones" in the new tongue of Europe, later named so by Hungarian xenobiologist Marco Bronstaff). An early version of what is un-officially known as a "Hawk" (a Tremist midrange heavy fighter, known for its speed and its heavy weaponry) is seen circling the installation in Neptune's high atmosphere, then disappearing.

2644: Second Contact. Three Tremist Hawks bomb the ESC main base on Mars, breaching a gymnasium and exposing thirty-eight cadets to Martian atmosphere. The ESC and the United Earth declare the Tremist hostile.

2644–2744: One hundred years of peace. The Tremist are not heard from again. Man continues exploring the galaxy. The ESC fleet grows by one hundred ships. Earth's already bloated population swells dangerously. Twenty million people are living off planet.

2735: A Tremist ship (one of their heavy carriers, later dubbed "Isolators") is seen in the Ursa Major system. No contact.

2736: Nori-Blue is discovered. Out of 144 known terrestrial worlds, Nori-Blue is the first capable of supporting human life. Life-forms are discovered, similar to those on Earth. N-Blue has the equivalent of livestock. None appear more intelligent than an ape.

2739: The ESC reveals plans to move those willing to Nori-Blue, or Earth II as some call it. A warp gate is constructed in Nori-Blue's atmosphere.

2740: The Tremist arrive in force and destroy the gate mid-construction. The SS Norway is hailed. A Tremist claiming to be king tells the crew of seventy that Nori-Blue belongs to them.

When Captain James Lee Burke objects, the leading Tremist Isolator fires at the Norway's engines, stranding them in low orbit. With no way to control their descent, the Norway plunges into

Nori-Blue's ocean. Many of the escape shuttles burn in the atmosphere, but 141 crewmembers survive.

2740–Present Day: The ESC wages war with the Tremist, an average of three skirmishes per year. The ESC wins an average of one in three.

2746: Ship production has tripled, as more and more are destroyed in battle. As the ESC's strength wanes, a massive recruiting campaign begins.

2756: It's predicted Earth will no longer be able to support humans by 2820. The ESC recruiting efforts triple, training soldiers starting at age seven.

2769: A record year for casualties. Fourteen thousand ESC dead in various engagements.

2787: Mason Stark, Tom Renner, and Merrin Solace are born.

2792: Mason Stark's parents are killed in the First Attack on Earth. His sister, Susan Stark, a cadet in the ESC, becomes his guardian.

2794: Mason enters Academy I, to become an ESC soldier like his sister and parents before him.

2800: Mason graduates Academy I at thirteen. He hitches a ride to Academy II on the SS Egypt, the flagship of the ESC.

The Planet Thieves begins.